Paris Syndrome

Paris Syndrome

Lucy Sweeney Byrne

BANSHEE
PRESS

First published 2019 by
Banshee Press
www.bansheelit.com

A CIP record for this title is available from the British Library.

Banshee Press gratefully acknowledges
the financial assistance of the Arts Council.

ISBN: 978-0-9956550-9-6

'Foley and the Wolf' and 'All My Exes Live In Texas'
originally appeared in *The Dublin Review*.
'Zeno's Paradox' originally appeared in *Banshee*.

Set in Palatino by Eimear Ryan
Cover design by Anna Morrison
Printed in Ireland by Walsh Colour Print

For my parents, Paul & Cathy

Contents

Paris Syndrome

That Sinking Feeling

Almost exactly twenty-four hours into my stay on *Ye Olde Americana*, a defunct ferry boat moored in Red Hook, Brooklyn, I discovered that Elizabeth, the woman who owned it (who was tiny and old, and had a springy walk, and who was intensely pious and chirpy and plucky, all in a deeply threatening way), had been sleeping on the bathroom floor with the cats for two weeks before I'd arrived, purportedly for warmth.

One of the cats was heavily pregnant and mewed a lot. The other two were one-year-olds who clawed up your leg if you stood still too long, or exploded in sudden bolts from hidden corners, tails askew and fur on end. The mother cat had birthed six kittens in the litter but the others had disappeared, presumably overboard. There were also two decrepit old sausage dogs on the boat whom Elizabeth *adored*. They smelled of piss and were overweight, red-eyed and coddled. Again, there had been three before my arrival. One of the first things that Elizabeth had insisted upon at the introductory 'mateys' meeting, was the terrible danger of letting them waddle untethered onto the gangplank. She'd found that out the hard way.

My first night living on *Ye Olde Americana*, I went to an Irish bar called Paudy Doyle's with the boat's general manager. He knocked on the door of my little cabin on the upper deck as I was unpacking. He helped me to tightly secure the last of my books and the framed Virginia Woolf postcard on their shelf, expertly knotting the white tasselled rope around the hook on the wall. Everything on board had to be secured in place like this. Disrupted cups and plates leaned against cupboard doors, ready to topple out in the mornings. It took a while to get used to. I sat on my bunk and pulled my boots back over damp socks with stiff, cold fingers. There was barely room for both my thickly layered body and his in the cabin. 'After you, missy,' he barked when I stood up, thrusting his work glove before him. We both had to duck our heads, walking in awkward single file back out into the cold through the tiny wooden doorframe.

His name was Gene Eisenberg. I'd met him for the first time about half an hour before, suitcase in tow. It was clear he hadn't been expecting me, and that my arrival was extremely inconvenient. He told me, shouting back over his shoulder as he strode briskly toward my cabin, that he'd give me a proper tour of the boat some other time, when things weren't so hectic. But things were always hectic, so the layout remained a mystery to me. There were doors I never opened. I just learned my particular routes from A to B, at most perhaps a quick foray to C, and stuck to them like a rat in the walls. It would have felt like trespassing to enter uninvited the stately rooms I glanced through thick porthole windows, slowly accruing layers of dust, giving a pale blue-grey sheen to all the inlaid silks and velvets, mahoganies and porcelains, lying untouched within. Besides, it was too cold to explore for its own sake. Movement had to be economized on *Ye Olde Americana*.

Consequently, in my three weeks aboard ship, I never quite figured out where Gene slept. He tended to just appear from corners or erupt through trap doors like an angry, dirtied badger from the earth. He only ever looked me directly in the eye when drunk – so after two or three in the afternoons – and he only got soppy or lusty after dark.

The bar was only a twenty minute walk from the boat, but in the freezing cold this was a trial. We slogged, heads down, too wind-whipped and frozen to speak, through the abandoned, slush-covered IKEA parking lot, lit in Venn diagrams of gloomy white light from the lamp posts. I could hear the sea sloshing off to my left, a faint sound of engines and the occasional plaintive, free-jazz howl of a truck's horn to my right. But they were far off in the distance, some place between the starless night sky and the dark huddled redbrick buildings ahead, the roofs of which outlined the limits of my immediate sight, and thus my knowledge of this place. Up close there was only our rustling clothes moving in quick, tight rhythm, bootsteps landing in slushy snow, Gene's hoarse breathing to my right, my own, and the hissing wind that felt like papercuts across my watering eyes.

It had been a nightmare getting to *Ye Olde Americana* earlier that evening: finding the train, the bus stop, the right bus, definitely going in the *right* direction, all in the snow and that January air that burns the lungs. I'd known it was going to be cold, but knowing never prepares you.

When I finally hauled my suitcase onto the squat, heaving 291 bus to Red Hook, black and Hispanic passengers, wrapped tight in thick layers of coats and hats and scarves, glanced up at me disinterestedly before returning to their phones. Every person under thirty appeared to be wearing headphones. Old women carried blue or white plastic shopping bags tautly bulging with fruit and tinned goods. A young guy across from me took up three seats, he spread his legs so wide. His jeans were enormously baggy and he wore a red leather coat over a huge grey hoodie. I could hear the tinny sound of bass and deep voices escaping from his headphones. I watched him, dazed, and thought, how funny, to look so exactly like someone in a film, or a music video; someone dressed as though in a costume designed to convey a particular style: 'gangsta'. But then, maybe I looked the same to him: 'lost white girl'. He turned his head and met my stare with cold indifference. He must've sensed my watching him. Embarrassed, I quickly shifted my gaze through the window behind him and squinted slightly, trying and failing to give the impression I hadn't been looking at him at all.

Grey hunched buildings, snowy streets blackened by tyres and coughing engines, poles, mail boxes, kids in bulky, multi-coloured coats with cartoon backpacks, *Nemo* and *Dora the Explorer* and *The Avengers*, sludging in twos and threes, heads down and chattering. An old white guy hovered in a doorway, staring down the street, long trench coat hanging open, revealing a loosely buttoned cardigan and jeans, all faded from endless wear into nondescript shades of grey and brown. I peered out the front windshield in the direction he was looking and saw nothing coming for him. What was he waiting for?

How must it be, to be homeless in weather like this, in a city like this, I thought. It would be so easy to get lost here. If I got lost right now, who'd ever find me? Someone pulled the bell to stop, and as our bodies heaved, I found my eyes resting absentmindedly on the strong, clenched jaw of the man across from me again. His head nodded slightly to his music. From the collar of his hoodie emerged the beginnings of a tattoo. I couldn't make it out, but the edges looked jet-black and jagged. Again, his eyes caught mine, and I smiled nervously, and he did not smile back. I quickly forced my gaze to my feet, submissive. I've always stared too much, been too smiley, too ready to catch eyes. I always seemed to be straining around as though expecting any minute to see a new friend, or someone who might know me.

The night before leaving, I'd lain in my single bed in my father's house in Wicklow, wondering what on earth I was doing. Leaving again, restless again, entering the unknown – alone, again. It may have been because I was lonely, but it was hard to know. What does loneliness really feel like, after all? What I was experiencing – the scooped-out hollowness, the dull ache, the longing for warm touch – these could have been caused by a number of things, I reasoned. Vitamin deficiencies, or the weather. Besides, I had grown so accustomed to my solitude that it was no longer recognizable. It carried no distinct emotional colouring, at least none that I could see. I had been single two years. In that time, I'd travelled alone a lot. I told myself that, after all, this was what I'd become single for: 'freedom'. To see foreign places, foreign faces, to taste exotic foods; to sleep with new, strange and poetic-seeming men.

Yet already, with every new place – every cramped plane journey, every conveyer belt groaning into motion, every samey-same bathroom cubicle, every lurching bus, every 'hi, hi, yes I'm Lucy, yeah, hi, yeah, fine thanks, how are you?' – the big, wide world was losing more and more of its romantic lustre. The men I had met were either less interesting than or bizarrely similar to my ex. I felt as though I knew them all already: their frayed jackets, their untameable cowslicks, felt their calloused finger-pads hardened from playing guitar for hours in their bedrooms at night. I was sure I'd heard their jokes already, their *Curb Your Enthusiasm* or *Peep Show* references, their obscure album recommendations and insightful opinions on the films of Linklater, or Kurosawa, or Tarkovsky. Their probing tongues and their tight, serious orgasm faces.

Depressingly, I realized that they must have felt the same about me. I was just another lost twenty-something, pretending to be above it, attempting to play the modern heroine. Pretending not to be confused, and ignorant, and terrified too. The wincing shame I felt in considering how they might've, at best, deemed me 'kooky'. At worst, utterly forgettable. In the space of six months I slept with three different men who professed *Moby Dick* to be their favourite novel, and I'd smiled to convey 'impressed' each time. I'd tell them I was a writer and they'd say, rolling a smoke or scrolling through their phones in bed, afterwards: 'cool, yeah, so am I, in my spare time like – I'm also a photographer/filmmaker/sculptor ... look, actually, I can show you ...' Each interaction only deepened my despair, which felt more and more as though it were bulging in growths across my body, like stalactites growing steadily from a cave ceiling. Sometimes, thinking of these men afterwards, walking home along unfamiliar streets at daybreak, stepping onto underground trains in grotty booze-scented clothes, I felt monstrous in my gaping need, and in what seemed in those moments to confirm its ultimate incommunicability.

It wasn't just the men though, or the sex for that matter. It was the realization that foreign foods could be bought at home; cooked just as well at home, in pyjamas, while talking happily with the dog. It was the discovery that views of exotic places looked just like they had on the internet, and tended only to be sweatier and noisier and more jostled when experienced in real life. I would arrive at beautiful landmarks and historically significant sites and find myself at a loss, not quite sure what to do with my own presence, with the fact of my body's being there. Invariably I ended up just wandering around, trying and failing to feel overwhelmed, or to have even just the slightest emotional connection to my surroundings, while in fact becoming increasingly irritated by the other tourists, and especially by the suggestion that my being in proximity to them could, to a layperson, make me seem like just another one of them.

La Sagrada Familia, the Shakespeare and Company bookshop, the Brandenburg Tor; these places had brought me face-to-face with my own ordinariness, my intense unoriginality. They forced me to recognize myself as just another camera-toting, notebook-wielding shit-muncher. I usually ended up trying to find a quiet corner in which to write to remove myself from the present; to relieve the humiliation of being there in such an agonizingly predictable scenario, by casting myself as an 'observer' of the scene rather than a partaker. If no writing spot proved available, I'd just end up taking photos. I'd attempt to find unusual-seeming angles, squatting down low or finding a small manageable wall to stand on, above the other plebs. These would be uploaded to Facebook for one or two bored aunties back home to hit 'like' on, or be forgotten in some digital pictures folder, and would never turn out as impressive as the ones I'd seen on TripAdvisor while lying at home in bed planning it all beforehand anyway.

(The other option, of course, would have been to attempt to travel 'off the beaten path', to seek out the 'local hangouts': some cool back-alley café, some little-known jazz bar. But these are simply the go-to methods and locations of the more deluded among us. The alternative holiday locations for the younger, more self-aggrandizing globetrotters. Better, I grew to realize, to give the peace sign towards a selfie stick in front of the Eiffel Tower, than to feign touristic originality.)

Yes, leaving again meant being a perpetual traveller, one of those people who treated the earth like a television, requiring a constant stream of newness and stimulation from the outside world to counteract all their various internal lacks. So why was I going? I shifted in my bed, moving my hands above the covers to relieve their clammy warmth. I could hear my father snoring through the walls – a sound I'd been hearing all my life, so familiar now as to be at one with the night's silence. I breathed deeply, and tried to calm my humming mind. Why go? Because what would I do otherwise? Stay here, in my father's house? Keep walking the roads I'd walked since childhood? Say hello to the same faces, have the same conversations about the unreliability of public transport, the increasing prices in the grocery shop on the corner, the weather? I felt as though to stay would be to give in to a life without variety, without the chance of surprise or grand horizons; to give in to loneliness and resign myself to a life of small and gentle disappointments. At least, in travelling, there was still the opportunity to hope.

Leaving provided a hope that was constantly disappointed, yes; but also a hope that was, in the face of all experience, continually self-renewing. With each new place; each new delicious scent on the air; each new city park; each new glassy skyscraper disappearing into sky;

each new gaudily packaged product in the aisle of each new supermarket; each new steamy-windowed coffee shop, with a new smiling barista with new and bizarre tattoos to study; each new street corner glimpsed aglow at dusk; with each introduction to a new way of walking through the world, there was hope. To forgo all these would be easier, safer and perhaps, all in all, less harrowing, but it would also be to forgo an infinity of potential futures, and to submit myself to a life so well-trod and easeful as to be a sort of living death.

And so, lying there, the alarm clock on my nightstand glaring 3.37 a.m. in illuminated, boxy numerals, I knew that in a matter of hours I would be on a plane to New York, to *Ye Olde Americana* in Red Hook, Brooklyn. I would work in return for room and board; the plan was to stay aboard for three months, although in the end I'd only last three weeks. It would be new, it would be different. Maybe it would make *me* different.

In the relief of the warm, glowing bar that night, I got drunk to console myself for all the travel and terror and cold and newness. There were shamrocks and *'Guinness Is Good For You!'* signs with seals and pelicans that I outwardly cringed at but was secretly comforted by. In the back room they were dancing jigs in neat pairs, high kicking and swip-swapping to music blaring from a cassette player; and afterwards, an earnest Irish-American man in glasses taught 'Gaelic' on a big plastic whiteboard using green and orange markers. On my way to the loo I fell into a chair at the back of the class and scoffed as I pretended to know the language better than him.

As the night's edges began to blur, I was bought drinks by two bearded Scottish men my father's age (I would grow accustomed to being bought drinks in this bar). Whiskey, I imagine it was. They said they came to New York and back here to Paudy's for a Guinness every January. As they spoke, I finished their pizza crusts. I hadn't eaten in hours, and I'm naturally greedy, which becomes more apparent when I'm drunk. I told them I'd come to live and work on a boat and that no, I knew nobody on it, nobody in New York, and nothing about boats. I leaned heavily on the bar, attempting to look less in need of its solidity to stay upright than I actually was.

'I was meant to – hic! – do a Skype interview, eh, once, but their – hic! – Wi-Fi wouldn't work, or something ... So here I – hic! – am!' I smiled and shrugged merrily in a vague *c'est la vie* gesture.

'Eh, right, wow,' they said, glancing at one another with their bushy eyebrows raised. 'Well ... good luck with that!'

Gene Eisenberg sat propped in what I guessed was his usual spot at the end of the bar, bantering with Martha, the overweight Irish-American barwoman, and throwing me glances whenever he thought I wasn't looking. He was huge and bald with a dark beard and brown eyes and a gruff Boston accent. Everyone in there seemed to know him. As the night progressed, he became increasingly full of layman's wisdom, full of 'experience' he wished to knowingly impart. After the Scotsmen left, I somehow ended up beside him, and worked hard on appearing to listen attentively to his advice (leaning forward and nodding at intervals) because he also bought me drinks.

Before we left he arranged for an old Irish-American man who'd emigrated to New York back in the seventies, 'with only the clothes on his back and God in his heart', to provide me with fifty dollars' worth of weed for only thirty. I don't really enjoy weed, but it had come up in conversation and I was playing the part now: the Wild Young Irish Cailín, up for craic and mischief. Some time after, as the night wound down to its end and time itself began to spin a little and the light in the bar turned a deep bourbon colour, I registered Gene's enormous hand running up and down my back, his hard-work callouses catching on my top's material as he breathed into my ear, huskily whispering that he kept vodka hidden in his cabin if I felt like joining him for a nightcap.

I found myself running back to the boat alone, because it was too cold and awful and sobering to walk. I almost slipped and fell three times on ice and snow but somehow, magically didn't. I also had the good sense not to slam shut the glass-panelled door at the end of the gangplank. I eased it into place with drunken theatrics, shushing it under my breath. The fire was going in the stove but, mercifully, I could detect no other movement beyond the boat's own slow and constant rocking. I hadn't met anyone on board except Gene so far and didn't think that, at this moment, I would make much of a first impression. I quickly escaped up to my cabin, trailing snow.

Shivering, I removed my boots, my fingers too numb with cold to bend properly. I couldn't bring myself to take off my coat. The temperature within the wooden walls was the same as that without, only more silent and compressed. Instead, with slow and jerky movements, I hooshed myself up and pissed in the sink of the little kitchen unit next to my bedroom. I did this because the only toilet on board was two floors below deck and I may have met someone on the way. And besides, I reasoned, it was too miserably cold, and Gene (who'd be home after me any minute now, and who I resolutely needed to avoid) had told me the pipes had all frozen before we left, so the loo wouldn't have flushed anyway. The piss made a clattering sound against the metal and I hoped nobody would hear. I breathed deeply, relieved.

When I finished, I sat and listened to the ensuing silence. At first it seemed deathly quiet, before my ears tuned into the sea sounds: the sloshing, the lapping, the creaking and clanking of the boat. Off in the distance I heard a siren wail, but faintly, louder, loud, then more faintly ... New York's out there, I thought, and with the thought a wave of ice water ran through me. All the people out there: breathing, sleeping, walking, snorting, eating, injecting, laughing, crying, dreaming, or just shivering too. Pissing in sinks, too. Babies whimpering, artists painting, celebrities showering, convicts smoking, old people coughing, wheezing, and someone, right now, dying. All strangers to me. Well, wasn't that what I'd wanted?

Before I could prevent them, my thoughts leapt quick as a flash across all that cold, sloshing, wide-open water back to Ireland. A stillness. It would be approaching morning there now, the sky quiet except for the trills of small waking birds, the first hint of white light washing out the blackness; January's fusty clouded skies revealing a calm, resigned day, just beginning. Yesterday, I was there. And now, here.

Beside the sink was a little dying cactus plant, frozen at the roots. I looked at it dazedly a minute, listening now to the lulling rhythms of ocean and thinking of my parents, sleeping soundly in their beds, my dog in his chair, listening out for movement; the soft-rolling grassy hills of Wicklow, blades of grass and wrapped-tight flower petals, stretching and yawning; and all the delivery men, breathing clouds of white, dropping bread and milk and bundles of newspapers, the *Independent* and *The Irish Times*, outside all the locked shop fronts and doorways, careful not to skid on the morning's hoar frost on all the little winding roads connecting all the villages, towns and cities; all as I sat slumped forward here, now, holding my coat bunched up on my lap, with my tights around my ankles, surrounded by strangers in the softly swaying dark.

White lights from the dock beyond glittered on the surface of the water through the porthole window to my left. As quickly as I could, I tore off my bulky coat and pulled on my pyjamas, over which I wore a jumper and a second pair of thick socks. All of my clothes smelled sickeningly of gasoline, which I would later learn came from the old-fashioned mothballs Elizabeth placed in the trunks of every cabin. As I clambered into my bunk, I couldn't tell if the heaving sensation was the effect of the boat, the smell, or the drink. Before I had time to be overcome by nausea at the thought, I tipped head-first into a heavy, blackened, dreamless sleep.

Elizabeth's age was unclear, with our guesses ranging from sixty-five to eighty-nine. She had the air of someone who'd been pretty once, in an elfish sort of way. She wore clothes in the cut and style of the 1800s, like someone from a Dickens novel, but in outlandish colours. She dyed her hair boot-polish black, but adorned it each day with ribbons, also in (carefully coordinated) outlandish colours.

On my second day aboard *Ye Olde Americana*, Elizabeth asked if I'd like to attend church with her, in a way that implied 'no' was not an acceptable answer for good people. She banned all swearing, smoking, drinking and 'premarital relations' on board ship. In practice, this meant you were strictly forbidden to find yourself alone with someone of the opposite gender, for fear of being overcome by temptation. Usually, she told us, there was a whole 'joyful motley crew' of volunteers on board, but it seemed those who'd been there only the week before had disappeared in the night. Now there were only two, including myself; although there was, throughout my time there, the constant vague promise of more coming 'probably tomorrow, maybe the day after'. She insisted on calling us 'mateys' and on making up nicknames for us. Mine, she announced, would be 'Lulubelle'. Mercifully, these didn't stick (in fact, I didn't hear mine again until my very last day aboard). She also insisted that all references to the boat itself, in conversation or writing, would *always* be as *Ye Olde Americana*, never 'the boat' or 'the Americana' or even 'Ye Americana'. She broke into laughter at unnerving moments. She revealed an underlying racism very early on, telling me conspiratorially, as though I would naturally understand, that she didn't take black volunteers because they were too lazy and smoked 'marijuana leaves', and didn't take Asian volunteers because they were too small and weak. I would discover later that it was quite something she'd taken me, an Irish person – usually she wouldn't, since we're all drunkards and, even worse, *Catholic*.

It was Gene who'd told me, swigging his secret flask, that Elizabeth had been sleeping on the bathroom floor. But then he also told me she didn't sleep at all. She stayed up all night pressing sheets in an antique presser with two huge rollers, because she didn't find ironing effective enough. She was meticulous about the appearance of the ship when it came to the folding of towels, the aesthetically pleasing placement of logs by the unused stoves, or the precise alignment of tassels and picture frames. Yet she managed to never see all the caking dust, the rot and rust, or the little hardening piles of sausage dog and cat faeces hidden in the corners. Her approach to the boat put me in mind of someone painting the nails of a corpse. The whole place looked like somewhere thoroughly enjoyed thirty years before, with its stunning chandeliers and long walnut tables and expensive lamps and furnishings. It had real hand-carved fireplaces and stunning Persian rugs and porthole windows and original paintings, landscapes and abstracts bought in Sotheby's and framed in gold, hung carefully on the wooden-beamed walls. All of which emitted now the pungent scents of sea-damp and dust. This, combined with the mothballs in the cabins, ensured that anyone who came on board soon began feeling queasy or complained of a slowly worsening, throbbing headache. But the most memorable thing about being on board was the cold. That's what stayed with me, after. The cold, and the whispering sense of dread.

There was no clear function to the boat. I asked Elizabeth, in that first meeting, what it was actually meant to be. What her plan was. Thinking of myself asking that now – the hopeful naivety, the belief in the possibility of a clear answer – makes me want to laugh (although I can't quite yet manage it). I had been brought on as a volunteer to market the boat, to promote it online and to sort out the paperwork for future grants. I was given the title of *Ye Olde Americana* Administrator. Usually volunteers were given physical labour and so initially, I was pleased. In our first meeting, Elizabeth told me with flourishing hand gestures – almost brought to her feet with the sheer enthusiasm – that *Ye Olde Americana* was a heritage site, a source of hope and history, a meeting place for great minds.

'I want,' she said, eyes gleaming, 'for all the great leaders of the world, for Mr Obama and Mr Putin, and whomever else' – she always said 'whom' or 'whomever', never simply 'who' – 'to come to *Ye Olde Americana* to meet, to talk, to navigate new, pure ways through these murky waters, and to altogether change the world, with *Ye Olde Americana* at the helm!'

I smiled falteringly, wondering, amongst other things, how a boat could be at its own helm.

'How does that all sound?' Elizabeth asked with a breathless smile.

I glanced at Jacques, the other new volunteer, a Parisian who arrived the day before I did. His English was poor but even so, observing Elizabeth's demented vigour, his eyes widened in a mixture of scornful disbelief and fear.

There was a pause. 'Oh, uh ...' I said, 'sounds ... great!'

Elizabeth and her husband Jasper had once been extremely successful in the home furnishings and interiors world. Back in the '80s, they'd been commissioned to design furniture and sculptural pieces for various hotels and corporate buildings, as well as the private mansions of the international elite. Elizabeth and Jasper's names were still recognized with respectful nostalgia by those who travelled in moneyed circles, especially on the Upper East Side. Now their designs were dated but seen as *the* representative style of that era when it came to bespoke home furnishings. They'd been in all the big magazines, won awards. This, though, didn't make them any money now. They'd been cheated out of their business and most of their various other properties by a financial advisor, an 'evil-hearted, Godless woman!' back around the time of 9/11. I could tell that, in Elizabeth's mind, the two events

were far from unconnected – her fate was deeply inter-
twined with that of the United States of America, which
she loved 'deeply and truly, cross my heart and hope to
die'.

Nowadays, Jasper lived upstate Monday to Friday in
their one other remaining property, an old school house
which he had converted into an artist's studio. He still
made designs, but fantasy ones, envisioning sculptures
for buildings he would never be commissioned to do. It
was unclear, but I got the impression that their current
financial advisor, a stocky, self-sacrificing woman called
Deborah, lived either *with* him or, at the very least, close
by. Deborah, I would discover from their vague financial
records, had given them incredible amounts of money
over the previous ten years to help keep *Ye Olde Americana*
(and, therefore, Elizabeth) afloat, safely out of the way,
moored down in what I began to think of as New York's
hangnail, the neighbourhood of Red Hook, Brooklyn.

Elizabeth showed me cabinets filled with boxes of yellow-
ing papers, old grant applications and legal documents
and scrawled minutes from meetings going back ten or
twenty years. (The ones taken by Elizabeth herself usually
featured floral scribbles and swirls, love hearts, crosses,
as well as lots of exclamation marks. There were even
some smiley faces with optimistically raised eyebrows.) I
was left to go through them, to sort them and to rebuild
the prospects of *Ye Olde Americana*. Instead I spent a lot
of time on social media and swiping through Tinder, or
looking up events for aspiring writers in Manhattan that
I never attended. At first, I worked aboard ship in a little
heated cabin near the back with the mother cat on my lap
for mutual warmth. But with increasing regularity, I took

to working in the café in the giant IKEA built on the docks, where I could get free coffee with my 'Family Benefits' membership card and which was, more significantly, far, far warmer.

Just over two weeks into my stay on board – perhaps as some sort of primal survival tactic, to rid myself of Elizabeth's Sauron's-eye-presence for a while, or to regain my own sense of perspective, which was growing more and more skewed by the day – I got sick. This is where Bobby Tzubowsky came in.

Bobby was a regular at Paudy's. He was small, early forties, with ferret-like features and poor posture. He was perpetually a little dirtied, in work clothes and scuffed leather boots. He always wore an old NY baseball cap that I had assumed covered a bald spot, but didn't. His hair was a little greasy and unkempt, but full and mousey blond.

The first time I noticed him, he was sitting at the other end of the bar, extremely drunk, giving mild abuse to Martha about feminism. He was explaining to her how a lot of it was, if she really took the time to think about it, horseshit.

Now, it's not that I don't think there's an argument to be made against many aspects of modern feminism – its militancy, its classism and racial exclusivity, its insistence on moral homogeneity – but somehow I doubted that Bobby, half-falling off his stool and gesturing excessively with his empty IPA bottle, was considering all of the myriad subtle nuances of the issue necessary to make this argument convincingly. Also, he was being obnoxiously loud, and ruining my attempts to read in peace.

'I'm not sayin' *all* of it's bullshit Martha, I'm not. I mean, you know me, I *love* women, I do ...' At this, I thought I caught him glance in my direction, but quickly darted my eyes back to my page so he wouldn't try to involve me. 'It's just that, you know, a lot of it, is, well, *bullshit* – alright?'

I immediately disliked Bobby. That way of speaking down, that righteous ignorance. Martha, assisted by her husband and son, both of whom were in the back cleaning out the ovens, sent him home. They were good-natured about it though. I got the impression they'd all done this before, including Bobby, who didn't put up much of a fight, except for show. The husband – a huge, hairy, red-headed man – stood at the door in the cold, watching to make sure he got down the street okay, telling him to sleep it off. It turned out Bobby lived only three doors away.

Soon after, Martha told me Bobby was harmless really, a good guy, just had trouble holding his drink was all. She also told me, winking, that he was loaded.

'I know yah'd never guess it,' she said, in her strange Crumlin-Brooklyn accent, 'but he's got the big bucks alright … construction … he owns the whole ahperation, a huge ahperation, he juss doesn't like to be showy about it, ya know? A good guy though, heart ah gold, a real good guy, mostly.'

The reason he came up at all in our conversation, and why she seemed to be trying to sell him to me, was because it turned out the last thing he'd managed to do, before being forcibly removed from the bar, was to pay her in advance for my next three drinks, to be served with a small green napkin on which he'd written: 'on me Irish, 23745638, love Robert x'.

The day I woke up sick, I went to the IKEA café in a daze and pretended to work for my allotted five hours, for lack of anything better to do or anywhere better to go. I sat as close as I could to the radiators and drank, in quick succession, eight or nine cups of piping hot free tea and coffee, which admittedly was taking the whole 'Family Benefits' thing a little far. Fuck it, I thought. I felt like I was dying.

I could barely focus on my computer screen. Everything blurred and melted, and my head pounded. My body felt icy cold and hot all at the same time – much like how it must feel, I remember hazily thinking, to be a baked Alaska, straight from the oven. At one point, throwing caution to the wind (Elizabeth could've walked in at any moment), I fell asleep, head resting on my crossed arms on the table before me. In retrospect, I realized I ought to have been more worried about my computer being stolen.

At the end of my five hours, I sent Elizabeth a short text message to say I was sick, and that I may not be able to work the next day. She wrote back a lengthy, seven-paragraph email about how sickness didn't exist, how God had given us perfect bodies, and how it was a human affliction to believe in illness, one that stemmed from vanity and the devil. She sent me links to various Christian Scientist articles that backed up the truth of her argument and strongly advised me to turn to prayer instead of medicine, 'for the health of your body *and* soul, whom is after all one's greatest concern and happy burden given from the great God above in his wisdom whom is with us and protecting us always!!' She concluded that she would need me to work the next day regardless of how I felt, 'for the Greater Good of our beloved *Ye Olde Americana* whom we dedicate our time energy and efforts to bringing forth into a dark world in need of light! Love Elizabeth xxxxx'. I decided not to go back to the boat. I went to Paudy's instead.

Bobby had never actually spoken to me, but he'd sent drinks my way on the following two occasions he'd seen me across the bar. I always raised my glass in thanks, and he raised his bottle back sheepishly. I'd never seen him drunk again after that first time. Since then he'd been quiet and polite, unnoticeable had it not been for the proffered drinks. He seemed to always have his meals there and to be very familiar with the proprietors, Martha and her family, as well as most of the other regular patrons. I got the distinct impression he lived alone and was lonely. I understood that, could empathize, and I could see he was kind and generous. Yet somehow the apparentness of his loneliness, the meekness of his eating there alone every night, of his buying drinks for me but not even coming up to say hello, disgusted me. To sit and stew in one's misfortunes, as Bobby did, seemed to me to be the height of selfishness. I was lonely too, I thought, but I didn't inflict it on those around me. I had the decency to leave, to conceal my condition. By being there at all, in a bar in New York, I felt as though I was at least trying, even if I was reading and not speaking to anyone. His being there, three doors away from his house, amongst people he knew, sending drinks to strange women without even asking their name, made it clear to me that he had given up. That, to me, was pathetic.

It was a glancing impression, admittedly, but I got the feeling that Bobby would be the type of guy who'd tell you a sad backstory at the earliest opportunity, and that he'd probably cry earnestly during, or certainly after, sex. And so I sat and drank the drinks, but didn't invite his attentions, and I never used the number he'd given me to contact him.

On this day I managed to meander – coughing and disorientated, through snow and slush – to Paudy's, and unwittingly fall into a free seat at the bar directly beside Bobby. (Did I do this on purpose? I don't know, it's certainly possible. I am equipped with survival instincts.)

'Jesus, you look terrible,' he said, startled into a familiarity we didn't actually have.

'I know, but thanks,' I said, annoyed at having exposed the real, snotty, un-mystical me to this man who'd been under the illusion I was beautiful.

'No, sorry, I mean, you just look, eh, sick – are you okay?' His eyes showed true concern as he turned towards me on his stool. He went to reach for my shoulder and stopped himself.

'Honestly, no,' I said, slumping. 'I feel like death … I think I have, I dunno, the flu maybe … I really don't know … I never get sick, I don't know what, or, if this, if this is what is …' Unable to formulate my sentence, I peeled off my coat, suddenly roasting in the warm bar, beads of sweat forming on my forehead.

'I know what it is,' he said, helping me free my right arm, which was stuck in the sleeve. 'It's living on that damn nuthouse of a boat is what it is – no proper heating, no insulation, the crazy work she makes you guys do.'

I decided not to tell him that I was the administrator, and so didn't usually have to do the horrible snow-shovelling and engine room-cleaning. I gestured to Martha's son, who was behind the bar today. 'A hot whiskey please,' I coughed.

'I'll get it,' Bobby said when it arrived.

'Are you sure?' I asked, pretending to be surprised.

He batted my wallet away, handing over a twenty. 'And get another, while she's having this one, she'll need it.'

I could've cried, but didn't. 'Well, God, you're very good … thanks.'

'Don't mention it,' he said, smiling shyly.

I don't know how the bath suggestion came up, but I was too muddled and sickly and desperate for kindness – for comfort in any shape or form – to resist. Yes, the idea of going to his house where he lived alone, for the sole purpose of taking a hot bath in his apparently enormous bathtub, with massaging water jets and a flat-screen TV built into the bathroom wall and candles and more hot whiskeys promised, may have sounded like a situation specially crafted to end woefully; one of those situations in a bad horror movie in which you, sitting in the audience with your popcorn, scoff at the bimbo's stupidity. But my other option was to return to the boat, to either be lectured on the non-existence of illness by Elizabeth, or die from shivering in my cold cabin alone, or be lured into vodka swigging somewhere below deck with Gene, where he'd no doubt take the opportunity to have his way with me. I decided to take my chances.

Bobby couldn't seem to believe I was even considering it. His eyes got all wide and he sat up straighter in his stool. 'Look, you're sick, you need it ... what we'll do is, I'll bring you back – it's right on this block, only three doors away, you know, real close – so I'll walk you back and let you in and all, show you the place – it's real nice, I did it myself, converted it, you'll like it, I think – and then you can take a nice hot bath, as long as you like, and while you're doin' that, I'll clear out, I won't even be there! What I'll do is, I'll go get medicine, lotsa medicine for ya, and then I'll come here, and then when you're done, you can call me, and I'll come back ... how does that sound?'

I tried to compute. I couldn't think straight. It all sounded too good to be true, like a fairytale. And yet, I knew I shouldn't.

He could see I was wavering. 'And tell ya what,' he said, leaning in, 'look at the menu here, have a look, see, and pick somethin' – they do lotsa things, pizzas and pastas and burgers, or salads or whatever, good stuff – and when I come back, when you call me, I'll bring whatever you picked out for dinner, sound good?'

And so I found myself having a bath in the most luxurious bathtub in D'Agata Bay and, afterwards, eating pizza and downing shots of expensive cough medicine on Bobby's soft, enormous couch. I was wrapped in a black and grey-striped dressing gown that Bobby had left out for me, watching some shitty Hollywood comedy about policemen in San Francisco that I barely followed. Bobby had wanted to watch *Goodfellas*, which I vetoed as too long and involved for my current feverish confusion.

He'd only really suggested it, it transpired, because it was a means to letting me know that he knew Martin Scorsese's nephew. 'Yeah, I grew up with him, went to school together … actually, I've been talking to him about producing something together soon … yeah, y'know, obviously he's interested in movies, 'cause of his uncle, and since I have a bitta money an' all, and I love movies too, y'know … yeah, very cool, very cool …' He went on to say that maybe since I was a writer, I could write a movie for them, and he could show it to Scorsese's nephew. 'Why not, right? I bet you're a great writer anyway.'

I looked at him in disbelief. His kindness – after my three weeks so far on the boat, which had turned out to be such a disappointment; in what felt like a lifetime, in some ways, of incremental disappointments – was startling, and so clean and fresh and white as to be almost too much to bear. Looking at Bobby's kindness that night was like looking into the face of God – a God that, in that moment,

I was sure Elizabeth had never come close to witnessing. For the second time that evening, I felt and fought the urge to cry. If I'd started crying then, I knew, I may never have been able to stop.

I spent that night in Bobby's king-size orthopaedic bed, covered in dark-grey pure cotton sheets that I guessed a cleaner must've ironed and changed for him. Bobby slept in the spare room. It was the best non-drunken sleep I'd experienced in New York thus far. Perhaps my best sleep in years, I thought. I didn't feel fearful or alone; the room did not sway, and I did not shiver. I woke at eight in the morning feeling refreshed and almost entirely better. It was a good thing too. Little did I know, but that would be my last day on *Ye Olde Americana*, and I'd need my strength.

I was due back on board to start work at 9 a.m. sharp. When I arrived at 9.04 a.m., cold but resigned, head down against the Atlantic winds and mentally bracing myself to re-enter the madness, Elizabeth was standing on the gang-plank, shivering, holding her ornate purple and gold-lined cloak tight around her tiny shoulders, waiting for me. Her eyes were on fire, her lips thin with fury.

'So *Lulubelle*, feeling better, I *presume*?!'

That last morning was a blur. Elizabeth screeching, Gene roaring. The pipes had frozen again overnight, and neither Jacques nor I had been on board to relight the fires. He'd made some French friends through a Facebook expat group, and increasingly slept in their hostel in Greenpoint with them rather than suffering the cold indignity of the boat.

Gene, when Elizabeth had gone to rouse him, had been dead drunk in his cabin, making teary phone calls to his ex-wife and son back in Boston. When Elizabeth had instructed him to go light the fires, to 'hop to it!' he was unable to get to his feet. 'Gene, have you been ... *drinking*?!' In his inebriation, when she wouldn't leave him be, apparently he'd told her to 'fuck the goddamn fucking off'. She'd nearly scratched his eyes out.

'Godless people!' She was now screaming at all three of us.

'Mad old bitch!' Gene was shouting back, still drunk, I guessed.

Finally, forcing herself to be still, to breathe deeply, all four of us sitting around the wooden table in her kitchen, where one of her lumpy sculptures served as a centrepiece, she quietly and calmly gave us an ultimatum: we could either dedicate ourselves to *Ye Olde Americana* wholly and unreservedly, and agree never to leave her in any hour of the day or night, for the greater good of God's earth and mankind, in the creation of a better, kinder, more peaceful world. If we chose to do this, she was sure – if we gave her concise lists and sufficient money – that she could do the food shopping for all of us while we stayed aboard ship, keeping the fires lit, and then we would soon be through the winter, warm and united and ready to face the future. *Or*, we could leave right now and never, ever come back, and doom *Ye Olde Americana* to a winter of hardship and trials in the face of her grand and noble pursuits, alone.

Jacques, when I translated as best I could in my appalling, broken French, burst out laughing, looked at her incredulously, and stood up to leave, throwing back a merry 'ciao ciao!' over his shoulder, before sauntering off to his cabin to gather up the little of his stuff that was still on board. He would go to live with his French friends, get construction work, no problem (he had no doubt been on the brink of doing so anyway).

Gene said fine, whatever, he was going to Paudy's, he'd be back later. 'If you need me to stay on the boat, fine, Elizabeth, *fine*, but I start tomorrow. I'm taking today off.' Elizabeth, glaring at his departing back, said nothing as Gene stormed out of the room. She could not afford to be rid of him yet, and what else was he going to do? For now, they were stuck with one another.

I, on the other hand, had nowhere to go but also could not stay. I could not commit to being on the boat 24/7. I really would be lost. I'd lose what was left of my sanity, and then I'd probably die – from the cold, madness, or in the dead of night, by Elizabeth's deranged hand. I had to choose my words carefully.

'Elizabeth, I understand you're upset, and that you feel we've disappointed you –'

'You especially!' she said turning on me, eyes ablaze. 'You *especially* disappointed me!'

I blinked, stunned.

'I don't know how things work back in *Ireland*,' she continued, 'but here things don't just happen magically, with *fairies* and *elves*, or *leprechauns*, or whatever it is you have over there! Here, in *America*, when you *believe* in something, when God's good will and graces are behind you, like wind in your sails, when you really want to do something *important*, like what we're trying to do here, on *Ye Olde Americana*, here in the *United States of America*, you work hard, and you do it! Now, maybe that's not what you think you do, back in *Ireland*, but here, by golly, that's what we do – we work hard, and we make our dreams come true, *yes we do!*'

I didn't know how to respond. She was pointing at me across the table, doggedly. Her eyes, honed in on me, were filled with a raging energy.

'Right, okay … emm, well, okay.' I didn't want to argue with her or to defend myself. I was worn out, and scared, and cold, and besides, there was no point. 'Right, well … I'm sorry you feel I let you down, Elizabeth … truly I am … that wasn't my intention … I guess I hadn't realized the, uh, dedication the job entailed –'

She cut me off, erupting: 'Job? *Job*? You see *Ye Olde Americana* as a *job*?!' (Not even, I thought, but dared not say. For jobs, you get paid.) '*Ye Olde Americana* is a *mission*! This is not a job – it's a *vocation*! From *God*! A task set by God for those whom he loves and treasures on his good, green *earth*! This is a holy *vessel* – *Ye Olde Americana* is a part of God's plan to save the earth, the good people whom live all across the entire planet – don't you *get it*?!'

She'd stood up fully as she spoke, her chair legs screeching against the wooden floorboards. Unconsciously, I'd stood too, preparing to be struck, or to run. I started backing out: 'Okay Elizabeth, well, good luck with it, really, but I'm gonna have to … eh, go, I think.'

'Of course you are,' she grimaced, collapsing back down into her chair. 'And good *riddance*!' she screamed through the door, as I fled to my cabin.

As quickly as possible, my hands shaking in cold and shock, I gathered and packed up my things, flinging them into my Nana's old and wrecked St Bernard's suitcase. Trying to breathe evenly, to think calmly, I silently marvelled to think of how I'd only unpacked it three weeks before. Well, I thought, trying to ignore my throbbing heart – I'd wanted to see the world differently, to become different. In that way, I reasoned, it had all gone pretty well.

I called Bobby to tell him what had happened and he collected me at the dock in his truck. He raced all the way back from work on a site all the way up in Queens. He let me crash in his spare room, and cursed Elizabeth and the boat repeatedly. 'I knew it was a fucking cult!' he said, pacing before me as I sipped a beer on his couch. He was enraged on my behalf, his arms flailing and eyes wide. I didn't know what to think. Had it been a cult? Maybe. All I knew was that I was very, very tired.

I managed to find a friend of a friend living in Greenpoint who had a fold-out couch I could crash on, at least until I could get myself back to Ireland. I didn't see anyone from *Ye Olde Americana*, or Paudy's, or Bobby again. I ignored his texts and didn't answer his calls. I wanted to forget the whole thing. I was barely able to think about it, let alone talk about it. Better to look forward, to push it from my mind, consider it a blip – to make it, at most, a short and funny anecdote, only mentioned after at least three drinks, and with all the terrifying, menacing and lonesome bits skilfully omitted.

It was only recently that I got back in touch with Bobby. All in all, I'd treated him terribly. I'd taken his kindness and run with it. I'd been desperately in need, but that didn't excuse my selfishness. Through his construction company, I tracked him down and found a work email address. I sent him a long heartfelt message, sitting at my old desk in my father's house in Wicklow, the dog beside me. I told him that I really didn't know what I would have done without him. I told him that things could have gotten pretty ugly for me, had he not swooped into my life just then and rescued me. He wrote back almost immediately, and said it was good to hear from me, he was glad I was well and safely back at home. He said he'd wondered what had happened to me, that yeah, he had to admit, he'd been pretty hurt, that he'd wanted to take me to Nobu, to meet some cool people he knew in the film world, but that yeah, of course, he'd been glad to help. He said I was a sweet girl and had clearly needed saving.

He also told me that a couple of months after I left, when the weather had started to improve, Gene had returned to the boat one night after Paudy's to find all his belongings in a pile out on the dock. Attached to one of his suitcases with a red ribbon was a note from Elizabeth, written in florid cursive, telling him that he was a drunk and a scoundrel, a devil in man's clothing, and that she'd filed a restraining order against him. He was no longer legally welcome within three miles of her, Jasper, their upstate property, or *Ye Olde Americana*. Gene had slept in the back of Paudy's that night on a blow-up mattress under some blankets, and left on a Greyhound the next morning. Maybe back to Boston, maybe elsewhere, Bobby didn't know.

I heard nothing from Elizabeth, and didn't expect to, until about a week ago, when I received a friend request from her on Facebook. I couldn't believe my eyes. I had almost forgotten – or forgotten as anything more than a funny story mixed with a bad dream, like some movie I'd seen once – the very existence of Elizabeth, let alone *Ye Olde Americana*. I glanced at her profile. There she was, ribbons and all, smiling enthusiastically. I scrolled down. There were lots of pictures of the sausage dogs, and lots of long, long posts. Some about *Ye Olde Americana* – a plea for volunteers, for funding, as well as messages of hope, her dreams of its future. Some about God, how he is watching over us, taking care of us, about how he is all we need, as a light in dark times, as a compass for our souls. There were also several posts about Donald Trump (referred to exclusively as 'our good, God-fearing Saviour President Trump') – about how he was exactly what America needed, how he was a ray of good and golden light, how he would surely see them through and how he, with the help of *Ye Olde Americana*, would undoubtedly continue to 'Make America Great Again!'

Her profile page background was a photo of a Trump election banner draped across the boat, with her standing on deck above it, thumbs high in the air, decked out in red, white and blue. I wondered if it had been Jasper or maybe some new volunteer who, embarrassed, had stood on the dock to take it for her. I shook my head slightly, momentarily saddened, declined her friend request, blocked her, and got back to my coffee and the book I'd been reading.

Once, as we polished the brass piping in the bathroom, Elizabeth had told me about her childhood. She came from the South, she said. Her accent thickened as she talked about it. She still called her father 'Daddy' and clearly idolized him. It seemed he'd been from big Southern orange and lemon grove money. She told me that she and her brother would make orange juice and lemonade and sell it for two cents a cup on the dusty roadside. Her mother had educated them until high school, when they'd both been sent away for private educations.

'Oh golly no, Daddy would never have let us go to school with those local children, my oh my, no – why, they, well … they had no, well … they were the children of our labourers, *see*? I mean, we could barely understand what they were saying half the time, honestly, even Daddy! And well, with their, with their – well, it was hard to tell how dirty they were, from looking, but the smell sometimes, if you got up close – my! No, no, Daddy would never have allowed it ...'

She herself had grown up on a large property a few miles outside of town; a place that conjured up images in my mind of lush groves, orchards, neatly kept lawns surrounded by rolling meadows – someplace from a film or a fairytale. She said every year a big howling April storm would pass through the local town. She said there was an old bowling alley that had a roof in the shape of butterfly wings, going down in the middle instead of up, and she said – laughing a little too much, bending her tiny frame over as though momentarily overcome with the memory – that every year when the storm came, the roof would fly off and end up somewhere over in the mountains, and every year when the storm ended they'd build a new one just the same.

'It was pink!' she said girlishly. 'And once the storm had blown itself out Daddy would drive us into town in the Cadillac – oh yes, he had a *beautiful* Cadillac, white, with white leather seats, and boy, were you in trouble if you scuffed those seats! – and we'd go to see it, see them rebuilding it just the same, and boy oh boy, we'd laugh so hard! There it was again, with the roof blown clean off! And there they'd go again, putting on a new one just the same! Well now, if they weren't just the stupidest people I ever saw in my life!'

She buckled over laughing, leaning on the enamel bathtub for support. Behind her, the mother cat sidled in through the door, propped open so as not to slam as the boat shifted. She stared at Elizabeth and me, sat down and mewed. Elizabeth righted herself, glanced at the cat, and then turned back to me, wiping non-existent tears of laughter from her dry eyes with the back of her hands, careful not to let the rag covered in dirt and brass polish touch her smiling face. 'Golly, that sure was funny.' She looked at me wide-eyed, awaiting confirmation.

'Yeah, I bet ... sounds funny.' I forced a smile, and with it, Elizabeth sighed, then bent down to return to work.

It was impossible for me, in my early twenties – all future, all potential, all still yet to be done – to remotely comprehend all that this woman had lost. It was a Friday and, as she'd spoken, in the back of my mind, I'd pictured the drinks I would order out somewhere (anywhere, everywhere) later that evening. I'd dreamt up all the people I might meet, wrapped in expensive-looking scarves, perched on bar stools, with beautiful hands or dark eyes or inner ears that curled gently toward me, like the softly worn folds of a seashell.

In that moment, with Manhattan in my thoughts and her voice washing over me, it had suddenly felt (and, in many ways, was true) as though my whole life could be changed in a night; could be transformed, realized, ignited by any passing chance. It had felt as though she – this ridiculous, racist old woman, with only her memories to sustain her – was wasting my time, and I was anxious to be gone. In my ignorance, I had assumed Elizabeth's story had nothing to teach me.

Just before we finished up, as I was growing more and more anxious to be gone, Elizabeth told me, quietly, that she could have married a man who was a big senator now – highly successful. But she hadn't. Taken aback, I paused to look at her. He'd proposed after a dance, just before he'd left for Harvard, and she had turned him down. He'd had a ring and everything, she said; beautiful, with a big white diamond – it had been his grandmother's. But he was long married now, and retired, living on a big ranch in West Virginia. He'd had six children in all, she told me. Four sons and two daughters, whom she'd seen smiling arm in arm in photos on his official Facebook page. All, I imagined, blonde; all with gleaming, evenly proportioned teeth; 'all so *handsome*,' Elizabeth sighed. He'd grown old now, she supposed, and somehow, without noticing, she must've grown old too. 'I guess it always happens like that,' she muttered, trying and failing to smile to herself, 'but, still, it sure is a surprise, when it does ...'

She told me all this in a voice barely louder than a whisper, squatting down and rubbing hard with the last of her might, the final section of the piping that ran along the wall by the floor behind the toilet. She had lost her Scarlett O'Hara exuberance. She seemed, suddenly, to have grown weary. Behind her, the mother cat mewed again, bored-sounding, and slowly waddled from the room. It was midweek, so Jasper was upstate in his studio. We were both wearing our coats because the boat was so cold. I stared down at her. I was struck dumb by the admission. Silently, I watched her blue-black hair, tied in lime green ribbons (Wednesday's colour), coming loose and falling askew with the motion of her cleaning. I wondered for the first time if she'd ever wanted children, or grandchildren, or if maybe she'd wanted to end up living in a house, or just somewhere warm, more like the South. If, in fact, she'd ever wanted something – anything, *everything* – else. Like I did.

'Whatever happened to the citrus groves?' I asked finally.

'Oh gee, all gone, all sold, when the business went bust ... probably a mall now!'

Her tone had changed, a forced lightening, as though only at the sound of my voice did she remember the fact of my existence, there beside her, listening. I asked nothing else. Her coat sleeves were rolled up, and I could see the muscles tense as her thin arm moved back and forth. The skin was papery and mottled, with small spots of pale brown and clearly discernible lines of thin blue veins.

'There!' she said, stopping suddenly. 'Beautiful!' Elizabeth was freakishly strong, and had done a far better job of cleaning, scrubbing and polishing than I had. But then, I didn't have to care about it. This boat, permanently moored, cold, damp and lilting, was Elizabeth's home. Whatever else, I reminded myself, gathering up the cleaning things – I was still young, still untethered. I had other places yet to find, other people to meet. Other, maybe better, ways to be.

Where Do You Lay Your Head
This Night?

The scraped-out silent hum of the city this night. Traffic far off, somewhere been to somewhere gone. Endless street lights, electrical appliances, lit-up overnight shop signs, humming, humming. Men standing motionless behind counters, waiting, still waiting, and church bells there, a bell for every hour – one, two, thr– ...

A truck manoeuvres the narrow roads across the way, heave and chug. A woman's clip-clopping feet coming, come, fading, following her for the rest of the long night but for me to silence fading, and the low groan of a bus turning at the corner there, tightly turning, its last round of the day.

The city is empty and full, stretching thin and already broken. A trickling out. Yellow air sneaks in under the bedroom blind, carrying a faint scent of burnt meat. A siren, gone almost before it arrived, soft and ghostly, and the mutter of two old women's voices passing slow below, the sound of a wheeled bag in tow, the day's few bits of shopping.

All out there now, and still the place holds nothing.

The graves in Glasnevin, the tombs beneath Christchurch, all the vacant office buildings, screens aglow. The water in the canals flowing, minnows darting, the swans asleep in nests hidden amongst the rushes on the banks. Foxes' tails flit thickly around the corners of alleyways before leaping soundless through gaps in back-garden gates, suddenly caught still, ears pricked, head low – the hum through glass of television, muffled voices lilting up and the bursting hiss of applause, undersea waves of coloured light across the lawn – deeming safe, nothing there, nose down quick to sniff the dirt before padding softly on.

All the burnt-up men, their skin puckering in folds like crisp packets on the fire, bulbous rose noses, only just balanced on the leather stools gone faded where they – from all the times before, their ashen, creaking bones – count out the last few euros, while the heartbroken, full of prayers or this-time-I-mean-it resolutions, thump down their salt-wet pillows, searching for hollows in which to sleep. Someone being born now a wrenching screech in Holles Street. Someone else home, the dark room, soft sheets, soft breathing, in Crumlin or Ballsbridge or Stoneybatter, dying, soft a fade the dying.

A dog growls in its sleep, legs twitching.

A girl somewhere out there now, not too far from here, with a free gaff for the week, Tallaght or Donnybrook or Rathmines, or a few girls maybe, in all three: the tear of her hymen and seep of blood onto childhood sheets. This'll be the night that she looks back on, a black or golden thing.

The cans and the bottles flung into the Liffey, smokes bummed or rolled all through Temple Bar. Tourists silent lying side by side impossible to sleep; the whoops and howls of the merrymakers, the pipes gurgling, a flush or the TV on next door, heard through the walls of the old Georgian house hotels, nothing at all like the quiet hum of home.

A bulb blows with a bang in a Vietnamese restaurant on Parnell Street. Everybody ducks.

Half a mile over again another bang as a man crashes to the floor. He is in the kitchen alone; the oxblood tiles are hard, he is frothing now, his body is convulsing and there is nobody else due home. As his body settles and stills, the kettle, frothing too, clicks itself to off.

The statue of Wilde lounges in sickly colours atop a rock as some young skin passes thinking who the fuck is he to me, fucking faggot anyway, full of frustration and rage at all that growing up is turning out to be, who later etches 'up d ra!' on the back of a cubicle door even though he's not really sure who they are and what it means – freedom, violence, history – but wanting anyone, anything, to pour all this dull and endless being into.

Someone injects their boyfriend first, then themselves, in a back alley not far from Connolly Station as the last of the DARTs trickle in, the Irish Rail lads bantering, keen to get off home, or not; stalling, a pint maybe, quick one at least, while small quiet men from the Philippines haul themselves up from the tracks to clean the coffee and cans and wrappers and whatever other dregs from the empty carriages, wiping away today to be ready for fresh tomorrows. One man, thirty-six, with three daughters and a wife back home in need of money, leaning down for an empty cigarette packet reads, in black and bubbled letters burnt into the carriage wall: 'J&F 4evr'. That's funny, he thinks, in a language I don't know – they're our initials too.

A runaway sits hunched on a bench along the boardwalk, a turmoil of pain and fear and gaping future, looking up from his silently flashing phone to watch along the far side as a woman he doesn't realize is a prostitute hurries by, clip clop those heels still following, heading for

41

a hotel bar not far from the Ha'penny (she calls herself an 'entrepreneur' when asked by her grandmother back in Montenegro, or by those she might actually want to love).

Further inland, seagulls are perched along the walls of the river near Heuston. The tide is low. Just discernible in the light of the lamps, each adorned with silver curling shamrock plants, is the river bed, bulging black and slimy with generations of waste: trolleys, buggies, car tyres, a chest of drawers. Here, the water barely gurgles.

Two lovers walk melting into one another across the bridge back along the tramlines, knees buckling in bleary want, towards a terraced house five minutes from the Lighthouse, where they'll find the air inside cold enough to see their breath plume hotly white together.

The paintings in IMMA hang still, faintly lit in green and blue security lights. Somewhere, the water of a toilet with the button pressed down won't stop flushing.

A man calls his brother in Canada – he'll be home from work there now – to tell him he has bowel cancer. Lying in bed, no music playing, a couple who got engaged in Stephen's Green earlier today scroll through their respective Instagram and Facebook likes.

Somewhere below my window to the left I can just make out a woman's voice softly calling '… *baby … baby … baby …*' when, at the pub on the corner to the right, men erupt out for a cigarette and shatter the night with raucous laughing – in my mind I see them, glasses lifted to their chests, buttons up and stances wide, tight definite gestures mouth to side, mouth to side, the smoke in white clouds rising, all the city brewing for them, all ready to go, while I sit here still, quiet, straining forward but not quite catching the outlines of their words. Their voices disappear inside, burst of sound as the door is briefly opened and I, sinking back into humming silence, wonder again how many steps your body is now from mine, and what you might be doing.

'… baby … baby … baby …'

Foley and the Wolf

On my first morning up there, I woke in a darkened, cold and filthy room, completely naked except for baby-pink Penneys knickers, with a hairy arm flung across my waist and a sticky substance on my chin that I initially took to be smeared food. I got up and tried to wash it off over the sink, which was covered in black smatters of mildew and frothy hairs, before realizing that what I was feeling was not marmalade or jelly, but an absence of skin. It stung and I realized I was shivering, exposed and barefoot on grey (once-white) tiles.

My godmother had called me back in May and asked would I be up for doing it. She and her girlfriend Maria, an Italian conceptual artist, were heading off to the Caribbean, island-hopping with an inheritance windfall. They just needed someone to feed the chickens, water the vegetables. Someone at a loose end. She said their part of Donegal would be lovely that time of year; the trees changing and the blackberries out and all.

I didn't need convincing. I'd just returned from an abortive stint living in Berlin, during which I'd become violently infatuated with a charming Lithuanian. Between bouts of vigorous, sweat-soaked sex on increasingly grubby sheets, we sat in his tiny kitchen in the middle of Kreuzberg, sirens wailing through whirling snow down below, smoking weed, eating carbs and drinking whiskeys neat. Walking hand-in-hand along the icy canals, we marvelled aloud at all the great things we were going to do; all the Art we'd make together. But it wasn't long before it all wore off. We gained weight, we barely slept. Somehow, between the sex, drinking and getting high, none of our big plans were coming to fruition. Soon we each grew to hate the lonesome, unwashed stench of the other, and so one morning, with surprisingly little difficulty and lots of expense, I booked a last-minute flight and left. I found myself, therefore, very much at a loose end.

I received the letter informing me of my results and upcoming procedure *and* saw a rat in work on my last day in Dublin before driving up. It was late September and uncomfortably warm. I'd worn my denim jacket to work and was sweaty and red-cheeked by the time I reached the café's heavy black shutter. I fumbled for the keys, dying for a piss, jigging around with my thighs clamped together. The lads from the tattoo studio above were smoking in the entrance next to mine. Smirking, they watched me struggle, leaning against the doorframe with their backward-facing caps, gaping ear-spacers and patterned arms and necks.

I'd woken up to the letter lying there in the hall, the dog wriggling excitedly in my way as I bent down to retrieve it. I read it through twice as the ring under the porridge pot reddened, and the first few surface bubbles began to rise through the gloop, bursting pockets of hot air. *Dear Ms* — ... *cervical* ... *cells* ... *growth pattern* ... *cancerous* ... *removal* ... *5 November, Holles Street, 10 a.m. Yours sincerely, Squiggle.*

I was due to come back from minding my godmother's house on the fourth of November. That's lucky, I thought, refolding the letter back into the envelope and into my dressing-gown pocket, out of sight.

The hairy arm that I'd found flung across my bare goose-pimpled stomach turned out to belong to a man called Foley. I'd met him the night before, although apparently we'd played together as kids when I visited Donegal with my father. He remembered and I didn't, but then, he was a few years older. We discovered later, in the kitchen-cum-living room, that the aforementioned arm sported grazes all up the length of it.

'Maybe you beat me up!' I joked from the table, attempting to tie my boots with stiff fingers. It hurt my chin each time I spoke, flexing the fibres of raw flesh. I kept forgetting, and wincing.

'Huhuh, yeah, maybe,' he said, hunching over as he filled his chipped Maltesers cup with four spoons of white sugar straight from the bag, the pot beginning to hiss quietly on the hob at his elbow.

I would discover over the coming weeks that Foley was fanatical about three things: weed, coffee and wildly implausible conspiracy theories regarding Jewish business dealings. I told him it was racist but he shrugged it off, saying it wasn't about the Jews, it was about the money; the people who had it all and ran everything just *happened* to be Jewish. He lived alone except for his pet wolf, Mika, who spent weekend nights such as this one with his parents, a few doors down.

'What d'you mean a *wolf*?' I'd asked him the night before, stumbling home. 'Like, a husky?'

'No, no, she's the real deal. A lad over the way breeds 'em ... but she's harmless like, mostly.'

Foley had black eyes and sallow skin. He was gaunt to the point of skeletal and wore baggy, unwashed clothes.

'Seventy euro, three-bed, not bad,' he said, when I asked about the house. The rent was so low, it transpired, because the place was technically not fit for human habitation. Asbestos in the ceiling, damp in the walls, icy cold everywhere in between, regardless of the weather. Whenever the uninhabitable conditions were raised, by me or by others, he just repeated his motto: 'Seventy euro, three-bed, not bad now, not bad.'

I'd come to write. That's what I told myself, and what I'd told many other people – usually family friends with children my age who'd studied medicine or law and were now buying first houses, or (intentionally) pregnant. Those well-meaning people with Orla Kiely bags and golf handicaps, who asked me with tilted heads what was I up to at the moment, what was I doing with myself: 'Oh, I'm heading up to Donegal for a few weeks, to write …' In reality, house-sitting in Donegal wasn't much, but at least it was a bookmark in the swirling blue nothing of my life; a definite shape to aim towards.

When I found myself back in Ireland after Berlin at the tail-end of spring, I was lost. Another relationship over, another possible future burned. I started at the café within days of landing – a good word put in with the boss by my dad, an old school friend (I hadn't actually been looking for work). Within two weeks, I had my first unpromising doctor's visit, and soon after, the first of many letters. *Irregular … will need to come back in … colposcopy.*

'Probably nothing!' the nurse said lightly on the phone, clearly doing something else that required attention while talking to me. Six weeks in the country sounded like just what I needed. It also meant that I could treat the summer as downtime until I got there.

A waiting-room summer; time put aside for mental magazine-flicking.

I decided that once I got to Donegal I'd sort my shit out. There'd be no drinking, no smoking, no anything, unless it was green and wholesome and tasted about as appetizing as the dirt it had been pulled out of only the day before. Once I got to Donegal, I'd go for a run every single morning down dappled, golden-leaved laneways, cows and birds and deer and rabbits all egging me on with earnest, happy eyes: 'You can do it! You look *wonderful!*' I'd run, then write the novel in the afternoon, and then maybe some yoga? Then a good uninterrupted night's sleep. The Atlantic air alone would set the connections whizzing through my brain in high-def mode. It'd all be sorted; my life would really start to take shape and come together, once I got up to Donegal.

Foley was footering around with his internet-ordered milk-frothing device (eight euro plus four for P&P, direct from Denmark): 'It's actually amazin' like, wait 'til yeh see, just like a café ...'

I could tell I made him nervous, but I enjoyed the power of it, and so didn't go out of my way to reassure him that it was okay, to take his time: 'Mmm, right okay ...'

He sprayed hot angry milk out of the pot onto the counter, splattering his top. I said nothing. He cursed, looked around, picked up a dirty kitchen cloth and wiped his front, before throwing it into the plate-filled sink with a clatter. I tapped my foot twice in my seat behind him, pushed air out in a sharp hoosh through my nose, and glanced around. I was trying very hard not to run my fingers back and forth across my chin. There was something wonderfully satisfying about the sharp, stinging pain of it.

*

I'd been in Donegal for less than ten minutes when my godmother suggested taking a dab. She didn't look how I'd expected. It was a small shock when she opened the door, the mental image built over years contradicted by the physical reality. Shorter, older, broader. I had remembered her as one of those integrated outsiders you get on the fringes of towns in the country; all flowing skirts and folds of colourful material, with heavy creative involvement in summer fêtes in the primary school car park and fundraising tea mornings, without going so far as breaking out tarot cards at a session or pontificating in pub corners about the effects of the moon. She had friends all over the world to whom she sent secular Christmas cards saying 'Happy Holidays!' or 'Season's Greetings!' She'd been briefly married to a man in her twenties, and later said it was seeing all the women on the beaches in Sardinia on their honeymoon that had made her realize she was a lesbian. Since then, she'd had a string of exotic, artistic-seeming girlfriends, all initially attracted to her idyllic home on the windswept tip of the Irish countryside. They came and went with the Atlantic tides, but she stayed put, and never seemed too distraught when things ended. She'd been with Maria two years. In my mind she'd always had sparkling black-brown eyes, chestnut hair and glowing, sallow skin.

But she looked different now. She wore jeans and a fleece hoodie that (she later told me with great pride, holding her sleeve toward me to feel) came from that central trough in Aldi, where they stock miscellaneous unbranded items like coffee-makers and non-stick woks, two-man tents and reinforced running socks. Her eyes were tired, almost matte, as was her skin, which reminded me somehow of sliced roast beef, left on display under heat lamps. She seemed excited to see me though, restless from waiting on her own, watering house plants and half-watching *Grand Designs* reruns all afternoon. She kept hovering around me, her movements erratic, flitting back and forth into my orbit. I could see the mischief in her fidgeting hands, slipping in and out of fleecy pockets. I'd been in the middle of filling the kettle to make tea, but then when she offered, I said sure, MDMA sounded grand instead.

She ran up to her and Maria's room and brought down a neat little folded-cardboard packet full of crystals from their knicker drawer. I filled two glasses with water while she smoothed some crystals into dust with the rolling pin between two sheets of baking parchment. We were standing with arms crossed before the fire, bobbing from side to side, eyes wide and catching up on family gossip at high speed, when Maria walked in. She raised her eyebrows at us and grinned. 'Pub?'

Sitting at Foley's table, awaiting my wondrous coffee, I tried to recall the night before. Heading out with my godmother and Maria, doing up the buttons of my coat in the porch, I remembered reasoning that I could start with all the health and productivity stuff the next day – the travel day didn't count! I was restless, itching for a pint after the long drive with only my thoughts, the dog, and two skipping CDs for company. I bought and drank a can of Druids when we stopped at the garage on the drive into town. The effects of the dab I'd had in the house were already fading and, as always, I wanted more. The sun was just setting over the Atlantic to my left, and I counted two flattened rabbit carcasses and one heaped badger along the narrow hard-shoulder as we sped by.

I remembered my godmother pointing out Foley to me the moment we entered. He was the town's premier drug dealer, the go-to guy if I was in need. Not that it would've been hard to guess. His eyes were red, he mumbled his words, chuckled just before the punchlines of jokes and, up close, there was the fragrant reek of weed from his endless, burrowing trouser pockets.

I vaguely remembered squeezing my way into a vacated seat on the bench beside him as soon as it became free. Introductions, little friendly explanations. 'Drink?' A smoke shared, another and another and then, skins loosening, comfortable in blurring warm proximity, a meaningful glance after a nose rubbed self-consciously between thumb and forefinger on his way back from a trip to the bathroom, pupils dilated. Finally, under thickened darkness, humming of bulbs and warmth of chatter surrounding, the beautiful little baggy, slipped between palms.

Ah, right, yes. There it was – the moment that led me to this one here: cold, confused and lacking chin-skin, in a damp-smelling house, on the outskirts of a small town, on my first morning living on the northernmost chunk of rock on the whole damn island.

The rat I saw in work was small, but identifiable as a rat rather than a mouse by his grotty damp fur, pointy nose, long tail and considerable claws. He tip-tapped across the kitchen tiles to my left as I stood hiding behind the cake display, reading my book. He might as well have had an eye-patch, this rat. I stared down vacantly, still more in the book's world than this one, as he dodged under the fridge. A girl, lounging over a coffee and swiping idly on her phone in the back corner, yelped and leapt out of her seat as he scuttled by her foot, my attempts to subtly shoo him out the door with the broom having gone awry. I gave her the coffee for free, apologizing unconvincingly as she fled, locked the doors behind her, and called the boss.

'A *what*? How the *fuck* did a rat get in?'

'Eh, the front door, I guess?'

He sighed pointedly. He'd be over in an hour or so, he'd bring traps and poison, and we could stay late into the night and kill it. At least there'd be no more customers, I thought. I popped on Frank Ocean, picked my book back up in one hand, a fork in the other, and started into the last few slices of carrot cake. Now that I had precancerous cells festering away in my cervix, I reasoned, I had every right to get as fat as I liked.

The morning after we'd staked the rat out, killed it, and lain small mountains of poison in every nook of the café for any of its friends and family, I left Dublin. I waved *byeee* to my dad, who'd followed me out to the path in his pyjamas, barefoot and frowning, pulling rogue leaves from the hedge and kicking neighbours' litter away to distract himself.

'Fucking kids, little cunts,' he cursed, catching his toe in a Tayto packet. The dog peered out the back window mournfully, ears pushed back and tail rigid, as though I was taking him off to a quiet field to be shot.

'Ah here, I'm not that bad, Max,' I said into the rearview mirror, not quite convincing myself either. He didn't even turn around to look at me.

The drive took six hours, with just one pit stop for Max and me to relieve ourselves (on grass and in toilet, respectively), in one of those big shiny Applegreen garages that I really, really love. I bought a wrap, chicken something, and stole a green 'raw' juice that promised to *NR-gize!* me by slipping it into the inside pocket of my burgundy coat. I didn't really want it and had enough money for it, but I'd grown accustomed to stealing. It made me feel like I was winning at something.

Until getting that letter, nothing bad had ever happened to me. Not *really*. I could walk, I had all my fingers. I had 20/20 vision, I'd never broken a bone. I'd never in my life been on antibiotics or even gotten a filling. I used to say, when people marvelled, that I actually was Bruce Willis in the film *Unbreakable*. I'd been in the Twin Towers a week to the day before 9/11. There's even a novelty photo of me, my little chubby hamster face smiling out merrily from dishevelled eleven-year-old hair, standing as a King Kong-esque giant with one pink Dunnes runner propped up on the left tower, hands on my fanny-packed hips. (My father had hidden the picture in the attic afterwards.) I was healthy, had friends, did well in school, got on with my family, could bake a mean cake. It was all a bit too lucky. A bit too *wholesome*. If the structure of all tear-jerking American films from the eighties and nineties were to be believed, it was clear that someone like me was destined for tragedy. And now, as far as I could see, it was coming. Precancer would inevitably lead to cancer, and then I'd die. And that was that.

I'd lit a joint the moment I got out on the open road, reasoning all the good health could start once I actually arrived in Donegal. But even lightly stoned, with the low autumn sun breaking through herds of showering clouds (fleeting patches of golden warmth shining over the road, the fields, the slowly erupting mountains of the north), I still couldn't ever quite forget that letter: still folded, untouched, lying in wait, back at home in my dressing-gown pocket.

*

There was a drooping Jamaican flag hanging on the wood-panelled wall of Foley's kitchen-cum-living room, a set of bongos in the middle of the floor, a huge black computer on a desk in the far corner, three flaking guitars propped against the couches (two, I noticed, with missing strings), and a truly enormous lunchbox of weed surrounded by Rizla packets, tobacco pouches and lip-smeared glasses of varying sizes on the table beside me. When I leaned my elbow on its surface, the wool fibres of my jumper adhered slightly to an unidentifiable spill that had left a thin gleaming pattern across the black Formica. I decided, upon reflection, that I didn't want any coffee and stood up suddenly to go.

I saw, gathering up my wildly strewn things from amongst the general squalor, that there were short, wispy white wolf hairs coating every surface. It would transpire that Mika was so strong and energetic that Foley had to wear roller skates when exercising her, and fell regularly doing so. He could be seen late at night, whipping along through the beam of a car's headlights on the black outskirts of the town, hunched over with knees bent, giant earphones stretched over his curly black hair. He had put videos of it up on YouTube (I still have no idea how he managed to hold his phone in place to film them) that were long and of poor quality. It was difficult at first to understand their purpose or merit. Later, though, I would watch them with him while on mushrooms and be utterly mesmerized.

The house was very quiet and the damp felt thick and green in my lungs. I got the feeling that being there for any length of time would make a person die sooner. (In spite of this, I would frequently find myself back there with

Foley over the coming weeks, curled up on the couch or passed out in the bed.)

If anyone needed anything from Foley they just popped in. Otherwise, they knew they'd find him in the pub. I couldn't understand at first how he didn't get caught, but then the Garda station in town only opened from 10 a.m. to 2 p.m. five days a week, and two of the six local gardaí were Foley's cousins. Any other time you might need police assistance, you had to call the station in the big town, about an hour's drive away along the winding country roads.

I needed to hitchhike to get back in time to bring my godmother and Maria to the airport. Foley was thirty-one and insisted he could drive, but didn't have a licence or a car. You could walk into town from his place, but my godmother lived seven miles out the road. As I retreated down his front garden, he gestured vague directions to me from the vampiric safety of his hallway, and said he'd call me later after he took a nap, if I liked. I wasn't keen, still believing at that point – despite this rocky start – that I might manage to stick to my clean-living intentions. I pretended I hadn't quite heard him and, banging shut the gate behind me, waved back at him with a big blank smile.

It was bright and crisp, the kind of morning on which, under different circumstances, I probably could've achieved something. Everything was new and strange and barely held together. Had the sky always been that *blue*? My godmother and Maria had their bags ready to go in the car, engine running, when I lurched in from the road. Their lips were pursed. 'What the *fuck* happened to your *chin*?'

When I arrived back from the airport, weak and mentally whitewashed by the effort of the drive, the house was emptier and more still than I'd anticipated. Their breakfast dishes lay neatly drying on the silver draining board by the sink. I stood staring at them. Six weeks, just me, the dog, the chickens. This was what I'd been waiting for. The house was completely silent except for the hiss of water passing through pipes, the hum of electronics. Without thinking I put my fingers to my chin and dug my nails, hard, into the sticky exposed surface of my wound.

My chin hadn't fully healed by the night we ended up in the Dutch yoga instructor's kitchen at the very top of the mountain, snorting coke and eating his freshly chopped pineapple. It was so fucking juicy, that pineapple, it got everywhere. It was on special in SuperValu that week: 'two euros only!' The Dutch yoga instructor had chopped it with a very long, very sharp kitchen knife on the counter while Foley measured out neat lines on a mirror with his Visa Debit card. I played Solange videos on YouTube and danced alone around the kitchen, smiling and chewing. The juices were ruining the make-up covering the thick dark scabs on my chin. It should have been completely gone by then but I kept absent-mindedly picking at it while watching TV by the spluttering fire at night.

I couldn't get it to light the way my godmother did, and so I'd grown used to wearing three jumpers around the house in the evenings, shoulders tight up around my ears and hands cupped inside the sleeves. My system was that I kept the TV on downstairs as I went up to bed, all lights blazing, to turn on the second TV in the bedroom, before going back down to turn the first one off; then I would work my way upwards, flicking switches, so that there would never be full silence or darkness, and so I'd never have to check shadowy corners or listen out for the thuds and creaks of all the murderers I was sure were watching me through the reflective windows and waiting with knives raised behind doors in all the spare rooms.

At that point I didn't care if they could see the scabs anyway. I was in bliss, dancing around with the coke running electric through me. It was so juicy! I really couldn't believe it; had a pineapple honestly *ever* been this juicy before? Besides, I was the only woman there, and they were only the Dutch yoga instructor, chopping industriously (these northern Europeans!), Foley, and a melancholy local called Ray who kept going on and on loudly about how it was 'absolutely grand' with him that his Russian girlfriend had decided to extend her holiday in Turkey by another two weeks, leaving him home alone.

His loneliness was sickening and I wanted him to shut the fuck up, for fear of it infecting me, but I acted vaguely sympathetic to seem the kind-hearted female. Foley had whispered to me in the back of the car on the way there, sitting close and giggling, our fingers interlaced, that I was his dream woman and that I should move up here and live with him. I'd laughed, a loud bursting guffaw, the inside of my nose already numbed and that metallic taste coating the back of my throat, and then held his face between my hands and kissed him to soften the blow. His teeth were black around the edges but I didn't mind, and he was a surprisingly tender kisser, his lips soft and tentative. Now his black pits-for-eyes were watching my every move from his quiet perch on a kitchen stool in the corner as he licked the seam of a joint, rolled to mellow out the edges from all the coke coursing through him. He reminded me of a spider watching a little silly fly buzzing around, perilously close to but not yet in its web. I just kept dancing, swaying slow, because I knew he was staring but didn't mind. If anything, I liked it.

Foley had met me outside the pub earlier in the night. He'd offered to pay for me to get a taxi into town, and so I'd taken a dab at the kitchen table and let him order one for me. While waiting, I'd gotten hot and bothered and overzealous, and emailed a few people. This included sending a link to a bad music video that seemed *genius* in that moment to my ex in Berlin (to whom I hadn't spoken since leaving) without any explanation or message attached. I carefully constructed (eyes unblinking, both hands holding the phone directly before my face) the text: 'Hi there, hope all's well. All good here, talk to you tomorrow. Lots of love, x' and sent it to my dad, to ensure I wouldn't have to talk to him later in the evening while off my face. I then blasted my hand-crafted 'Hot B*tch' playlist through Maria's Bose speakers and stood up on the cold fireplace, studying the dilation of my pupils in the mirror and muttering quickly to myself and giggling, until the call from Foley came through that my taxi was outside.

The pub was the one we'd been in on my first night, and it was called The Harbour Bar, but everyone in town knew it as Stone's. It never got tourists and had the air of being barely legal. It consisted of a single room with a bar along the back wall, a frosted-glass window at the front that somehow let in no light whatsoever, a few stools, a bench over to the left and a modern flashing jukebox in the corner. A too-big pool table took up all the space in the middle of the room. The women sat along the bench to the side, chatting amongst themselves or watching the men win and lose; except for the more outgoing ones, with lower-cut tops and blue eyeshadow, who stood at the bar, chatting and laughing with the lads. The men lined up their two-euro coins on the table and the winner could stay on for three games max.

As the night went on, people started openly smoking inside, no longer arsed with standing over by the door or with a hand hanging half-heartedly out the window. Behind the counter stood one or other of the couple who ran the place. Both now in their early seventies, they had inherited it from his parents, who had in turn inherited it from one of their parents. They seemed friendly enough and knew how to carry a chat, but they were also aware down to the last peanut just what everything cost and who owed them what. Their daughter was supposed to be working with them by now, learning the ropes so as to take over the place in a couple of years, but she was off in Belfast, still 'studying' well into her forties, and had developed a heroin habit. She only came home every now and then for money and to steal bottles of whiskey from behind the bar to bring back to her friends in the city.

The old couple – along with everyone in the bar – knew this, although it was never spoken of in front of them. The wife of the couple had dyed black hair with a blinding white strip of roots along her parting, giving her the appearance of a badger. She was extremely thin, requiring at least two fleece jumpers to maintain a bearable temperature, even in that steamy, congested room. She silently despised all the women who came in, not actually approving of female drinking. She especially hated the ones who stood at the bar, and sometimes she even forgot to put alcohol in their orders of vodka and coke or gin and tonic. She liked to ask them seemingly innocuous questions about their children – where they were, who was minding them tonight: 'Oh, your mother, again? God, well, isn't she very good now ...'

Her husband, on the other hand, was a tall, once-impressive man who talked about the good old days of the IRA, when Ireland dealt with her own troubles, but who now had yellow in the whites of his eyes and trousers perpetually just about to fall down. Sometimes his shirt buttons mismatched with the holes, exposing pockets of fleshy white belly and making his collar droop. It gave him the appearance of a body melting or (in stoical, northern fashion) suffering a slow and silent stroke.

When I'd gotten out of the taxi, Foley'd passed a tenner in through the car window and said 'cheers Henry, sound' to the driver with an overly effusive thumbs up that told me he was already drunk. He then kissed me on the cheek (another liberty he wouldn't have taken soberly) before we, and a local gay fisherman called Monk, walked straight to the ladies' bathroom and each snorted a generous line of coke off the discoloured cistern through a five-euro note.

'So what do you do?' Monk asked me, wiping his nose and checking his hair as we trickled back out to the bar.

'I'm a writer,' I said.

'Oh really?!' He turned to face me and took my hands in his, stopping us in our tracks with his sudden enthusiasm. 'Maybe you'll write about this – about me, all of us, down here, ha!' His hands, which were slightly too warm, smelled faintly of fish. The coke was just hitting me. I looked at his face, his smiling face, with the smoke snaking around us, and the roaring sounds of life just through the door: sounds and movement and heaves of people. It felt like so many, too many, all of a sudden – drunk, progressing, slipping, the night in full swing, all dark blues slit quick across with burning reds and yellows, and for a second I couldn't, I didn't – where was? How did, *how had I* –?

I thought of the Lithuanian, back in Berlin, not thinking of me. Sitting with a book and a glass of whiskey in his room, or with a girl maybe, in the hidden corner of some dark quiet bar, hand working up her leg. I thought of my dad back at home, sitting at his computer working, or downstairs maybe, eating cheese and crackers at the kitchen table reading *Private Eye*. I thought of my grandparents asleep side by side, my grandfather's snoring accompanied by the crackle and hum of the radio left playing through the night. I thought of my best friend, out dancing in Dublin maybe, or on the couch, pyjama'd, nestled into the crook of her boyfriend's arm, watching a comedy or a sad romance, a mug of tea cupped in both hands for warmth.

I thought of all the skies, clouds drifting slow, blacker shapes against the black, and fields of sheep, and empty roads with humming yellow streetlights, and sleeping children in their beds spreadeagled under patterned sheets, dreaming. All the world between us across the black, and that empty house waiting for me down the road: the chickens in their coop, fluffed up, silent; the dog waiting patiently on the mat by the door, head on crossed front paws, sighing; and the sea out just beyond, swaying, the belly of it, the fish, the cold, swaying; all the way to myself, there, in that body, right then, swaying. And there I was. There I was, with precancerous cells, spreading, metastasizing now, deep down inside me. And one day, maybe soon, I was going to die. I blinked hard, and took my hands from his grip back to my sides.

'Huh, yeah,' I said. 'Maybe.'

'Well, if you do,' he said, shouting back over his shoulder as we entered the wall of noise, 'make sure to make me really handsome, right?'

Monk, the local gay fisherman, was, I should mention, *extremely* handsome.

Sometimes people my age, people much younger – brighter, sweeter, kinder – really did get cancer. They might find out about precancerous cells like I had; they might see signs, feel a lump, or it might just hit them out of the blue, fully grown and deadly. Of course I was thankful that the latter wasn't what had happened to me. I still had time, I still might be alright. But I also might get cancer.

Cancer, when I tried to conceive of it – write it down, control it – overpowered me. It couldn't seem to fit out the nib of my pen. The letters used to make it buckled and lost their shape under the pressure of coming together to form the word. It was just *wrong* – a monstrous thing that my mouth didn't feel large or brave enough to release as sound. It was like a thick black tar coating my tongue, the roof of my mouth, my soft inner cheeks, caking itself across everything. *Can-cerr* ... I tried to say it, to let it out, but the black just trickled forth from my lips down my front in a long glutinous stream of no sound, no sound, no sound, cutting off my air in panic. No sound, no meaning. If I heard it on the television or caught the word written in a book or online, I flinched. Now that I wanted to hide from it, to never see or hear it, it was everywhere. All anyone ever seemed to talk or write or think about was cancer.

One time, on my usual walk with Max, a seal came to the beach. I'd brought a joint to smoke once I got there. Something to do. It was approaching nightfall, but I decided Max and I would make it down with a moment to pause there, while still allowing for enough lingering light to see our way home. Our after-dinner excursion had become one of the few routines I managed to maintain in all the time I spent alone down there. A linchpin on those days when otherwise I wouldn't have left the house (after all, what would prove the world beyond the door was still even there, if I didn't go out to check on it?). On that particular evening, I'd roasted a whole chicken with the intention of eating it over the coming two or three days. After my initial sensible plateful, I'd wandered back into the kitchen and eaten the whole thing, tearing the warm wet flesh from the carcass with my fingers, allowing the greasy juices to stream down my (still not entirely healed) chin, as the dog sat hopefully by my feet. So a short walk, at the very least, was necessary (needless to say, the daily run hadn't been going to plan).

I was sitting on a large grey rock, trying to cup the flame of the lighter and the end of my joint against the hooshing Atlantic wind, when from the corner of my eye I spotted the seal. I stared. It stared back. The seal opened its mouth wide, making a circular motion with its head as it did so, as though yawning or calling out soundlessly, before going under the water again. I waited. Thirty seconds later up he popped, slightly closer to the shore. He was looking right at me. I called out a sound, a sort of friendly roar. He looked at me. I waited. He opened his mouth wide, and let out a sound back. '*Aaawwwwrrrghhhaaewwrrrgh.*' He went under, emerged, and the exchange was repeated. He came closer and closer with each surfacing, to the point where I wondered if he would actually come clambering ashore, and if so how I would respond, although really I knew I would just sit there and see what happened. Do seals attack? Or would he befriend me?

Finally he submerged, and I waited and waited, but there was nothing. The surface, now a deep steely-grey, rippled unbroken. After some interminable length, heart emptying out, I finally accepted that he'd lost interest in me. With that sinking resignation, I was reintroduced to the sounds of the world outside of our exchange. The sloshing ocean, the breeze through leaves behind me. Otherwise, silence. Finding myself bone-cold, I stood to go. It was only then that I realized the darkness that had crept up around me. My eyes had adjusted there on the beach, but on the walk back up, sky covered over with growth and hissing leaves, it was pitch black. With Max already gone off ahead, it took me a long time to feel my way – toe-testing the ground, hands outstretched – back to the softly lit windows of the empty house.

Every now and then over the course of my time there, alone with Max, I'd catch him looking fixedly at me – as I sat at my laptop typing, or reading, or stood waiting for the kettle to boil, or watched TV, or twisted buttery spaghetti on my fork at the table, or threw oats out to the chickens, or mopped the white kitchen tiles, or hung out wet socks by the fireplace – and I'd meet his round black-brown eyes, and even though I knew that he was probably just hoping for some sign of food or a walk or attention coming his way, I still couldn't help but wonder: can he smell it off me? The unhealthy cells, growing? Does he know?

The sun blazed right into late October, giving me a swelling sensation of guilt and anxiety: I had written nothing. I didn't understand where the time had gone. I'd thought there was going to be so much *time*. I started furiously taking notes on Taylor Swift for a fantastic essay I decided I would write entitled 'Blank Space', comparing my life to hers (we're the same age): talking about the problems of millennials, the emptiness and vacuousness of our concerns in a post-postmodern era, newspeak, virtue signalling, and I'd somehow work in something about my ex in Berlin, who I felt I might as well write about, since he was always lurking in the shadows of my mind. It'd be a sort of covert love-letter, very subtle and intellectual and impressive. I'd write it in a seemingly random polyphonic style, to suggest the layers of distraction and numerous levels of awareness necessary to live in this multivalently digital and drug-fuelled era. Taylor would be its queen, the overarching symbol for all of the amazing yet terrible concepts I would explore. It would be brilliant, as brilliant as her pearly-white teeth, and its completion, in these final days before my godmother and Maria's return, would justify my time up there in Donegal. Would justify everything – my entire life thus far, especially since it might end up being all I had to show for it.

Two hours into the project, I hit a wall. I had six or seven pages filled with a diffuse selection of quotes and facts from the internet which I told myself I would include. Then, clicking through links randomly, Ryan Adams's *1989* covers playing on YouTube in the background, I read that Taylor Swift's mother had been diagnosed with breast cancer. Taylor had announced it to her fans on her blog, taking credit for making her mom go get checked. She closed the post by asking them all to respect the family's privacy at this time. Reading it made me feel a strange ache in my lower stomach. I scanned through it again two or three times and the nausea increased. How could she put that online, I wondered? It's a real thing. Does she not understand that it's a *real thing*? It's cancer. *Caaan-cerrrr*. I put my hand to my belly. I hadn't even been able to tell my own dad about my *precancer* results, about the procedure, let alone the whole world.

Eyes refocusing, I looked out the window at the startling brightness of the garden. The dog was lying on his stomach, head up, ears cocked, raptly watching the chickens as they bustled along in nervous single file behind the cockerel who proudly stalked ahead, pretending not to be scared, occasionally pausing to scratch and peck at the earth. Vacantly, I noted that when the cockerel acted as though he wasn't frightened of the dog, it didn't seem to occur to the dog to chase him. The dynamic didn't allow for the possibility – he was bluffing his way to safety. As I watched, the cockerel stretched up and flapped his wings and hollered. He seemed to have realized that I was watching him too, his beady eye watching me back, and was now showing off. I looked beyond him to the sea. A fishing boat, red against white-sparkling blue, was passing left to right. Probably heading back to town, to the harbour. I wondered if they'd caught anything. Maybe Monk was on it, working. Living, doing, working. My shoulders fell slack and I closed down the lid of my laptop. I decided to abandon the Taylor Swift project. Fuck it. She was probably a cunt anyway.

I wandered into the kitchen, rolled a spliff on the marble countertop, poured myself a glass of cheap Pinot Grigio from the fridge and went into the living room, switching on the TV to watch a repeat of *The Great Irish Bake Off*. I texted Foley to come over with some drugs and he replied saying he'd be there in half an hour – he'd get a lift from his dad. While waiting, I ate the last of the Aldi extra-crunchy peanut butter from the jar with a teaspoon. It was a Tuesday. My godmother and Maria were due home on Saturday morning. I'd written nothing, and I was probably going to die. On the television, the contestants were making trifles.

By the last week or two of my time in Donegal, I had become somewhat obsessed with Foley. I saw him almost every day. I'd drive out to his house unannounced with ingredients and a bottle of cheap wine from SuperValu, and we'd hang around watching YouTube videos and movies while getting drunk and stoned (we usually waited until nightfall to take anything harder). Things never got especially sexual, beyond some half-assed heavy petting, which I could write off – if I'd ever bothered to address it – as a side-effect of the copious amounts of love-happy drugs and drink. Mostly we'd sit side by side under a smelly blanket, or I'd lie with my legs across him, or we'd pull on some wellies and go hunting for mushies in the fields around the house with Mika and Max. I wanted company, and he was there; and at first he seemed, in his own strange way, to genuinely adore me. I was a novelty, an eccentric girl up from the Big Smoke, who swanned about in dresses and lipstick and called herself a writer. I cooked him nice dinners, fretted over his torn clothes, laughed and joked. I was, initially, a possible source of salvation.

For me, being with him made me feel good, because he saw me as valid and solid, and so for a while I could believe myself to actually be valid and solid. I could be a real thing, a person with a life plan and goals and all that other stuff. More importantly, he was kind. Even more importantly though, I felt good with Foley because he gave me lots and lots of drugs. Drugs lit up my mind a clean, gleaming white, so bright I couldn't see.

Yet as things progressed, I found myself mistreating Foley. I texted him when drunk, writing mad pointless things, just to be writing something. To be communicating with another breathing human. I kept him up at night when I couldn't sleep – from the drugs or the terror or the anxiety, and was bitingly cruel to him sometimes, in spite of (or because of) myself.

'How can you have no *dreams*?' I prodded, the night I'd given up on my Taylor Swift essay. 'How can you not want something bigger than this shithole small town, selling drugs from that house?' I was sitting beside him on the couch not really watching a pirate DVD of *Gravity* he'd brought. I was feeling especially malicious, my self-loathing seeping outwards, by now locked off my face on the white wine and sadness.

'I dunno ... I don't mind it like ...' he answered after a pause, hurt and sheepish.

'Huh, okay, wow.' I adjusted my position beside him to angle my body, pointedly, away from his. Okay, sure, maybe I was achieving nothing; maybe I was a failure and maybe I was dying; but at least, I told myself, I wasn't as bad as Foley.

On my final Thursday house-sitting, I had one last wild night. I didn't really want to, but I'd said a couple of weeks back I'd have a few people round, and now I didn't care enough either way to stop it going ahead. My whole mind was scrambled and days were beginning to blend into one continuous stream, punctuated with fleeting moments of darkness and light. I was out locking up the chickens in the last light of that particular day, one drink in. I was proud of myself for remembering to do it – I'd been forgetting to do it most days, and was lucky none of them had yet been devoured by foxes in the night. The sea looked calm out beyond.

Rum and Diet Coke in hand, I was weaving back through the flowerbeds to the house when I heard the voices rippling through the soft evening air from inside. They'd let themselves in and were taking up positions in the kitchen.

'We're making pizza and cocktails!' Monk shimmied towards me with arms outstretched as I walked inside, shy from a day of silence. I knew his effusiveness was in part a way to counteract any reluctance I might show at their taking over the house. But I was beyond giving a shite. They could've been setting the place alight for all I cared – I was just glad of the distraction.

I gulped down my drink and proffered my glass: 'More of anything, please.'

It was myself, Foley, Monk and another girl whom I didn't actually like (in the sticks, with one warm body per mile, you realize you can't be picky) called Jane, who worked cash-in-hand as a waitress in the big hotel two towns over as well as collecting the dole. She had two small children but tonight they were with their grandmother.

An hour or so after dinner, the lads played cards and Jane and I discussed her most recent arsehole boyfriend (another fisherman, from the island out beyond – once, back around 2003, he'd accidentally selected 'Raspberry Beret' on the pub jukebox, so now everyone in town referred to him exclusively as Prince). Foley, getting up to refill his glass, slipped a small powder-filled plastic baggy from his trouser pocket and put it down on the table in front of me. It was filled to the brim. I smiled up at him, eternally grateful. We ended up dancing wildly, climbing on my godmother's kitchen table (the engraved one she'd had shipped especially from Morocco), stripping and kissing, all four of us, sloppily giggling and groping.

Foley and the Wolf

Foley and I woke together in the garden between layers of duvets. I was confused. The blanket below me was damp and I was cold and shivering in spite of the early morning sun. The dog was lying at our feet, looking up dolefully when he noticed me stirring. Foley lay curled up beside me, fully dressed, his body compacted tight for warmth.

I tried to connect this time of waking to the night before, and I recalled, in white-noise-coated flashes, images of myself insisting to him that we sleep outside so that we could watch the sunrise. Thinking back, I was pretty sure it had already been light out by the time we lay down, but this hadn't affected my determination. I put my hand on his shoulder and shook him gently. He opened his eyes slowly, blinking, and groaned. We lay in silence for a while, not able to face moving just yet. I wondered what state the house would be in, and for a moment I felt like crying.

Jane and Monk had driven home, completely twisted, at around four in the morning. Monk had to report for work at the harbour at eight. He'd probably already be out on the water now, I thought, and grimaced. Foley reached into his pockets under the blankets and tried to roll a spliff while remaining horizontal. I lay as still as I could, paralysed by fear and shame and regret and the pain throbbing in my head. I remembered, in another series of flickering images, that I had broken a glass and stepped in it, and had found the whole thing – the glass and the realness of the blood, the astounding vividness of its red colour – very, very funny. I wondered if there would still be glass in my foot when I tried to stand, and felt intensely weary at the prospect.

After what seemed like twenty minutes or so, we rose. I would have lain there forever if I hadn't been so thirsty.

The cockerel was going apeshit out in the coop, and I went to let him and the chickens out. What time was it anyway? The whole thing was filthy, covered in huge round lumps of white shit. I hadn't cleaned it once in the five weeks, in spite of my godmother's detailed instructions, stuck to the fridge under a magnet I'd given her of Frida Kahlo. I picked out three fresh eggs, careful not to touch against the wet, marbled globules, then walked into the house through the back door after Foley, who'd wrapped the duvet over his head like E.T. at the end of the movie. It was chaos – glasses and tobacco and spills, empty bottles and dirty plates, pizza crumbs and bits of tomato sauce and cheese mashed into the rug and all the lights burning.

'I'll deal with it later,' I said curtly, when Foley asked did I want a hand. I couldn't face it, not yet. Not ever, maybe. If cancer was going to kill me, you'd think it'd have the decency to get it over with before I had to clean up. Fuck it, I thought. Just fuck it.

After a silent breakfast, with our plates empty and second cups of coffee growing cold, it became clear that Foley was anxious to leave. He would need a lift from me, but didn't want to seem rude by asking. At first I pretended not to notice, avoiding his eyes, lips pursed.

'Right, well, I'll just clean up and then I'll drive you in,' I finally sighed. I got up and started clanking plates around the sink, scrubbing furiously.

He stood cringing off to the side, watching me. 'D'ya want help wit' anything?'

'Nope!' I said, still avoiding his eye.

He paused, thinking for a moment about whether, or how, to address it. 'Here, what's wrong wit' ya?'

'Nothing, nothing!'

'... Ah no, go on, there's somethin' like, I can see it by ya... what's goin' on?'

'Ugh.' I paused in my cleaning but kept my eyes on the sink. 'It's ... it's nothing ... like, I just ... you come out here, you sleep over, and then first thing you just want to leave? Bit, I dunno, rude like? I mean, d'ya not want to hang out, spend the day or something? We could just get high and I dunno, watch a film or whatever, chill like ...'

I didn't understand why I was suggesting it. I didn't even like the sound of it. I had things I needed to do. My godmother and Maria would be home the next morning. I had to sort everything. Organize the chaos: wipe surfaces, vacuum stairs, restock loo paper, empty ash from fireplaces and ashtrays, change some pretty grimy sheets. I couldn't have hung out even if he'd suggested it. I was just picking a fight for nothing. Causing anguish for nothing. Instinctively, my hands went to my chin for the distraction of a more simple pain, but no, nothing there – it had healed. Finding that nothingness – no relief – I suddenly felt an overwhelming nausea at the idea of even one more long day stretching out before me with only the fields, the sea, the dog, and these cancerous fucking cells, growing in writhing blackness inside me, for company. I couldn't do it. I needed him to stay. Anyone to distract me, to be with me, to just please stay. Foley looked at the floor, uncomfortable.

'Oh for fuck's sake. Never mind, forget it,' I said, slamming down a pot on the draining board and walking past him towards the door. I grabbed my keys from the hook.

In the car, we sat in silence. Incongruously, almost mockingly, Van Morrison's soothing tones poured forth from the stereo while manic rage seeped out from my pores towards Foley, who sat squirming in the passenger seat. I drove recklessly, skidding on corners along the winding stretch back towards the town. The sun was out and I cursed it and everything under it, the stupid blue fucking sea and the sheep and the green trees and all the fucking people in all those cunty little bungalow houses along the way. We sped past a shrine to the Virgin Mary carved into the rock face and I cursed her too, the dozy cunt.

Foley glanced at me and I, compounding my raging shame and misery, pressed my foot down a little harder. What did I care if I crashed? I'd achieved nothing, I was useless; I'd already wasted my whole fucking life.

'Careful, for fuck's sake!' Foley shouted, grabbing hold of the dashboard as I screeched around the corner only to be met head on with an enormous truck, forcing me to swing suddenly into the green bank of the road. The truck driver honked, probably assuming I was some idiot boy-racer flexing road muscle. I slammed on the brake, whipping both our bodies forward and back in a violent slingshot motion.

We sat suspended for a moment, breathing heavily over the hum of the engine and Van's silky voice on the roadside. From outside, birdsong. The bleating of a sheep. Slowly, Foley turned to me.

'What the *fuck* is *wrong* wit' you?' he spat. I'd never seen him angry. It was frightening, the strange unfamiliarity, eyes wide and teeth bared. It snapped me back from my rage into the reality of the moment, of myself and this man, hearts racing, sitting there.

'Jesus … Jesus fucking Christ, I'm sorry … fuck, sorry, holy shit, fuck, I'm so sorry Foley, holy shit, I'm sorry ...'

'Sorry? *Sorry*? You're fuckin' *nuts*, you know that? You seem sound, like, but really you're fucking batshit!' He was sitting erect in his seat, still gripping the dashboard with both hands but staring straight at me, his whole body blazing. I nodded and said nothing.

Shame, deep ugly heavy shame, was building up like wet concrete and hardening in my stomach. Fleetingly I thought about telling him everything. About falling into a strange love in Berlin and it failing so abruptly, leaving me dazed and hurting. About how I wanted to be a writer but secretly knew I couldn't be, not really, because actually I was talentless and stupid and dull, just like everybody else. Even, maybe, I could tell him about having a letter in my dressing-gown pocket back at home, a letter containing words that said I had precancerous cells, cancerous cells-in-waiting, or whatever the fuck it was. About how I was shit, a fraud, a terrible person, a bitch, and one who was probably going to die soon anyway. But I didn't. I said nothing and when he was finished talking, when his breathing was beginning to steady, I muttered 'I'm so sorry' again, before putting the car into first and, indicator clicking, carefully pulled back out onto the empty road. He said nothing more. He slammed the door as he got out.

I'd be collecting my godmother and Maria from the airport at half-eight the next morning. I didn't see Foley again.

When I got back to Dublin I had one night at home before my appointment in Holles Street. My dad's eyes welled up with joy when he saw Max, who'd erupted out of the car boot towards him the moment we pulled in.

I drove myself into town for the appointment, telling Dad I was off for coffee with a friend. I'd been told not to drive myself, due to the anaesthetic, but hadn't been able to bring myself to ask anyone. That would have meant telling someone. I cut out four times trying to park the car.

The blocked traffic sat waiting patiently, engines chugging, as I waved, panic mounting, turning and re-turning
the key as the little red light lit up on the dashboard, over
and over again.

The procedure took approximately twenty minutes,
with another ten minutes for recovery. They gave me a special pad to wear and told me I could expect soreness for
the next few days and some bleeding. I laughed nervously
and said yes, of course I was grand – sure it was nothing! I
thanked the nurse and doctor for everything and pretended
to have someone outside waiting to collect me. Afterwards,
I sat in the parked car and bawled my eyes out.

I was oddly disgusted with myself; with how easy, in the
end, it had all been. If anything, the nurse and doctor, both
comfortingly practical brunette women, seemed a little
taken aback by my unconquerable trembling as I hooshed
myself up onto the bed. Their demeanours implied that
this was really not significant enough to even have to put
a brave face on it. To them, it was routine. During the procedure, they'd talked about good mountains to climb in
Connemara with the family. I felt like a fool; relieved, yet
still utterly terrified. It was only when I saw the portly
uniformed traffic warden sidling towards me in the wing
mirror that I finally wiped my eyes and, moaning quietly
in self-pity, pulled back into the city traffic.

When I got home, aching and exhausted, I went straight
up to bed, citing illness. 'Lazy-bones!' Dad called after me
good-naturedly as I shut my bedroom door. Fuck you,
Dad, I thought. I slept straight through to the next morning. I slept like the dead.

It was three weeks later when the next letter landed on
the hall floor, and another two after that when I went in
to be checked and told by a different smiling doctor that

I officially had the all-clear. I was stunned. I smiled back and thanked her and said how wonderful, that's so wonderful, what a relief, I'm so happy ... I'm so happy.

'Of course you are!' she said, professionally delighted for me, already considering her next patient. She looked only a year or two older than me at most. I walked out, grinning emptily at all the nurses and doctors and patients and secretaries, and even the tired-looking man standing outside the entrance smoking.

It was late November now. There had been storms, biblical floodings. On certain nights it seemed almost apocalyptic. My godmother and Maria lost power for three days. They had to cook everything on the stove and use candles and torches at night. 'Sort of an adventure!' my godmother said on the crackly line from her mobile phone, making the most of it.

A week after returning, I emailed the Lithuanian to say hello, how've you been, and he replied to say it would be better to never be in contact again. Better for both of us, he said. I was back in the café, watching out for rats. Two rejections had arrived for stories I'd written the year before, and I was writing nothing new. I started walking aimlessly towards the city centre. I had no plans for the afternoon. I hadn't brought my book or my laptop, and so couldn't go to a café and pretend to work on something while actually surfing the internet, as I normally would. I had been expecting bad news; I hadn't thought beyond the hospital.

A small white pony followed myself and Max one evening on our nightly walk to the beach. I was a little scared as I walked ahead, hearing it breathing and plodding close behind me on the narrow pathway through brambles and whipping branches, catching my hair and clothes, leaving damp splatters. But I liked it too – the company. The path was shadowy under the growth and surrounded by fields on one side, dotted with cows who raised their heads to watch us pass, and a river and forest on the other, rolling down to sea.

When we got to the beach, the pony lingered in the lane behind while Max ran out into the shallows to startle off the seagulls, who rose silently, light grey against the darkening grey sky. 'Aren't you coming?' I asked, pausing to glance back. The pony lowered its head, and started munching on the grass rise in the middle of the pathway. I wandered around on the stones for a while, my eyes lifting to the pony's white shape every now and then. The tide was out, and I studied the exposed brown fronds of seaweed lying limp in gleaming fanned-out clusters. I always felt guilty for not looking out over the water, appreciating the grand expanse, but I could never seem to keep my eyes from finding their way back downwards, to study the chaos of pebbles and wrack and washed-up sea litter beneath my feet; searching for bursts of colour, jewels, the peeking necks of bottles; or for life, little creatures hiding, pearly shells to pocket. I always seemed to want to find something that someone else might have missed. I collected up anything that caught my eye: shell fragments, russet or translucent orange or blue-flecked stones, bits of sea-smoothed glass, and never knew what to do with them once I got home. Often I abandoned them in little piles on stone walls and wooden posts on the walk back up, hoping that another person would see them and wonder.

After a time, growing cold, I whistled to the dog who was sniffing further along. Lifting his head with raised ears, he obediently began padding in towards me from the shallows. Turning inland, I looked up to the mouth of the laneway where the white pony stood waiting. But it was empty. There was only a darkness surrounded by the breeze-ruffled hedgerows, and an unexpected wave of grief passed through me.

And We Continue to Live

Lucy travelled alone but with strangers (so, more alone) to the site of the Chernobyl disaster in the March of 2019 for a two-day/one-night expedition, and got her period in the little toilet cubicle on the plane on the way there. She had no sanitary towels or tampons, because she was never prepared for her period, even though her cycle was pretty regular. Every new month she reached was unexpected and unwelcome. She was always startled by the realness of the blood – evidence of her body working, moving in cycles, ageing and changing, all going along without her. The blood dyed the blue walls in the bowl beneath her purple and came away in smears of dark and bright red on the toilet paper and on her fingertips. She didn't especially like to look at or think about it. She stuffed some folded tissue into her knickers, pulled them up, and pressed the button for the terrifyingly loud, sucky flusher. The fasten seatbelt symbol dinged as she did so, glowing orange. A tinny female voice came from a hidden speaker up to her left. She hiked up her tights, straightened her skirt, checked the mirror, sighed, and returned to her seat. They were beginning their descent.

Lucy wasn't sleeping well. The dentist told her she ground her teeth at night.

'Tell me about it,' she said.

'Well,' the dentist replied, 'as you sleep, you clench your jaw, and move it back and forth ...'

It was a package deal. She shopped around the various travel companies providing trips into the zone. She was briefly surprised that competing companies for this service even existed. But along with everything else Lucy learned now, her disbelief dissipated as quickly as the time it took for the pages to load. She clicked through. One website had the men from *Top Gear* on the homepage, looking surly/respectful, straight to camera. They must've done a show from there – could they have? Could that be a thing? A *Top Gear* episode based around the zone in Chernobyl? Again, rather than checking the facts by simply clicking a few more links, she immediately accepted it as true. Why not, she guessed? Cars zooming around the zone, horsepower, leather, all slick and shiny. She imagined Jeremy Clarkson: 'I know it was a tragedy, terrible' – his tone the whole time somehow intimating that this could *never* have happened in Britain – 'but Christ, all these open roads – it's *fantastic*!'

This was what Lucy's chosen operator had written on their homepage:

Chernobyl travel for you:
- Experience of guiding into the zone, all the way back to 1986, the very first months of Chornobyl disaster
- In-depth knowledge and experience of the disaster mitigation, research and success-story survival
- The research unit
- Most important to us the radiation safety of the tourists

- Teaching and applying of most important skills of radiation survival
- Option for breath-taking bird-view of the zone using drone and helicopter technology
- Unique tour programs on demand to meet needs of the most inquiring minds and international press
- Option to contribute charitable support for Chornobyl zone self-settlers (includes meet & greet)
- Option to contribute to ultimate goal of establishing the Chornobyl national park / turn the zone into UNESCO world heritage site.

'Is that not … I dunno, immoral?' Lucy's sort of boyfriend but not really (we'll call him 'James') asked her the night she'd booked, lying in bed, in that brief space of goodwill when they sometimes actually spoke to one another – post-sex, pre-restless.

'Lots of people do it, go there.'

'Yeah … I guess. Although, to be honest, I'd never heard of anyone doing it. Going to *Chernobyl* like. But still, I thought you were against all that stuff? Didn't you go on about people visiting Auschwitz that time? In the smoking area that night, with your friend, eh …?'

Nora, Lucy thought. *Her name's Nora, and you've met her three times.*

'Yeah, but … that's different.'

'How's it different?'

Smiling, he rolled over on his side to examine her, propping his elbow on the pillow, his head resting in his hand.

'Because …' she sighed, as though exasperated by having to explain something so obvious, but really to buy time to think of something – something that wasn't the truth, which would've been *I don't know why I'm going,*

because I definitely am against all that stuff actually, that dark
tourism bullshit. In fact, I don't know what I'm doing in general,
which is kind of the whole problem, I'm lost, but y'know, maybe
if someone, maybe you, would just love me, or impregnate me, or
if I had cancer or couldn't use my legs, I wouldn't feel the need
to go to Chernobyl, just to actually possibly experience some-
thing, feel something of life being a gift, life being precious, or
even just, I don't know, worth persevering with – because that
truthiness would've made the whole conversation a bit
too fucking *real* and frankly a bit fucking *awkward*, lying
there in bed after sex with 'James'. So instead, after her
elongated sigh, she said:

'... Because I'm not going for stupid *voyeurism*, to like,
porn-out on other people's pain. I'm going for *research*;
I want to understand why people *go* on trips like this. I
want to see what kind of people are even *drawn* to trips
like this. Like, Chernobyl is so recent, so *devastating*, and
the zone is still dangerous – you have to get, like, X-rayed
going in and out – it's insane! I'll have to go through this
metal scanner thing, like. And still people actually *pay
money* to go and take photos of themselves outside the
reactor' – Lucy's mind flashed to all of the saved photos
in the 'Chernobyl' folder on her desktop of people crying,
deformed, suffering, in the wake of the disaster – 'It's kind
of sick, but it's actually fascinating that people are drawn
to it, y'know? So I'm, like, going *for the idea* of going ...
I'll write about it then, of course, an essay or something,
probably, after.'

'Right, right ...' he said, rolling away from her and out of
the bed as he spoke, reaching for his phone. 'So you're not
actually going to visit Chernobyl on a package tour, you're
meta-going to *meta*-visit Chernobyl, on a *meta*-tour ...'

*

Here is the itinerary Lucy was provided with upon booking:

Your 2-day tour to the Chornobyl!
For our 2-day Chornobyl tour we limit the group size to maximum 12 participants! This is gives us great flexibility in our itinerary and we can adjust our tourings depending on your interests!
- 7:45 a.m. – Meeting at the Independence Square near McDonald's
- 8:00 a.m. – Our minibus leaves for Chernobyl
- 9:00 a.m. – Coffee break at gas station
- 10:00 a.m. – Arriving at the checkpoint Dityatki at 10:00 a.m. (the earliest possible when the gate is opens for visitors!)

The first Day in the Zone includes:
- The village Zalissya
- The Main square of the town of Chornobyl
- 'Fukushima' memorial
- Statue to Lenin
- The only active church in the zone
- Abandoned Synagogue
- Dock
- Local shop
- Monument to the Firefighters
- Exposition of the remotely operated machines
- Hills of the buried village Kopachi
- Rustic Kindergarten
- Panoramic angle of NPP
- Stone road sign of Prypiat
- Bridge of Death
- Lenin Street

- The main square of Prypiat
- Supermarket
- Amuzement Park
- School #3 (with gas masks!)
- Swimming pool
- An existing sarcophagus
- NEW sarcophagus!

On second day we explore:
- Duga 3 (so-called 'Russian Woodpecker', military over the horizon radar and its base named 'Chernobyl 2')
- Barrack
- Cooling towers on the side of the unfinished reactors 5 and 6
- Fish farm
- 'Red Forest'
- Panel buildings with Soviet emblems
- Palace of Culture
- 'Jupiter' factory
- The ruins of the School #1
- Morgue
- Hospital
- Pripyat passenger boats River Port
- Cinema 'Prometheus'
- Music School
- Athletic stadium
- Laboratory in the former kindergarten
- Greenhouses
- Abandoned checkpoint
- Garages
- Contaminated ladle
- Tree of Friendship
- Bus Station

*

A day after she'd arrived in Kiev, they met early, as planned, outside McDonald's in Independence Square. It smelled of petrol and the mustiness of early-morning city and Big Macs every time the glass doors swung open. There was a tan short-haired dog rifling through plastic rubbish bins down the side of the building. The bins leaked crumpled McDonald's packaging and lettuce and bits of burger buns and meat and fries and coffee dregs and various stinking juices. Lucy watched it, standing slightly apart from the few other early group members. The dog paused his foraging to look up at her, ears back. She wondered could he smell her period blood, for which she had still not purchased sanitary towels. Lucy felt a whisper of deep, aching pity pass through her. Then it bared its teeth, emitting a low growl, and this feeling was replaced immediately by fear. Lucy felt her body clench tight against the dog. She moved closer to the tour guide.

Their guide, holding a sign and smoking enthusiastically, was called Victor. He was not one of the guides advertised on the website, the faces, names and qualifications of whom Lucy had inadvertently memorized. For a split second she considered letting this upset or even enrage her but, like all others, this feeling too quickly dissipated.

Victor was squat and dark-haired and had eyes so black it was almost impossible to tell the pupil from the iris. His skin was wetly smooth and tanned, with sun spots on the backs of his hands and on his upper cheeks. He had the smile of an insurance broker, or perhaps of someone second-in-command in a powerful prison gang. He seemed to Lucy like a good enough guy though. He was jovial and chatty, and clearly knew how to command a shy and sleepy tour group. She overheard him tell another of the men present that he had a wife and four children, three girls and a boy. Lucy assumed that they had kept trying until they had the boy, but no; it would later transpire that the boy was fifteen, the second eldest.

Victor eyed her through the smoke of his cigarette. He walked over and offered her one. She declined, but he stayed close. As they made introductory small talk, it became apparent that he was a little perturbed by her lack of companions. For the first ten to fifteen minutes he peered at every passing man expectantly as though he were about to join her and announce himself as her husband/father/brother. *What are you doing here?* his presence began to ask. *Why would you come here?* Eventually, his discomfort made her uncomfortable in turn, and she lied into a weighted silence between them, saying that she was a journalist for a national newspaper back in Ireland, doing a piece on Chernobyl, the landscape and people and all that, over thirty years on. She quickly made up some vague detail about the Chernobyl Children that used to come to Ireland, that actually still do, probably, for summer holidays, whom her neighbours had taken in for three summers in a row when she was a child. She didn't tell him that they always took boys, and that each and every year she fell madly in love with them, but the memory jolted her. They always had such beautiful sallow skin, those boys … She said, on a roll now, that after this tour, she was planning to go track them down, although this had actually never occurred to her before, and besides sounded like something that would prove both awkward and tiring. At this explanation, Victor let out a huge 'aaaaaah, of course!' and winked, as though to say, 'I knew I'd figure it out'. Knowing her purpose, he loosened up.

'Is warm.'

'Yes, very.'

'You can leave coat on the bus, it's safe.'

'Okay, great, thanks.'

'So you are interested in Chernobyl?'

'Yes, very.'

'Hah, yes, good, good.'

'... you?'

'Oh yes! Well of course ...'

'Yes, of course –'

'Most important event in the twentieth century! Most important!'

'Wait, really?'

'Yes, well, Chernobyl, Holocaust too, of course, but yes, Chernobyl ... changed everything. The nuclear, nuclear destruction, this disaster, changed everything, you see?'

Victor gestured loosely at the world before them, trailing smoke; the city square, grey, streaked with long, dark shadows retreating quickly from the butter-warm light of the rising sun, people trundling in criss-crosses, heads down, plugged in with wires from ears to pockets, the stall and jar of traffic around the edges, red car blue car silver reflecting gleams of light, a truck's horn, another, and the dog crouched and nervous, scuttering away from them, cutting a straight line across the centre. It was strangely quiet, all in all.

'Yes. Yeah, I see ... I see.'

Victor gave all the members of the tour a small booklet provided by the tour company as they mounted the steps to the minibus. It was simple black font on A4 pages that had then been folded in the middle and stapled. On the front, in large italics, was printed *'Your Chernobyl Experience!'*

below which, in smaller font was written *'useful information, statistics and tips'*. It contained some basic information on Chernobyl but, disappointingly, no tips.

Lucy was first to board the bus, then immediately felt uncomfortable about choosing a seat. She worried about whether or not anyone would sit with her; she didn't want them to, but also didn't want to face the stigma of rejection. She also found this distressing because she knew she ought not to be at a point in her life where these things still flustered her. It made her feel small and pathetic and somehow more alone. After panicking a moment, holding everyone up, she sat second from the front, and stared out the window, pointedly avoiding catching the eye of any other tour group members. Lucy wasn't here to make friends (but then, why was she here?). In the end, Victor plopped down beside her. She was grateful and frustrated all at once; her usual feelings associated with the benevolence or attraction of a man.

Lucy did not retain a direct transcription of the information on the leaflet. Here though, is her own approximation of the opening paragraph:

On the twenty-sixth of April 1986, an accident occurred at the Chernobyl Nuclear Power Station in the Ukraine, in reactor number four. (It was supposed to be a routine safety check.) It was then still within the Soviet Union. Initially, the Soviet Authorities tried to cover up news of the explosion in Chernobyl. They played down the severity of the accident, even to those working at the station and living in the surrounding areas. In Kiev, on the thirtieth of April, the May Day parade went ahead. People took to the (secretly contaminated) streets. The children in their colourful costumes, made especially for the celebration, waved to proud parents as they marched.

*

All the other people on her tour were men except for one middle-aged French wife accompanying her aggressively short, aggressively muscular, French husband. She was small and blonde and clearly unhappy to be there. She was clutching a McDonald's takeaway coffee cup in her lap and wore an expensive-looking teal-grey Hugo Boss coat, boxy DKNY sunglasses and tight jeans. She took photos a lot, many of them selfies, alone or with her husband, beside whom she crouched slightly to minimize the apparentness of his minute stature, smiling or kissing his cheek. Lucy didn't notice what the men wore because men's clothes don't matter – although no, one guy, an extremely tall and bulky blond man from Norway did wear a bandana, which was notable for its awfulness. He looked to Lucy like he was trying to be David Foster Wallace. He asked Victor would he be comfortable with being recorded, to which Victor shrugged, sure. For the rest of the trip he held up a compact audio-recording device with a little red light. Victor asked him if he too was a journalist, but he said no, no, the recordings were just for his own personal use.

The rest – a pair from the UK, three guys from Germany, one man from the States and another but separate Norwegian – blended into background figures.

The day before the trip, Lucy went to the doctor to get something to take for her insomnia, i.e. for the fact that she stayed online all night until her eyes were red raw and her brain in a permanent state of fizzing distraction, all bright colours and quick edits.

'And are you pursuing healthy sleep habits?'

'Sorry?'

'Like, no caffeine in the evenings, not eating too late, exercising, making the bed, consistent bedtimes, maybe some lavender oil, and no screens for at least an hour or two before falling asleep?'

'Eh, yeah, pretty much.'

'Hmmm, okay ... well, it could be your anxiety acting up maybe, do you think?'

'Em, yeah, I think that's it.'

'Okay, well, I'll prescribe you some more Zorclone ... now, this stuff is heavy –'

'– I know –'

'– so only one a night, and only when you really need them, okay?'

A pause.

'Okay?'

'Okay.'

By the end of the trip, Lucy's copy of the tour leaflet was so thumbed and sweaty and underlined and starred that it was utterly unreadable. She threw it in a bin in the bathroom at Dublin airport. She still had her period, and she still had not bought sanitary towels or tampons and had, as a result, permanently stained various pairs of baby-pink, blue and floral-patterned knickers. Here, again, is some of the information provided as Lucy recalls it:

The zone around Chernobyl is thirty-two kilometres wide. The reactor was number four. Fifty people died in the immediate aftermath. Many more after. Nobody is sure about the precise number, but people offer helpful estimates. Four thousand, twenty thousand, eventually millions affected. Six thousand children with thyroid cancer, at least.

Nobody was told. Europe detected the plume themselves, and traced it back to the source before they heard any word.

*

They visited Pripyat, the abandoned town built especially for Chernobyl workers. There was a swimming pool, a cinema, a school. Apartment blocks containing furniture. From all the town's tar and brick and concrete surfaces there erupted wild, jungle-like foliage, thick and verdant and shockingly alive. Back on the bus, the group compared photos. Norwegian David Foster Wallace carried a collapsible tripod in his rucksack that he took out, clicked into shape, and spent a lot of time perfectly positioning. Every single one of the photos Lucy was shown afterwards on the bus were astoundingly beautiful – so beautiful that they looked unreal, or as though they'd been digitally altered.

Victor told them stories. It was unseasonably hot and he was sweating, with dark patches spreading under the armpits of his t-shirt. He told them that one of the men who turned up for work the morning following the explosion, ignorant of the severity of the accident, was forced to wade through some of the surrounding flooded cooling waters to reach his work station. He didn't know. Nobody told him. It looked, smelt, felt just like water. Soon after, Victor said, as he lay dying, the skin of his calves, shins and feet peeled off like socks.

After a pause to wipe his brow with a folded tissue from a small plastic packet, Victor told them that the sand that they poured over the fire that had erupted in the reactor, melted into glass. Lakes of molten glass. He said it had all happened because of a simple test – procedural. They had delayed this test at the request of the controller of the Ukraine electricity network. Victor looked at them conspiratorially, before saying that they still do not know, *officially*, why he asked for the delay, but that there are rumours it was because he didn't want them to lower the output of power for the necessary ten hours before-hand, because he was having a party. A big party, Victor smiled, waving his arm. 'But this, like many, many things from Soviet history, is just one of the stories people tell!' Victor winked, and an awkward chuckle rippled through the tour group. The test was carried out later that night, Victor continued, suddenly serious again; but by then, the engineers were tired, and the day shift workers had been replaced by the night shift workers, who were less experi-enced, and less prepared.

'And then, as you know,' Victor said solemnly, sweat still beading and dripping, 'it all went terribly wrong.'

Naturally Occurring Radioactive Material is referred to in the industry as NORM. According to the World Nuclear Associa-tion, if buried directly in the earth – after the necessary fifty-year waiting period – highly radioactive waste materials from nuclear power stations will take an estimated 300,000 years to reach as safe a level as the original ore. To reach the levels of NORM. Sci-entists guess that, in fact, it could take up to one million years.

Victor told them, standing with his back to the glass wall of the observation building, erected especially for tourists, that the new structure designed to contain reac-tor number four at Chernobyl is three and a half times heavier than the Eiffel Tower. He said it was completed on the twenty-ninth of November 2016, thirty years after the explosion. It is designed to contain the 'sarcophagus', the term given to the original structure built to hold the con-taminated reactor. The sarcophagus was erected hastily, and in the meantime had been supported by extra scaf-folding to counteract deterioration. It was in the process of collapsing. The new structure is designed to last for one hundred years. It was built nearby and slid into place upon completion. Victor told them that it is the largest movable land-based object ever constructed. Digital videos celebrating it were released online. It is immense and silver and curved like an egg. It is a feat of modern engineering, Victor explained. It will, for now, securely contain the highly radioactive substances still inside the reactor.

'It is a marvel!' Victor declared triumphantly.

That night at dinner, in the only hotel in the zone, Norwegian David Foster Wallace, mouth full of the delicious but greasy stew (served with potatoes grown, the menu proudly boasted, within the zone), asked Lucy if she would like to interview him in his room for impressions of what they had seen that day.

'You might want another perspective for your article? I also have taken some very interesting photographs, if you would like to see? I am actually a writer myself, you know. Yes, yes, not published yet, no, but only a matter of time, yes … yes, well, you know Knausgaard? A bit like him, yes, but mixed with crime-thriller … You know Stieg Larsson?'

His eyes were so icily blue that they were almost painful for Lucy to look at. She decided, looking down from them to her dirtied plate, that they were wasted in his face. She could smell the onion and garlic from the stew on his breath, invading the air inside her nostrils, filtering into her bloodstream. She politely but firmly declined his offer.

Later, alone in a scuffed red leather booth near the back of the hotel bar, she regretted doing so. She was experiencing that scooped-out feeling in her stomach that she often felt when left too long to sit in her own aloneness; that feeling that no amount of eating or drinking could ever seem to fill – and yet, she persevered in trying. She was almost finished a bottle of surprisingly delicious Ukrainian red wine that she had been 'sipping' while pretending to write impressions of the day in her journal. These impressions were mostly to-do lists and doodles, before the descent into open-ended questions on the topic of what she was doing with her life, how she had ended up here, increasingly followed by two or three question marks. She wondered, swirling the last of the wine in her glass, if there was any way she could track down the Norwegian after all, but realized she'd forgotten his real name. That and the language barrier prevented her from risking the humiliation of asking the warty but homely woman behind reception: 'Norwegian man, yes? Hairy? Huge? David Foster Wallace-y? Ban-daah-naah? Where now please, for fucking?' Instead, she sent an ill-advised drunken text to 'James' – some unfunny witticism about the other tour members, finished with a kiss. She redrafted it three times before sending. The two ticks immediately lit up blue on her phone's screen, showing it was seen. No response.

On the morning of the second day, they clambered back onto the bus. Victor stood at the front, holding a cup of coffee with one hand and the gleaming silver bar above his head for balance with the other. He told them, straining over the engine, that on the morning of the disaster, calm and warm – just like this one, in fact – when everyone turned up for work as usual, one woman, getting off the bus to start her shift, accidentally dropped a tampon from her purse. It landed on the highly contaminated graphite-strewn ground. But nobody told her. She didn't know. Later, she would insert it.

This story reminded Lucy, cursing internally, that she *still* hadn't bought any tampons or sanitary towels, and now she was worried that blood would seep through her knickers to her jeans over the course of the next few hours. She wondered if there would be anywhere to stop and buy tampons in the zone and, if so, whether they'd now be safe to use, thirty years later. She then realized how silly and selfish this reaction was and felt guilty. She was groggy from the wine and the two Zorclone tablets she'd taken the night before.

The tour members all sat very quietly. Today, the French woman was wearing a tight white top with a mid-length royal blue skirt, a large gold necklace and red lipstick. The outlines of her tan-coloured t-shirt-bra were highly visible and caused her breast flesh to bulge slightly beneath her top. Lucy had seen Norwegian David Foster Wallace gazing at her from behind as she walked ahead with her husband to the bus, and hated him for his betrayal.

Lucy lowered her head, trying to appear lost in thought, while the bus itself, trundling along over the potholed dirt road, was deafeningly loud. She found it hard to concentrate, and decided to stare in a contemplative-looking way out the window instead. In every direction were miles of flat green fields that ended in a distant dark strip of woodland. Every now and then, along the side of the road where dust flew up from beneath the tyres, yellow poles stuck out of the ground, indicating where houses would have been, and thus where the ground was even more highly contaminated (Victor told them that, in their panic, the clean-up operators had quickly knocked and buried these houses directly in the earth, rather than effectively containing them). Crows that perched on the top of every third or fourth pole flew off, startled, as the noisy engine approached. The low morning sun sent a shadow from the bus stretching down to the left-hand side, reaching across the border between road and field, fleetingly blanketing all in its wake in darkness.

Studying her own bloated belly, warding off motion sickness, Lucy wondered could she slip a hand down under the seat of her jeans to check for damp without looking like she was scratching or pleasuring herself, but decided that no, she couldn't. After a respectful minute or two, Victor shouted across the engine, all smiles again, to ask did they want to hear more stories. Lucy looked up. After an awkward pause, not wanting to seem too keen – indecently keen – they all shrugged and said yes, okay, sure.

Victor told them, as the bus passed by a stooped elderly woman digging in her garden (wrinkled and brown, long purple-patterned skirt, sleeves rolled up, chickens circling), that some people have refused to leave. Mostly elderly women like this, he said, gesturing towards her. She continued digging with her back to the road, showing no signs of acknowledgement of the roaring engine of the bus.

Victor said they're called 'The Babushkas of Chernobyl'. A film has even been made about them. He said that a few of them are visited by tours now, as an attraction, although he personally doesn't like to do it because they tend to be 'difficult', telling long, complaining tales of woe, and to plead with the tourists for extra money. He said that really they are perfectly contented, and that they are all called upon once a month by soldiers, who check to see that they are still alive. The soldiers bring them firewood and water and flour from outside of the zone, but they grow their own potatoes and apples and keep chickens. There are generally only one or two old women every seven to ten miles, at most. In response to a question, Victor said that yes, it is very isolated – but everyone else has died or is long gone, and this is the only place they know.

Some say we are entering a 'nuclear renaissance'. It is being cited as a clean alternative energy. A way to counteract global warming. It is coming back into fashion. Hinkley Point C has been officially approved by the British Prime Minister, and is currently under construction. Other new reactors are being built all across the world – in France, Finland, America, China, India, Russia, South Korea and Britain, to name but a few. In 2015 alone, ten reactors – eight in China, one in South Korea and one in Russia – connected to the grid. Combined, their capacity was 9.4 gigawatts: twice as much new capacity as the year before, and the highest increase in twenty-five years. By the end of 2016, there were four-hundred-and-forty-eight active reactors around the world. Fifty-nine new reactors were under construction at the beginning of 2018, eighteen of which were in China. The hope of the World Nuclear Association is for nuclear energy to provide twenty-five percent of the world's energy by 2050. The pace of nuclear growth is only increasing. The only problem the W.N.A. foresee in pursuing these targets is finding suitable locations on Earth or in outer space to put the waste – but these issues can easily be overcome.

Victor happened to tell Lucy, as she bent down to pet the German Shepherd belonging to one of the machine gun-toting guards stationed around the exit building at the edge of the zone (where Lucy and the other tour members were about to be scanned for radiation poisoning, before being allowed to leave), that all the animals and pets belonging to the residents of the areas around Chernobyl had to be left behind. The horses, chickens, goldfish, the rabbits and gerbils, the cats and dogs.

'Oh yes, many dogs abandoned here, *many* many,' he said, making a dismissive gesture with his hand. Just like every other time, the moment they'd stepped off the bus he'd lit a cigarette. It was lit before his foot left the bus's bottom step. The pleasure he took from that first drag, the second, the third, made Lucy ache with a terrible desire to take up smoking. She looked up at him now, while still absent-mindedly petting the dog. He told Lucy, flicking flaked ash off his chest, that the people were told to tie them up and to leave some food and water out. No, no, they were not told that they would not be returning to rescue them. They were not told they were tying them up so that they'd be trapped there, unable to run off and infect anywhere else with all that soaked-up radiation. That they were being left behind, alone, to starve to death. 'They were left to die, yes, but you know, the people, even if they told them, they had bigger problems, you know? Is just animals. Animals, they die all the time.'

Victor told her this as though it were just a funny little anecdote. It was an afterthought, something he could easily have forgotten to mention had she not happened to pet this dog, who was nuzzling its face wetly into her palm. As he spoke, Lucy snapped her hand back from the dog to her chest as though she'd been burnt by its fur, causing it to start too, its ears pricking upwards in sudden fright. It considered whether or not to bark, eyes unsure, and the guard wrapped the chain lead another loop around his palm to reassert control, soothing it simultaneously under his breath, a low mutter in a language Lucy didn't understand. She straightened up quickly and took a few steps away towards the safety of the building. The dog watched her back up with its big black doleful eyes. The guard watched her too. Lucy wondered, suddenly unsettled, what other stories Victor had not thought to tell her, and for a fleeting moment she was deafened, overwhelmed by the din of all that unspoken silence: the dogs, the slow, agonizing pain; all the endless stories, forgotten, wordless stories; the women, with their periods too, their heartaches too, the men, their hunger, their loneliness too. All the lives lost and ruined right here, lives like hers, measly and nothing and everything too, for a short time, to them at least, and all those poor animals who had nothing to do with any of it, who wanted only love, walks and sleep and pettings and food and more love, barking and straining, the sounds of their barking, their howling, all through the emptied, earth-spun days and nights, left behind to die here, alone, all thundering all around her.

'Are you okay?!' Victor asked, alarmed, as Lucy, her knees weakening, lost her balance and fell back gently against the whitewashed wall. He jerked his hands out towards her, the left still holding the butt of his dwindling cigarette, trailing a gust of grey-blue smoke that quickly disappeared to nothing in the warm evening air.

'... yes, yeah, I'm fine, thanks, sorry ...' Lucy smiled, trying to brush it off. 'Just tired, tired, I think.'

The other tour members had walked ahead into the cool shade of the building already, and Lucy was initially thankful – and then, later, a little regretful – that they hadn't seen her stumble. Victor, standing by her, pursed his lips in a mixture of concern and disapproval. Silently, his eyes said: 'I knew it was no good for a woman to come here alone.' Somewhere, off to the far left beyond the fence, a dog barked.

'Let's get you inside,' he said, stubbing out his cigarette under his heel and taking hold of her elbow. The guard and the dog were still watching them closely, intrigued by Lucy's sudden weakness. She, enjoying the physical contact, avoided looking back at either of them, and instead silently allowed Victor to guide her into the soft safety of the exit building.

Thirty years after the event, Yukiya Amano, Director General of the IAEA (International Atomic Energy Agency) released a statement to commemorate the tragedy. He said: 'But the key lesson from both Chernobyl and Fukushima Daiichi – for everyone involved in nuclear power-plant operators, governments and regulators – is that safety can never be taken for granted. Complacency must be avoided at all costs.'

For the rest of the journey back to Kiev, Victor stayed close to Lucy, as though readying himself to catch her in her next inevitable, feminine fainting fit. He made sure she drank plenty of bottled water on the bus, saying 'no, go, drink' and tipping his hands towards her, whenever she politely intimated she'd had enough. He didn't tell her any more stories. In fact, other than insisting she gulp down the water, they didn't speak at all. Nobody on the bus did. Everyone seemed worn out.

Lucy hooshed herself down into her seat and stuck in her earplugs. She felt strangely contented. Happy, even. She rested her head against her backpack, which was pressed against the glass of the window, wedged into place between her shoulder and the chair. In the seat directly in front of her, Norwegian David Foster Wallace was reading a book on his Kindle, digitally highlighting passages of interest with his finger. Lucy thought idly about what she'd eat for dinner that night, what might be showing on the Kiev hotel room's TV, what time her flight home the next day would be, and what time she ought to get up and leave the hotel to be in plenty of time at the airport. Thinking over details like this could keep Lucy awake all night if she didn't go through every potential unforseen setback with minute precision. Yet, in spite of all the planning, she still often found herself frantically rushing for buses – to appointments or through airports – so as not to be too late. She kept taking out her phone to Google Map the best public transport route, and kept remembering, again, that she had no Wi-Fi. She reminded herself to buy tampons first thing when she got off the bus. Oh, and to buy and send some postcards, although what would she write? *'Hello from Chernobyl! The weather is here, wish you were beautiful!'* She supposed it would be better not to send one to 'James'. To be fair, she didn't even know his address. Or actually like him.

Lucy took her phone out from her pocket again and selected some sad music. She closed her eyes. She then trained her thoughts, concentrating on all those poor, poor animals left behind. At first, there was nothing – her own mild hunger maybe, unconscious attempts to identify a certain smell rising from the seats of the bus – and so she shook her head and forced herself to focus even harder on their sorrowful eyes, their straining muzzles, their low, pining yelps, their emaciated bodies, losing strength. She felt a sudden violent surge of emotion, and she breathed in deeply through her nostrils, relishing it. Yes, this acute sympathy, this feeling of their pain – this is what she'd come for.

*

When Lucy got home, everything was the same. For distraction, she took to researching the Chernobyl disaster further, telling herself it was for the essay she was going to write. She found a short interview online with one of the surviving children who'd lived in Pripyat. In the video she is a grown woman, beautiful and sad, with cropped brown hair and brown eyes. She describes her experience thus:

'You look around and you see nothing, as if nothing happened. When there is a war, you see the war. But the sky above us is clear, no one is shooting, everything looks like it used to be. And we continue to live.'

A detail Lucy would never have thought to tell, whether it were true or not: that night, in the hotel in Chernobyl, there was one small cream-coloured stain on the corner of Lucy's bed sheets. She found it when she pulled back the covers and inspected the entirety of the bed with the flashlight on her phone. Lucy did this in every hotel she visited, always hoping to find something. She was more drunk than she'd realized and so her motions were forceful and jerky. She kept stumbling over nothing. Then there it was. She did a double-take, blinking slowly. The stain was small and down near the foot of the bed. If it was cum, it would be difficult to explain how the guy managed to ejaculate all the way down there, at the very edge of the corner of the bed. Unless he was sitting on the corner while s/he gave him head from a kneeling position on the floor, Lucy realized. She was both appalled and jealous at the thought. Her mind flashed to Norwegian David Foster Wallace, then to James, and then to Victor, sucking on his cigarettes that day. His wife and kids at home.

All the people in the world, fucking and coming in their beds. Lucy heard the person in the room next to hers flush their en suite toilet. She leaned down to sniff the stain. It didn't have any odour strong enough to exist above the synthetic rose-smell of the sheets themselves. She considered calling down to reception and demanding someone come up to replace them. Then she realized how absurd, in the circumstances, it was for her to even care about this stain – and standing there, alone, in her hotel room in the zone, Lucy burst out laughing.

Montparnasse

I went to visit the grave of de Beauvoir and Sartre and felt as though, when I saw it, I would be truly moved. It was a sunny day in September, probably ideal – hot with a soft breeze, pleasantly sweaty, in the quiet scented air of Paris on a weekday afternoon. We were lightly hungover, in that drowsy warm way, where everything blurs a little, the whole day vignetting in memory even as we lived it.

My friend – who has never read de Beauvoir or Sartre, or even Camus for that matter – came too, and I fell into the usual rôle of presenting myself as someone with depth, someone who had felt something special when reading their philosophy (of my own volition!) and who simply *must* see the grave. I gave a vague, inaccurate summary of Existentialism on the Métro from our Airbnb, keeping it loose and low (something about God and sex and cafés) in case someone who actually knew overheard me.

We arrived at the cemetery walls after walking down a narrow street lined with crêperies, where we agreed we'd eat lunch afterwards. We were having one of those continually hungry days, our stomachs washed out by tiredness and copious amounts of house wine. My friend was also very excited to show me photos of her sister's new couch, which could naturally be appreciated better sitting down. It was from Habitat and a bit *chichi* but also, she had to admit, perfect for the space. Her sister had just gotten engaged, which she was genuinely very happy about, although she kept asking me, but honestly, did I not agree, really, that a man who doesn't hold the door, or pay for the first round of drinks, or who reacted badly when their girlfriend – for example, her sister – just happened to bring up baby names at a *christening* for God's sake, is not a gentleman? And I would say, sure, yeah, definitely not, and she would tilt her head and smile in a sad way and nod to herself, and maybe even look off into the middle distance behind my head. Then she would lift her glass and, after a deep breath in, somehow find the inner strength to smile and change the subject.

De Beauvoir and Sartre were right by the entrance, which was somehow disappointing. I'd wanted meandering time, to acclimatize, to get in the mood. There was another man there already when we arrived, and so my friend kept back, giving me space to have this moment to feel a connection, to be truly moved in peace. After a solemn smile, the man and I hovered at the foot of the grave, both swaying slightly, unsure, not wanting to muscle in on the special moment of the other.

I stood and looked and heard my stomach rumble. I wondered had the man heard it too, and cleared my throat, as though that would somehow retroactively cover the sound. He didn't show any sign of having noticed. He was staring at the grave. Was he praying? I watched him from the corner of my eye and, perhaps sensing my scrutiny, he glanced at me. I quickly shifted my focus to the grave. I squeezed my eyes closed. God, it was actually very hot. A bit too hot, really. And my feet were beginning to hurt. I shook my head slightly, and tried to summon a picture of the little rotting feet of de Beauvoir and Sartre, buried there together. I wondered if they ever got sore feet. I wondered if he'd been buried in his glasses. She in her chignon, perhaps. Images pressed themselves lightly against my mind – the two of them lying there, grey corpses, full heads of immaculate hair, cigarettes hanging from their indifferent, rotten lips. This made me laugh nervously, an impulse I often experienced in graveyards, or when supposed to be feeling deeply. My laugh developed into a cough, brought on by the cigarettes bummed from moderately attractive French men the night before. Maybe they'll think it was a sob, that I'm overwhelmed, I thought, this man and my friend, who I could feel getting bored behind me.

I flicked my hair and shuffled from foot to foot, feigning concentration. My mind that day, in that humming city heat, was like a watercolour painting spattered with constant fine rain, any hope of discernible images blurring in circles and streaming off in soft swirls of mixed and fading colours ... That morning, it had taken me at least eleven minutes to choose what jeans to wear, and I'd only brought two pairs. I'd sat on the bed while my friend showered, and stared at them. One pair of blue denim, one pair of black denim, both Topshop. It was impossible. Standing there in Montparnasse, a pigeon cooing above my head, I found myself thinking about what kind of crêpe I'd order at lunch (sweet or savoury, another impossible decision), and whether or not it would be too early for a beer.

I glanced over the little notes people had left on the grave, written on used Métro tickets, weighed down with pebbles from the gravel pathways. French, English, Japanese, other languages I didn't recognize. All with their own special connections. Some with little happy or sad smiley faces. The man looked too, and I decided to sigh deeply, trying to encourage some tiny hint of blocked emotion up from my chest. The sigh moved trapped air around inside me and I had to suppress a burp. Caught inside my mouth, it tasted on my tongue of Pinot Noir and strong white cheese.

But I didn't know these people. The notes made me feel sick and silly, the love hearts and quotes, and I hated the man for being there too, ruining it, and my respectful friend for expecting something of me. I glanced around and she was texting, probably her boyfriend back in London. They had been together for three weeks, nothing too serious, yet, although she was delighted by how much he was keeping in touch – he'd asked her to update him on every activity and vice versa, although he was just home as usual, working as an accountant for PwC in the city. Last night as we were getting ready to go out for dinner I'd seen her phone light up with a message telling her his gym stats, followed by four emojis of smiley faces with their tongues out and three of a muscled arm, flexing. Later, when I came back from the bar, she showed me a selfie he'd sent of himself and the guys having after-work drinks in Leadenhall Market. He told her they were planning a work-sponsored charity bungee jump for orphaned Syrian children, which seemed to make my friend weak at the knees. Along with the photo he included the hashtags #charity #goodcause #dotherightthing #orphansinsyria #nomorewar #savethechildren #peace #bungeejump #pwc. In return, she asked me to take a photo of her with every meal, because he was *such* a foodie and this was Paris after all.

I stepped back from the grave and smiled thinly at her, quiet and withdrawn, to convey 'overcome' and said something about how wonderful, how beautiful it was. I repeated for the man to hear (although he wasn't even handsome), how I'd just read their letters, how they were so personal, so intimate, even though, actually, a lot of them had been surprisingly bitchy and shallow (making them a far more satisfying read than I'd been expecting).

Walking our way around to Beckett (because it would be embarrassing to go all that way and not to bother with Beckett), my friend taking photographs of the dappled pathways for Instagram, marvelling over the grandeur of some of the graves and the decrepit ruination of others, I allowed myself the luxury of giving up entirely. I emptied my already-seeping mind. I thought about where we'd go for dinner and which lipstick I'd wear, and felt a tinge of worry because my feet were sore in my new heeled boots, but they went best with the slinky black dress I'd been saving for that night. Beckett's grave was suitably plain, which we commented on before leaving.

'I must try to read more of him,' I said after a pause, as a way to conceal without outwardly lying that I'd read almost nothing. A fly buzzed by my friend's eyes and she agreed, 'mmm, yes,' swatting it away with the hand holding her phone and frowning. 'He's with Godot now,' I joked limply, sickened by the utterance before it had even left my mouth, but she didn't seem to hear me.

A siren passed somewhere to the left of the graveyard, fading into the low hum of citied silence. Into this lull, we heard before we saw the older American couple approaching along the pathway, querying directions loudly, graveyard maps held out before them. Sweat spread flesh-coloured under the armpits of his white t-shirt. She wore small, rectangular semi-tinted glasses – no doubt, I immediately decided, the kind whose lenses were specially designed to react to light. They both wore tight, three-quarter length jeans, and backpacks.

'Hey, maybe these nice girls will help us … hey there!'
A big, gleaming smile. 'Hey, you ladies know where we
might find Sontag? Susan Sontag? My son, our son, he
went to college with her son! Told him we'd stop by, haha,
get a photo! … God, is it hot today or is it just us?' The man
cartoonishly pretended to mop his brow with the entire
length of his forearm, still beaming at us. 'Here honey,
your water …' The woman turned and started working
the zippers on his backpack, at which he bent his knees
slightly in a sort of emasculating curtsy, to facilitate.

Rolling our eyes at one another, my friend replied that
no, we didn't know, sorry. I hadn't even realized she was
buried here, and cursed myself. I couldn't go visit her now
– they'd be there, this couple, they'd probably make us take
their picture, and then make some joke about *On Photography* or something. Being there at her grave would bond
us together, encourage fellow feeling. I'd have to give her
grave a miss, although, I consoled myself, I could always
say I'd seen it. I wasn't taking photos anyway, because to
me a lack of holiday snaps implied depth, authentic experience, although I did enjoy when I had to reluctantly pose
for the ones my friend insisted taking of the two of us.
Every time I went to the toilet, I found myself compul-
sively checking her Facebook page to count the likes.

'Oh, well that's no problem – we have these maps, we
just can't make out a thing! My wife reads French, read
Proust first year in NYU, didn't you, honey? Life-chang-
ing! Oh, and look, here's Beckett. Catherine, look, can you
believe it? Wow … and he wrote in French too, right? Do
you girls read French? Have you read him? We just love
his stuff …' My friend smiled weakly. It was difficult to
tell who this man was talking to, us or his wife, or who he
was talking for – us, or himself. It was demoralizing, too,

to think of him reading Beckett. The thought of it made me want to swim to the exact middle of a big, cold lake, and stop. Instead, I cleared my throat, a signal to my friend, and then before they could engage us in further conversation, our body language a little stiff, we nodded to them, the smiling couple, and began walking back the way we'd come.

'Well ... that was beautiful,' my friend said as we walked back out through the gates.

I had been thinking of a guy I'd visited in Paris the year before. It had been his birthday weekend, 'the age of Christ', he kept saying. On my first night there, at three in the morning, after trying and failing to score some pills along the canals of the 19th Arrondissement, he'd tried to make me watch *Enter the Void* by Gaspar Noé when we got back to his place. On the morning of the day itself, after fucking, he'd shown me a video on his phone of sharks eating one another in the womb. 'Fuck nature,' he'd concluded, and the next day I'd gone home with chlamydia, although I wouldn't find that out for another four months.

Now, I could sense my friend looking at me. 'Yes ... Yes, wasn't it?' Keeping my gaze downwards, I endeavored to make my eyes appear a little misty, and then blinked as though attempting, embarrassedly, to clear them. But of course I was in complete control. I remained utterly unmoved. Had I expected it to be any different? And this realization of yet again feeling absolutely nothing when there ought to have been something caused a slicing of sharp, reddish-pink heat to rise in my chest. I flexed my fingers and worked hard on remaining calm. Not to shout out, to howl, to start banging my chest or pulling out my hair or scratching my nails deep into the soft, well-moisturized skin of my very kind, very good friend or – even better – to lie down right there on the white dusty path; to curl up and stop altogether.

Luckily, in a matter of seconds – under the warm sun, with hunger, sleepiness, the sound of languorous traffic outside the high surrounding walls, people eating sandwiches and drinking coffees outside the cafés, the promise of more drinks tonight, slow and merry obliteration, the delicious process of shedding skin – this feeling too, passed. And I was left with my familiar, easy nothing.

Zeno's Paradox

She has the thought, unbidden, over and over, catching her quick through the chest; ever since that first time; then, right when, heave gasping overbent on grass out, front-fallen knees, not knowing, how knowing; door open flung, light pouring limbs out into cool air somehow moving, not hers, nothing now hers known, all; upon hearing, the phone's screen still aglow with it there on kitchen floor, dropped a clatter, still ablaze with what, irrevocable, voice calling still Lucy are you there are you alright Lucy I'm so sorry Lucy, now known, no; howling out ow out with it now, convulsing out hands wet down from it green evening dew cold beneath her, white breath spilling out, the thought:

How easy short there forever looked, from freckled dappled days under swaying shade lying, warm red soft through foldover eyes, bright dozing, whispers slipped, sipped butterwarm in soft, fluttering dares to keep, fingers interwoven, for better, clam clap clamp palmed in sacred matters only, mattered to them, two, ownly. All promise. Why not yes, alright then yes let's give it a whirl so, yes.

At least that's how she remembers it now. Now that he is not here with a memory to contend, to complete. Mix colours in with, all colours turning to brown, round and round, muddied. The way a pot, spinning, just a lump, nothing, spinning, then fingers from two hands round mould up to form, a shape, a thing, definite. A shape designed to hold things together. The history is hers now, and the colours are hers; and she, let loose, is choosing reds and blues and yellows and greens for it. She fears she's running wild with it. She doesn't know how she got here.

Lucy is on a train travelling forward, rolling on into the city to collect the keys from his sister. His sister works in an office right in the centre, just west of the river (Lucy has never been entirely sure what his sister does, but it seems important and tiring. His sister pauses conversations to purse lips at her buzzing phone's illuminated screen and pinches between her eyes, and says no, I'm fine, really it's fine, what were you saying? And Lucy can never quite remember.) Lucy hasn't seen her since the funeral, and before that, not for a few months. Certainly not since she, bags packed, closed softly the door behind, while he slept. They have arranged to meet in a café called La Belle Époque, which serves teas and coffees and small, intricately glazed desserts that in fact taste dry and bland.

The café is around the corner from his sister's large mirrored office building, and they are meeting at thirty-six minutes past five, after his sister finishes work. His sister has told Lucy in advance that it will take her six minutes to get there and that she has to collect her son from a piano lesson at seven, so they can both rest assured that they won't be obliged to stay long. One precursory hot drink, the required exchange; keys and words, all small, and she'll be done. Finished.

Lucy is alone on the carriage, right at the back. Waiting. As she breathes long through her nose, she smells stale coffee rising and musty train, familiar. She is trying and failing not to think. Don't even, she instructs. No. It's okay, she soothes herself; she cannot reach, it's okay, she can't. To get there, Lucy must first cross from A halfway to B, and then halfway to halfway to B, and so on, and so she will be stuck forever in the halfways, suspended still. And so she will never have to face that welled-in, just-like face.

The train is silver, clean and bright, with shining yellow poles and a man's gentle voice making announcements along the way, telling her all her halfway points; towns that she knows she can never reach and yet is passing steadily. A person there before her, gone now, spilled their coffee. Bitter smell rising. The cup rolls. It is small and dark red, polystyrene, with a white plastic lid. One end is larger than the other so it rolls in lurching circles, getting nowhere. Brown liquid curls in lines, expanding out in widening rings, up and down across the floor with heaves of movement as the train brakes and accelerates. How many times will it travel to the city and back today? Round and round.

A month ago Lucy awoke, packed two small suitcases from the attic with clothes and a few personal belongings from the spare room, the few items left unshared (so few, by the end: some childhood photographs, one or two CDs, old books, jewellery, a razor, toothbrush ...), and left: softly easing the door closed behind her, the shock of summer's morning light shining in, momentarily blinding, in a collapsing triangle on the hall's pine floor as she pulled gently, so as not to wake. She left a note on the kitchen table. She thought it would be easier that way.

Lucy has now been set a task. She must meet his sister and collect the keys to the home they shared. Empty now, waiting. Lucy thinks of the teabags in the dark press, milk

in the fridge spoiling into thick white lumps. Bills collecting in a pile in the hall, DVDs lying haphazard on the
shelves by the television, left out of cases. Coins wedged
down the side of the blue couch cushions still bruised
with indentations; toothpaste stains on the pale green tiles
along the wall above the bathroom sink. The heating, she
thinks. Probably still on the timer. Six in the morning, five
in the evening, chugging into life, water gurgling. The low
constant hum of electronics; a thickened silence.

When she thinks of their – his, now her – house, it's
like picturing a place suspended underwater. Preserved.
She imagines swimming through it in a wetsuit and mask;
pushing off door frames for propulsion, carefully kicking
out her legs so as not to disturb all of the too-familiar items
as she drifts from room to room. She sees the blue Turk-
ish vase on the mantelpiece, brought back from that street
market in Kalkan; the watercolour of the lakeside cottage
at dusk her grandmother painted; the wobbly kitchen
table with a folded napkin stuffed under the leg by the
door; the towels folded in the hot press; their two white
pillows ...

When she pictures them now, they all seem to float;
to be held still, static and untouchable. Like items in a
museum or pieces of fruit in jelly. She does not like the
sensation this causes and tries to blink the images away.

And now she must collect the keys (jingling), front two
gold and for the back silver (jangling), with that miniature
yellow-faded plastic sandal from Vietnam – 2010, was it? –
all up in her fingers (jingling), her hands, all the memories
(jangling). She would give all she owns, she thinks now,
sitting and looking out at passing pale yellow fields rolling off to greyblue sea, everything she has to never have to
see it again. The house where they, where he. To strike a

match and walk away. But she can't do that. She has been irresponsible enough. Caused enough. Now it's all on, in, through her. This is her task.

He and his sister share the same eyes and way of tilting their mouth to the left when something amuses – a lilting face, they – and the dread of what she will see, when she sees those well-known so transposed, makes her shudder down in the very ashen black pit of her, and she coughs up smoke and soot nothing, raw in her throat at the thought.

A month ago Lucy left, gently pulling behind her the door to the house they shared, leaving only a note on the table, propped against the fruit bowl, to explain. Two weeks ago, he committed suicide. This is a thing that has happened now.

The train heaves to a stop, lulling her upper body forward, holding her there suspended before collapsing her back into place. A dark line of coffee, broken free from the circles by the heave, trickles towards her shoe. Lucy's stomach contracts. She has been unable to keep down food and the strong bitter smell is making her nauseous. But she sits still; she doesn't dare move. The silver disks on either side of the doors, surrounded in green, sing out. Nobody gets on or off. Two teenage girls are chatting somewhere further up the carriage, out of her field of vision. She didn't notice them embarking. They talk excitedly, interrupting themselves, volume and pitch building in heaving waves. They are discussing boys in their school. A text message, a party. Their chatter reaches climax and they shriek in a fit of nervous ecstasy over a joke made; something read out from a phone. An allusion to a kiss, a touch maybe. Lucy listens absently, the words only sounds, glancing off her mind. She is now twenty-eight. She doesn't know how she got here.

Lucy has mousey hair which she usually dyes blonde every month. She has not dyed it in a long time, and so her roots are long. She has freckled skin and bitten fingernails which crack in pointed shards of colour when painted. Reds, purples, blues. She has muddy green eyes, one of which contains three black dots in the iris. She is of average height, perhaps slightly smaller.

He always said she was small, but only to tease her; poking at her, grinning. She pretended to mind. He was so tall. Tall and gangly. He looked like his limbs were going to come loose and break free when he ran. When they were younger, she hoped that once they grew up he would fill out; that his body would eventually thicken and catch up with his height, and so they would match better. That was what she consoled herself with when they walked into restaurants, all squeaky clean, brushed and shining, playing at being a real couple. Or when she saw them reflected back through the eyes of others: friends, her family, the men, uncles and grown cousins, sizing him up. Yes, their eyes would say. Yes, they could take him.

Once they grew up, she thought. But he didn't. And he was oblivious. He remained thin, boyish, right to the end. When he lay naked beside her she would turn over to face him, her round breasts sagging down sideways toward the mattress, her tummy pouring forward, round too, her hip curving up in all the rolling hills of her. He never ceased to find the existence and proximity of her body a wonder. He ran his palms across her, disbelieving. They were calloused from lugging bricks and wood and digging on site, and from strumming guitar strings. His touch was tough and grated against her softness, at the pads. But she didn't mind. At first she liked it.

Lucy thinks now of how he ran his long fingers down her stomach, her hip, into the soft curls and gently inside along, loving soft. His movements were slow and tentative as though not wanting to frighten away a small bird, a rabbit. He inspected her all over. His serious wide eyes. It was like she'd appeared out of nothing, a magical thing. He ran his hand up, large and thin and clumsy, so young, placed it gently on her breast, held, as she looked back at him, willing, open; such soft yielding flesh, and a shudder ran through him and passed into her like a taut string plucked.

Dozing quiet after, his eyes half-closed, she used to trace her fingers along the edges of him like she was drawing him into life. His sharp ridges; hip bone, ribs, shoulder. His new pink skin. His limp dick, soft, a wonder. A real one, there, all hers, to play. Another body, a foreign body, outside her own. Cool cupped balls, filling her palm. All hers, all freely offered. Or if he faced the other way, curled up half-asleep: the rungs of his spine, the tendons stretching across the back of his knees. The line of his bum, the perfect round cheeks against her thighs, warm. Spots, freckles, dotted across his shoulders. All hers, given to her. The first ever she was to see, to feel. And for – they thought then, so young – forever. And now, she thinks, she really has become his forever. His only ever.

Lucy breathes deep, pulls herself up, and places her ember-hot gaze outside. Find something there, please. They crash-land into the bluegrey hum. Sea there, out. Ever out, to the line, the tide. In out, inout, innoush ... Can do nothing about the sea, she thinks. Just a bigger thing. A Bigger Thing. This thought momentarily reassures her. She was small in that sea once, and now she is big, and then she will be gone and it will stay the same. Is this the self-same skin, stretched across her bones?

Lucy feels stretched, memories expanding, making her skin taut and thin and easily torn. Would she taste the same now, to the sea? All connected, all water connected, going round and round. The cup at her feet. The train sways. Nothing new, just filtered throughout again; sea rivers the sky the earth. Through her, her body, drink it in and piss bleed cry it out, in out, inout, innoush ... Every drink drunk an infinite amount of times before, filtered through. Maybe Shakespeare drank the coffee at her feet, or Sophocles, or Hitler. Hitler's last sip of wine; da Vinci's early morning piss. Steam liquid frozen, all the same, a set amount, round and round. None of it goes anywhere, all here, always. Matter too, all the same, flesh of my; sinking into the earth, more earth, again, around. His now, too, the earth. Her breath catches hot in her chest. His, the sea, she. She doesn't know how they –

The train heaves and shudders to a halt, and the two girls jostle one another out the doors, their voices echoing down the carriage to Lucy before being lost, dissipating to nothing but disconnected peals of sound on the warm September evening air. But they understand one another. They walk in unison up the platform, arms linked. Lucy is left in silence. Off to the beach for the evening, she thinks. To hang around, to mess, and sit on railings; pass around poorly rolled smokes and hunch their shoulders against the sea breeze; chat and kick their legs back and forth, suspended in the just before. To spend another evening impatient for something to happen.

The first time they met was at the seventeenth-birthday party of a boy he went to school with on the far side of the city. Took all night to get there, Lucy remembers, she and two other girls; the train and two buses, and a room full of giddy strangers, dark smoke and noise and sex lurking red in corners. Lucy vomited from marijuana and vodka, combined in wild swirls of grey inside her. He brought her water and travelled in the taxi with her all the way back to her town, she crying softly, lying in his lap, hiccups. You're alright now no worries nearly home now you're okay. Then – lifting her under the elbow, ever-respect-ful – carried her stumbling heeled feet to her very front door, before walking the two-hour journey back home the way they'd come. (The taxi cost him all his money. He was young and poor and teetering on the brink of love.)

He texted the next afternoon to see how she was, and she, wrapped up still hidden in bed, full of self-loathing, felt shamefully indebted. And, she supposes, touched. He always was described as kind. He used three smiling emoticons, and misspelled 'then' as 'than'. Even so, they were together for just under ten years. They were happy, she thinks. They were. As happy as two separate, wrapped up in skins, trying to reach across, to build a life for two, together, can be. How short there forever looked, then. But it hadn't been enough. And now ... she doesn't know how she, how they.

Someone in the water, she sees. A man. Sitting on the train stock still, she passes, or seems to. Really she knows it's okay, she's going nowhere, she cannot reach B. He is swimming in a line parallel to the shore. Parallel to the train, trajectory – same and different. His own infinity of divisions, As to Bs, to travel through; each stroke, all. The weight of them, Lucy thinks, weary. How can he bear? Further along, the man's black dog paves the way, pad-dling. It is crisp clear bright out, the sun's heat thoroughly melted into the dark cliff face, seagulls squinting in their perches, and she thinks the sharp salt cold against his skin must be a wonderful thing, and envies him. He looks content, from Lucy's elevated view, trundling by the shore. It looks like a routine, a known back and forth, round. He wears a red cap and it is a shock against the rolling blue-grey. It marks him out as a definite thing.

A daily ritual, a way of being. To swim, to place oneself in the big and be small. To affect. Yes, she sees. Each stroke a splash to her, reaching out across, the water and air in waves; each arm lift and down, a wave to her. She watches, awaits each wave, a wave coming now, another wave, round and – all goes black thunder hum, and Lucy starts in her seat. They've entered a tunnel. It hushes past beyond her nose. She sits back from the window. The light approaches, white. When they emerge, the sea is gone. The man and his dog are gone. There are high hedges, the banks, swishes of green and dirt flitting. They have turned away inland.

The man and his dog, back there, swimming right now, still. Lucy feels herself longing, needing to go back to watch them, back and forth, forever, and feels a strange aching grief rising. She wants to sit on a wooden bench in her coat in the low September sun and watch the man and his dog swim back and forth, back and forth, with the sound of the sea hooshing as evening falls, shadows stretching tired out across towards her, back and forth, and never leave. Stay and swing her feet a little too; scuff the earth, scratching grains of sand, and watch his strong pink arms turning purple in the dark; and lights, small and yellow, appearing all along the coast left to right, people readying for night, the day closing soft; back and forth, the waves waving round and round, hooshing and hissing back, with her hands in her pockets, fading too, to nothing; back and forth, breathing into the neck of her coat, warm and moist, as darkness thickens all, blanketing round around her.

But she can't stay back there, back where things are contained in a certain space, and she is safe. The train is travelling on. Lucy is on her way into the city. She has been set a task. She must breathe evenly and steady herself. They are slowing now. The man's gentle voice announces somewhere coming now, along the line, and they slow. The circles by the doors sing out and the button is pressed and they slide open. Lucy sees that she is almost at B. How has that happened? Couldn't be, she doesn't know how she. And he is back there, still swimming. A woman steps onto the carriage with an empty buggy, a small child pulling from her side, big step now, on. She catches Lucy's eye, quick, glancing, and pulls the child, come on now this way up the carriage, the other way. Lucy sits still. She doesn't know how she.

That public loo she was in, in the garage a few days ago, on the way to the funeral. Filthy, encrusted from those before, stains splattered across the walls, and what was the toilet roll dispenser called again? 'Big Willy'? She laughed out loud when she read that, smarting hot red eyes, hurting her to shape her face that way, squatting holding up her black skirt and knickers forward at the front – out of the spray, over the bowl, not touching anything. And worried then maybe her mother or father had heard her, waiting outside, both huddled, lips thin, worrying. Mother smoking again with the stress, trying not to cry herself – they loved him too, of course, all those years, like a son to them – plumes emitting in fitful bursts, lingering in white lazily rising clouds on the cold stark air. Thinking she'd be in there crying, again and again, over. And there she'd been, laughing at Big Willy. Big Willy, with a picture, a little living toilet roll dispenser on the real dispenser, concentric, with a big smile and wide eyes and legs and waving hands. Waving at her, watching her piss. He'd have found that funny too, to be fair, she remembers thinking, pulling up her knickers and carefully letting down her skirt, no longer smiling.

And to think Lucy thought she knew pain before. Had relished it before. When it was all romance, all manageable. Thought they'd caused each other, before. With mean looks and dripping tears and all the biting words they'd used to test the soft eggshells of one another. And then there he lay, arms crossed. Serene. In that suit they bought for his cousin's wedding the year before. His mother there too, overbent womb-clutching. Sedatives, they'd had to, barely seemed to recognize, under elbow led, after the service. And without knowing whether her feet were rooted on the ground the shape of the room the sounds, she found herself talking in her head, looking down at him, her turn now, her parents either side, warm bodies shielding, telling him how she'd left and there he'd gone and left one better, wasn't that just typical, a place too far for her to follow. What was he at, she asked, and then she waited she reached out to him thought he'd let out a smile or something, some sign, a laugh, sit up, and on they'd go arm in arm out of that place a big dream some joke, ha, tell the grandkids and all that on to the future bright light shining just a hop skip now two ticks, but no, where was, her hand touched, cold, oh, no, eyes still closed, his skin, clam, clap, clamp, palmed, and she stumbled, her parents catching felt herself sink the deep water coming

up around her sink into the thought, how easy there
forever looked, but now, no, oh, forev–

The child down the carriage cries out, a piercing yowl.
Lucy is jolted up. What happened? Nothing, nothing.
The here and now. Her eyes focus outwards, the world;
the inside images sinking heavy back down below. Roof-
tops outside, flashes of streets. She breathes deep. Tall
smoking chimneys from the factory to the east where the
river meets the sea. A crane, slow moving, rotating over
beyond, mustard yellow. Building up or knocking down.
People there on the path below, now crossing in a flood,
released, green man. The low-buzzing sticky honeycomb
of city evening with the night ahead. She must step into
it soon. Her task. How did she get here? The man and a
black dog, the sea, hooshing. Red cap, back and forth, the
waves. All the divisions through to B. But now. The gentle
voice tells Lucy her stop is approaching. She must alight.
She doesn't know how she. His sister, keys (jingling), that
well-worn face, approaching now (jangling).

As it stands, two weeks after Lucy left a note on the
kitchen table – to explain easier, after all they, their bodies,
how they fit, no more she – and two weeks ago from this
moment now, long gone, irrevocable, he shot himself in
their room – his, her room – and was found lying on his
back, long limbs thrown asunder, after three days of not
turning up to work and the phone ringing out. He was
found by his father. He'd left the house unlocked. There
was a note on the bedroom door saying not to come in, to
call the police instead, but his father, desperate hoping,
had ignored it.

Lucy looks out at the streets, the roofs, gleaming warm
white on slate grey in the low light, the movements darting

colours, and she sees him: splayed out across their made bed, the white sheets stained in fireworks, dark red and crusty, out from the heart of him. It was in the chest, not the head, so they were able to have the open casket. His calm pale face. That welled-in lilting face. Hands folded. Those hands on her breast, a shudder, like a string plucked. So considerate, right to the end.

They did fit well together, Lucy thinks. In spite of everything, they did. Her breasts would fall forward towards his mouth when she sat above him, across him, reaching. And he would sit forward, body lurching to her, his fingers clinging hard, trying to melt right into the sides of her, pulling her down, all of her onto him, to lick and suck, slow, as she rolled up down. She would feel his sharp hip bones press against her soft, fleshy inner thighs (the first time – the first for both – they had left stormy bruises), and his large knuckles reaching around the round of her, up and down, those calloused hands, hard gripping nails around the dipped bowl of her lower back, to hold, snaking up and down the curling fern of her, to pull her in close, close now, close. He had been all jagged peaks, young, she soft hills, worn down and rolling. But they did fit, she thinks, somehow.

There was a dip between his neck and shoulder in which her head fit perfectly, after, when they, panting, flush hot-skinned, quiet. Fingers laced loose, not yet broken. The sounds of the world out beyond returning. They always left the window open in summer. A car passing, a neighbour's radio, voices muffled. A pigeon maybe, from the tree beyond, calling over and over, the sound rounding around in slow swirls towards them in the last light. He'd said, suddenly shy – the first time they came to see the house that late spring and the daffs beginning to sag a little, some broken at the necks – how perfect that tree would be for a swing. And she'd taken his face in her hands and kissed him hard, because she hadn't known what to say. That sinking feeling, her stomach, heavy; her whole life rolling out there before her; the swing, back and forth, perfect, from that tree. Back and forth. Somehow it wasn't enough. She wonders now, could he tell by her?

Lucy thinks now that she was happy. Mostly happy. It was like they were made for each other, just the right fit, she liked to tell herself then. That's what people always said, too, smiling over them. Young love. Not that she ever really believed. Did she? She's lost the, doesn't know how she, how they. She doesn't know now. He had been all concave to take her, and she had been all convex, reaching out, to fill.

And she still so young, they tell her now, in circles back rubbing. Perhaps in days, she thinks. But all her living done now, all her trying; done back then, back together, aching blissfully. How could she live on now, go on beyond, without him? She is his forever now. He has given her that. But here's her stop, and she has to get off. Task, meet his sister, keys, round and round. The coffee cup will travel back, all the way back now, spinning round, the smell rising. She can't help but envy it. The doors are singing, she has to go, her feet, up, go. But A cannot reach B, all the in-betweens, and the man back there still, black dog and red cap, back and forth swimming, as the evening light fades a thinning blue gold haze. All promise, so long there forever looked. Standing at A, fingers interlaced, loose, looking off at B, thinking yes, yes, alright then let's give it a whirl so –

All My Exes Live in Texas

There were four phones on the dashboard of the Azerbaijani driver's car: one for music, one for Google Maps, his official work one as a luxury car driver, and his personal one. On the personal one he showed me photos of his life, and on the professional one he spoke in an unfamiliar, harsh-sounding language, presumably Azerbaijani. I chose to blast 'Love On Top' by Beyoncé because it popped into my head, and because I was in Houston, her hometown, and because it was celebratory. I was giddy to be there after nigh-on fourteen hours of travel (to save money, I'd flown from Dublin via the pure unadulterated misery that is Manchester airport). But I regretted my choice almost immediately.

'You like this? Black music?' he asked me. After a moment of disapproving listening, he said 'I suppose is okay,' but then turned it down to tell me that all the trouble in Houston, no, Texas, no, *America*, was caused by the blacks. All the trouble. He said yeah Obama had been fine, but he wasn't really black. He also said that yes, he carried a gun, but that he had to, because all the blacks did.

I asked Karl what the city was like, the night life, the food, and he said Houston was now eighty percent Mexican. He said it with a tone of significance I was supposed to comprehend. He said he and his friends liked to go out to the clubs on weekends, but that no, he never danced himself, he just watched the Mexican girls get drunk on tequila and shake their hips. He said they always got so drunk on very little, just a few shots, because they were so small, and then they danced like crazy until they fell over or the night ended and they got kicked out by the bouncers.

I also chose 'Love On Top' because he'd made it very clear from the outset that this $100 lift he was giving me, from George Bush Intercontinental Airport north of the city to the distant south-eastern suburbs, was pretty much the most incredible favour anyone had done for anyone else, *ever*. I was also very aware that it was only even happening because he thought it might increase his chances of fucking me. Therefore, I thought something poppy and playful would keep him appeased; make him think I was a nice, fun girl, potentially up for nice, fun times.

There was some cause for him to feel he was doing me a favour. I had landed without any clear idea of how I was going to get from one side of Houston to the other, to the library where my friend (well, my ex-boyfriend, so my 'friend') was to meet me. Meeting at a library had initially sounded quaint and romantic, and now seemed like an awkward fucking nightmare.

At the airport, I spent what felt like an interminable amount of time loitering by the entrance to the ladies' bathroom, bags abandoned in a pile at my feet, cold armpit sweat just beginning to emit that acrid smell. I was trying and failing to download Uber on my phone, because my phone was incredibly shit – so shit that I couldn't store any photos or music at all, and the only app beyond Chrome and Gmail that it could support was WhatsApp. Not even Facebook, let alone Messenger.

In most scenarios this smart-ish phone, this phone of a semi-resigned Luddite, was a source of smug pride for me, because I'm one of those dickheads who believes that a visible resistance to the technological trappings of modern life indicate to others that one's thoughts and leisure activities must be on a higher plane. Like, that everyone must assume I'm always reading Marcus Aurelius or Sartre instead of scrolling through the Instagram feeds of near-naked pouting celebrities. Also, I was perpetually broke and tight and unwilling to spend the little money I had on a proper phone.

Because of this, feeling trapped, Uber failing me, I found myself becoming a bit teary and high-pitched and needy. Looking around for a saviour, anybody to help, I could sense myself becoming all wide-eyed and girly and *I have always depended on the kindness of strangers*-y, and that is when this Azerbaijani driver – whom I have decided to call Karl, but whose real name I genuinely don't remember – swooped in and offered me the use of his luxury car to get wherever I was going. For a moment I thought he was just some rich guy there to rescue me, not unlike Richard Gere in *Pretty Woman*, but almost immediately it became clear that nothing about Karl suggested a life of great success or pleasure. He had the practical yet wary, unconsciously resentful demeanor of a person who must work doggedly to survive – that slight stoop and malnourished sheen of someone who struggles just to eke out their barely sufficient share of the American dream. I, on the other hand, in spite of being quite poor, generally manage to look quite rich in a shabby, thoughtless-seeming way; because I'm intimidatingly tall, work little and half-assedly, and wear red lipstick. I guess this must've been what fooled him into thinking I'd be the kind of feckless moneyed woman worth approaching.

Karl had a neat white shirt tucked into black slacks, Neo-from-*The-Matrix*-style sunglasses (that he kept on indoors) and incredibly pockmarked skin – almost like he'd had some terrible disease as a teenager. I guessed he was only in his twenties, probably around the same age as me, but I could see his smooth scalp clearly through his oiled black hair. He was tanned all over, with dark circles I could just discern underneath the rim of his sunglasses. He had moles on his face and neck that I imagined spread in constellations all across his tight little body.

I explained to him that yes I would *love* a 'ride', yes I was a bit lost, haha, yes silly me, but he needed to understand I wasn't going to the city centre, I was going south of Houston. Or did I just say 'south Houston'? Regardless, it wasn't until we were sitting side by side within the incredibly shiny and bulky black car in the multi-storey car park, with the air-conditioner whispering out soothing air and the engine purring, that he comprehended how far away my destination actually was. He kept looking at the screen of the Google Maps phone and shaking his head. Unimpressed, but not quite willing to abandon me entirely (my thigh was *just* visible – my skirt must have accidentally hiked itself up), he half-heartedly tried to order me an Uber from his phone, until we realized the payment would be too awkward and that he'd have to wait for it with me.

I began making a song and dance of clambering out, my voice all squeaky and childish but resigned to my new life stranded at the airport, full of 'oh don't worries, not your faults and thanks anyways' before he said with a defeated sigh 'No, fine, no, come back, get back, I won't leave you, I will take you, I will take you'. I was delighted. We'd already agreed on the $100 fare. He told me repeatedly, especially when we got caught in traffic taking the free-way over Houston's endless smoking oil fields, that the journey ought to have cost at least $200 – $250 probably, if not more. It was important, therefore, for him to think it was ladylike foolishness that had made this situation occur, not any manipulative sharkish survival skills on my part. Hence: '... *love on top!*'

The pictures Karl showed me were mostly of him alongside his exclusively male and Azerbaijani friends, standing beside nice cars in matching shirts, slacks and sunglasses, or holding beers and smiling. There were some selfies taken from above in clubs with one or the other of them giving the peace sign, and other photos of them standing around a grill with lots of different kinds of meat on it, again holding beers and smiling. He said they loved to go to the lake and barbecue on their days off. Weirdly, though, the photos looked like they were taken inside a garage – there was indoor lighting and a cement wall behind them.

Still, the men appeared happy enough. One held a string of sausages aloft in his tongs and I imagined the various phallic jokes that would've been made. They all looked like photos contrived to impress people back home. Ex-girlfriends who could go fuck themselves, just see how well they were doing in America without them, maybe. He told me that he had come alone from Azerbaijan when he was seventeen to stay with a distant cousin and that he'd spoken no English when he arrived. He said he was the eldest of eight, one brother and six sisters, with two left to be married. He said his father was 'a coroner … no, wait, a, what is it …? Ah, a military judge'. He said that I would never guess that they were father and son – his father had gotten married at fifteen, and a month after he turned sixteen, Karl had been born. He said they were more like brothers. I couldn't tell whether this likeness to his young father was a source of sadness or pride for Karl, whether he expected my reaction to convey 'impressed' or '*aawww, that's tough* ...' He was hard to read because his voice was pretty monotone, as though all communication was an effort he was overcoming especially for me. Also, I was mildly frightened of him – of his machismo, of being alone with him without anyone knowing where I was, without a working phone. I tried very hard not to think of my loving parents.

I was distracted, too, by the giant sand-coloured highways, the beating sun, the enormous honking trucks all around us and the flat, lifeless green fields; the water towers and the lingering oil smoke befuddling the sprawling emptiness; and the miles and miles of billboard advertisements: McDonald's, Whataburger, Burger King, Once You Pop, Holiday Inn, Just Do It, Girls Girls Girls, Beautiful Friendly Naked Girls, Investing in your Future, Insuring You And Your Family For Whatever Life May Bring, I'm Lovin' It again, Your New Home In Texas, Don't Miss Out!, Mmmm, Food Network, some Hollywood film with Emily Blunt, another with Channing Tatum, Be All That You Can Be, the United States Army, the *Houston Chronicle* App, Starbucks, McDonald's *again*, Applebee's, Motel 6, Coke again but Zero this time.

Trying to focus, returning my gaze to the slick inside of the car, I asked Karl did he ever miss home, his family, and he said yes and no – in some ways life was better here, in some ways not. I didn't ask him to elaborate. When we finally pulled up to the library, I felt Karl's body preparing for something beside me – a slight shifting and settling in my general direction. Luckily at that very moment I spotted my ex-boyfriend (let's call him … Charles) walking directly towards us.

'Oh, that's my friend!'

'Where ... wait, the man?'

'Yeah!'

Karl was not happy. I had not specified the gender of my friend, leaving him to assume it was a female. Now his tight frown told me I was clearly a lying whore, a traitor just like all the others. But oh well, too late – I was already gone.

Before this goes any further, I ought to explain, as concisely as I can, the history between myself and Charles. He and I had fallen madly in love two years previously, when we were both living in New York. Not to put too sickeningly idyllic a spin on it, but loving him had been breathtaking. He was *that* one. But I don't want to write about walking hand-in-hand through snow, or about watching Bill Murray movies in bed on Saturday mornings, or about home-cooked meals steaming up all the windows in his teeny-tiny Chinatown apartment. You probably know all that stuff already, in some form or another; love like that's the same for everybody.

It died quickly. He lost his job. I was running out of money. We found ourselves approaching the time when my visa was due to expire, at which point I'd have to go home to Ireland. His life was in America. Too soon, the distastefulness of reality began to leak onto our bed sheets, into our clothes and skins. Drunkenly, between soft kisses, we discussed getting married so as to be able to stay together. Soberly, we wavered.

The pressure grew debilitating. I wasn't sleeping. We began to hate the sight of each other, for all the loving pain it caused. Finally, he – the realist – made the call, and I boarded my flight home the following week. This sort of thing had happened to me before, although not with such intensity of feeling. I'd thought this was it. You'd think repetition of failure would make it easier, but it made it worse. Clearly, I was proving to be the common factor in love's implosion.

In the intervening years, there'd been a few casual emails back and forth, all friendly, all saying nothing in particular, but we hadn't seen each other since. I never really understood what had happened exactly. It remained a murky bruise hidden somewhere on my body; a bruise whose dull pain, when touched, I imagined I'd grown used to. But of course I hadn't. And now, out of seemingly nowhere, I'd come to visit.

I'd said, as though it were all entirely normal, that I was coming to see the South, Trump country, and told Charles I'd be driving to Austin too, to make the fact of this trip being about Texas – and most certainly *not* about him – clear. I presented it as though it were a funny coincidence that he lived there – almost as though I had been sent to Texas on a work trip, compelled to go, rather than visiting the precise place where he lived of my own volition. I think when telling this version of my motivation to Charles, to friends and family, or when repeating it over and over like a mantra in my mind, I'd almost believed myself.

Charles's apartment was sparse and clean. There was a pleasant lingering smell from the scented candles his younger sister had bought him for his birthday in January, and none of the usual underlying male smells. Even in the bathroom, around the sink and in the shower, there was no hint of that warm, savoury semen tang. I was impressed and disappointed. The floors were a cool light wood, and the few pieces of furniture came either from IKEA or from relatives: his grandmother, who had recently moved to a nursing home, and a wealthy Republican aunt with possessions to spare. A grey couch that would serve as my bed; a beautiful deep oak dining table, round, with four matching chairs; an antique carved coffee table; and a small compact piano with real ivory keys.

This was the Life of Charles I was presented with:

In the mornings, after an early half hour in the gym, Charles came back and made a flask of drip coffee and ate a banana and a protein drink that, when I sniffed the glass he left in the sink upon rushing off for work, smelled of absolutely nothing. He packed a quinoa salad he made in bulk on Sundays for lunch, and came home to a simple, usually vegetarian meal, which he ate before an early night to bed. He sometimes drank a glass of wine, sometimes didn't (it wasn't always worth the sugar content). He indulged, occasionally, in Netflix – mostly documentaries and foreign films. On weekends he read books and worked on his music, not using the piano but an electronic keyboard in his bedroom that he plugged into large, noise-cancelling headphones, so as not to disturb the neighbours.

On our first night in his apartment, chatting, Charles's grandmother called him twice. When he called her back, it turned out she had a Subway sandwich coupon for him. He doesn't eat Subway sandwiches but thanked her profusely, his Texan accent thickening. His mother called too but he answered her straightaway, walking quickly into his bedroom and gently shutting the door.

In his room – which I guiltily took in from the doorway while he was at work – along with the keyboard, was his bed, as well as a closet and a small desk upon which he had recording and mixing equipment that I recognized from our tiny bedroom back in New York.

On my second evening in Texas, Charles wanted to take me out drinking. When he emerged from his room, ready to leave, he was wearing awful sneakers and rectangular reading glasses. Back when I'd fallen wildly in love with him, back in New York, he'd been so stylish, so effortless, so sexy. He'd throw on a white t-shirt with a hole in the underarm and an old grey marl knit and I'd loved how he looked so much I'd tear them straight off him again and pull him back down into our tiny sweaty bed. Now he looked like an office worker from the Midwest, someone who would go on to suffer a mid-life crisis in a Jonathan Franzen novel.

I don't know what I wore, except I know I would've been trying to look as insanely attractive as I could manage, allowing for the fact that the humidity was not agree-ing with my hair, and that I was jet-lagged and bloated ('bloated' being what I like to call being fat, as though one day I'll drink some water or take a big shit and drop three dress sizes). Probably some sort of flowing flowery dress, to distinguish myself from the natives, but in a pretty, non-threatening way. And red lipstick, of course.

On the roof of Outriggers Seafood Grill & Bar we knocked back beer after beer and ate fried crawfish from a red plastic basket, watching the locals or the lights glinting on the water while chewing, or when conversation lulled. It was right on the ocean. And I mean *on* the ocean – the place was built on an extended jetty.

We had to walk the jetty, my heeled boots clomping against the boards, because we'd arrived by land. But we were in the minority. Most of the patrons had come by boat. They'd come from all along the shores of Texas, getting lit on bottles of beer all the way there, blasting music from their speakers. Some arrived in fleets of four or five boats, each carrying anything from one to seven or eight people, yelling and joking back and forth, trying to create waves to rock and topple one another by turning sharply and at speed as they pulled up. All along the jetty and around the edges of the wooden, creaking building itself, were these gently listing, white speedboats, all in varying sizes, rigged out with Texan flags and confederate flags and American flags, with names like *Little Missy* and *Freedom* and *the howdy-do*! One that Charles silently pointed out to me was called *Kyle, Kelly & Kaitlyn*, the initials of which it was hard to ignore.

After our food, Charles and I moved downstairs to the bar. It was incredibly crowded, roaring with bodies. All the patrons that I could see were white. There were men in black, long-sleeved t-shirts with the Harley-Davidson logo on the back, others in luminous short-sleeved button ups, others in t-shirts with the names of football teams or beer brands printed in cursive across the front. Many wore their sunglasses inside the building or rested them on their heads. There was an abundance of crew cuts and ponytails, as well as a few with long, thin rat tails at the back. Some wore baseball caps to cover bald spots, others cowboy hats, although many of those had been hung on hooks beneath the bar, due to the many-bodied, swampy heat.

Stuffed in one especially sweaty corner, a band of black men played funk classics. The singer's silk burgundy shirt sported two enormous sopping patches below the armpits and another across his back. The drummer wore a little black beret from whence sweat poured down his face in slick streams. He was so large that his girth spread out far

beyond the edges of his small round stool, almost stretching the width of his kit, and his arms, belly and neck
rippled as he played. He kept his eyes closed the whole
time, his face scrunched in concentration.

'I need another drink!' I shouted into Charles's ear,
before heading for the bar. Two men made a point of
graciously standing aside for me as I approached, one
lowering his cowboy hat, the inside seam of which, I
could see, was also drenched in sweat. I smiled thinly and
quickly signalled the barman for two beers. To ensure the
men didn't engage with me, I angled my body away and
studied the crowd as I waited.

The dance floor was inhabited front and centre by a
gaggle of older blonde women. The ones at the very front,
five in all, had identikit figures consisting of tiny waists and
large fake breasts bursting out of tight, v-neck t-shirts or
tank tops. They were, at least from where I stood, difficult
to tell apart. Above the din I could hear their high-pitched
voices encouraging one another to drop it like it's hot. All
five wore tight, flared jeans, platform heels and had little
leather purses perched on their shoulders.

One layer of bodies back, three very drunk women
kept trying to draw men in from the surrounding crowd,
shimmying to the edges, hands reaching out. The men
either refused outright, shaking their heads, hands up, or
reluctantly allowed themselves to be led out for twenty
seconds or so, bopping a little behind the woman who
dragged them, and then retreated back, bopping again, to
the safety of the bar or the walls. Directly in front of me,
the backsides of possessive husbands swayed slightly as
they watched over the dancefloor, at most doing a small
two-step back and forth, beer in hand or thumbs looped in
the belt hoops of their jeans.

Just as one particularly trumpet-heavy Motown number finished up, one of the drunker women fell over a bin as she was tottering back to the dancefloor, Bud Light in hand. For a stretched heartbeat, she lay unmoving, splayed in the puddle of her own beer on the wooden floor, before her friend came forward, tottering herself and giggling in nervous embarrassment, to attempt to help her up. Slowly, the woman heaved herself up onto all fours, her friend pulling at her arm. One of the men who'd stood out of my way at the bar stepped forward and, grabbing her other arm, pulled the woman shakily to her feet. 'There now! Y'alright?' The fallen woman looked around a moment, confused, hurt, before loudly, pointedly, joining in her friend's giggling. Fair enough, I thought. What else could she do? Her white, low-cut t-shirt was stained dark and transparent all down her front, the wetness clinging to her lime green bra and her belly.

When I came back, Charles mouthed thank you for his beer, then leaned forward into me, shouting above the din to ask was I having fun. I nodded an enthusiastic God yes (!) before putting my lips to his ear to say 'no really! Seriously, this is amazing! But like, I love it and, well, not to sound like a dick here, but I love it, like, *unironically* – know what I mean?' We both sat up straight so I could see Charles's widest of wide eyes as he shook his head enthusiastically, eyebrows up. We leaned back in, his lips to my ear, 'Oh my God, exactly, totally! Totally! Unironically, like, the music, the people, the whole thing – it's so good!' We sat up again, almost laughing now, to shake our heads again in disbelief at how much we were enjoying it all *so* unironically. I leant in once more, enjoying the familiar scent of his sweat, 'Exactly, so good! It's so fucking good, like, the music, everything!' We shook our heads, shook our heads again, smiled, shake smile, smile shake, so fucking good. I turned back then to face the music, trying very hard not to let any sobering self-awareness seep in and ruin my completely unironic pleasure of the moment.

One day in the series of hot blended days I wandered into a Milky King near Charles's house. I had been trying to find a pharmacy to buy some Dioralyte because I was dehydrated and hungover. There are no paths for pedestrians in suburban Texas. People don't walk. Drivers and passengers and children strapped into back seats leaned out of cars and trucks to stare at me, the oddity, as I plodded along the blackened grass verges. In the roadside heat, I got befuddled and lost, and became desirous of any sort of cool comfort ASAP. I didn't mind much of what happened to me in Texas – after all, to have notable things happen to me was purportedly the whole point of being there – but it did seem like a bad place to die. I could feel the heat of the ground through the soles of my shoes. An empty grey parking lot emerged in the haze to my left, and some bright comforting colours: a Milky King.

I already knew, from endless ice cream expeditions in the summers spent in and around Illinois with my Irish-American cousins as a child, that the manager of any particular Milky King branch is free to decorate the walls however they please. Much like Starbucks howling out your name when your coffee is ready, this tactic is designed to add a personalized touch to the customer's experience, as though each Milky King branch were independently run – just your local, wholesome ice cream parlour – rather than one in an infinite number of uncaring, money-hungry corporate outposts. Understandably, most of the managers don't bother decorating. The few

I've seen who actually did usually just put up pictures of celebrities, or maybe their families, or maybe (as in one particular branch about half a mile from my uncle's house in Wheeling that was run by a single middle-aged woman) hand-painted inspirational quotations surrounded by flowers. As it turned out, the guy who ran this particular branch in suburban Houston was one of the few who did decide to decorate.

It had been so bright outside, it took a moment for my eyes to adjust to the darkness of indoors. When they did, after a few red-hot blinks, I felt as though I had flown into a conceptual spider web. All the walls were covered in arrows and long red lines made with tape, connecting, say, a picture of a benignly smiling JFK with crudely drawn lines of blood pouring from the corners of his lips – cut roughly out of a book or magazine, or printed off Google Images – to the Twin Towers, with a hand-drawn picture of a plane flying into them surrounded by flames and smoke etched directly onto the wall. That image was then connected to numerous other images, such as a chicken coop packed with unhappy-looking white hens, or a young, scantily clad Reese Witherspoon sprawled on a beach with red devil-horns and a tail drawn on. He'd also pasted and drawn things like upside-down Hebrew script and those triangle symbols for the Illuminati.

There was no one inside, but the door had dinged as I entered and eventually a young man (I'll call him 'Steve') emerged from a dark room behind the counter. He was still chewing something and was wiping his large hands on his Milky King apron. He also wore the required Milky King hat and t-shirt, but in a way that made the perky apparel seem somehow transgressive. They weren't dirty, per se, but wrong somehow. They didn't seem to quite fit him, pulling in awkward directions, like clothes poorly placed on a doll. The sight of Steve – after the heat, the roadside, the engine fumes – made me shift uncomfortably in my own clothes, sweat-drenched and clinging. Looking at him, at his not-quite-rightness, I felt as though I had stepped into a deeper gorge in uncanny valley.

Steve was young, raw, scrawny. His skin was pinkish white and he had angry red bumps on his neck, chin and cheeks where he'd shaved closely over unsmooth skin. Studying him, too hot and disoriented to hide my curiosity, I decided he had the face, build and demeanour of someone you'd imagine travelling in the back of a pickup truck across America in a Steinbeck novel – distinctly Southern, with previous generations of labour and undernourishment leaving him bony, proud and embittered-looking. I would find out that he had studied biology but hadn't finished his degree, that he was applying to enter the army reserves but that, for now, he was this particular Milky King's proud branch manager.

'Hi there,' I said. And then, 'Howdy.'

He didn't look at me. His eyes darted to the counter, the ice cream selection, the walls, or in little nervous upward glances through the glass behind me. Finally he settled his gaze on an advertisement to my left offering any coffee for ninety-nine cents before noon on weekdays, subject to Terms & Conditions. His eyes were blue and clear with the glazed conviction of a preacher's.

'What can I do for you?'

'Mmm ... a large Diet Coke please.'

He nodded. 'Ice?'

'Sure.'

146

He filled my cup, placed a lid on it, indicated where to find the straws, and rang it up. All without looking at me.

When our exchange was completed he lingered, swaying slightly, unsure of me, of whether he could retreat again to his back room. I wandered around the Milky King slowly, sucking up the cool, restorative liquid through my straw, and inspected the walls. After a minute or two in silence, only the sound of the air-conditioner and the faint hum of traffic outside, he spoke:

'You like it, huh?'

'Yeah! It's fascinating ... did you do this?'

His shoulders lowering, resigned, he slowly leaned his weight against the back counter, crossing his shins. 'Mmhm, that I did.' There was a moment of silence as he looked around, considering where to begin. Then, methodically, in his deep Southern drawl, he began telling me how he'd been creating the wall for the last three years, ever since he took over the branch from his predecessor, who had died unexpectedly after a fall from a ladder when installing a satellite dish.

'God, that's terrible!' I said, looking at Steve with wide eyes.

He looked at the walls, expression unchanged. 'Yeah, he was a good guy, bud it made me the youngest ever Milky King branch manager in all of Texas.'

'Oh, wow,' I said, '... congratulations.'

'Yeah, thanks.' Steve went on to tell me that the walls pretty much explained how the American government was a farce, and how the pharmaceutical industry was running the world, and how they answered to a 'higher force'. He didn't specify what he meant by 'higher force'.

Steve said the walls showed how 'their' control was perpetuated by brainwashing, via our food and advertising and social media and Google Maps and the banks, and actually pretty much everything we're exposed to as functioning humans on Earth.

'Even them straws you use,' he said, gesturing loosely at me without actually looking directly, 'they lace 'em too, the insides, to stupify the people.' Even though he was forced to provide these straws, to work from within the system, Steve said that he had created the display in order to simultaneously educate his customers, to give them the opportunity to see the light, and to help fight the tide of ignorance overwhelming the United States of America, 'even in Texas'. As he was speaking, he'd started cleaning, even though everything was – to my eyes at least – sparklingly clean already.

There was a sudden interruption to Steve's calm yet forceful monologue: the growl of a truck's engine pulling up right outside and the blare of Latino music. Steve paused. For a moment, he and I seemed to be waiting for something to happen, a reckoning, but nobody got out of the truck. The windows were tinted to protect against the Texas sun, so even though the truck was facing us, we couldn't see who was inside or what they were doing. It was slightly unsettling, and made me only just creepingly aware of my own body, visible to the hidden driver through the glass-fronted Milky King. Batting away the discomfiture, too fascinated by Steve to leave just yet, I sucked up more of my drink, clinking ice chips with my straw. Steve, propelled into action by the sound, squeezed his cloth over the sink, grabbed a different cleaning spray, and came out from behind the counter to start wiping down the empty tables. I sensed that this gesture, crossing over into my space, meant that he now wanted me to stay. When he emerged, I could see that his blue jeans were bootcut, and slightly too short for his legs. His shoes were red, Converse-style but brand-less. His movements were strangely compacted, coming in sudden awkward bursts, like a teenager hiding an erection. I guessed his age as twenty-three or twenty-four, but he easily could've been younger.

Steve told me that he'd always had ideas, ever since he was a boy. He said they were always developing, every day, metastasizing with every story on the news, every new encounter or Facebook post he read or dream he had. I was surprised by his use of the word 'metastasizing', and, no longer walking aimlessly around but standing still, glancing from him to the walls, endeavoured to listen more closely.

He said it was people like him – visionaries – who changed the world, and that he intended to do the same. 'Don't matter how exactly, I just know I got things inside myself that need to be heard.' He stood erect a moment, staring vacantly out the window toward the low dry hedging by the road, and then continued the thought: 'Ways for us all to live, ways to be *better*, and most importantly, ways to fight all this that's happening.'

Steve sighed and stopped talking. I worried he was finished and asked him to go on. I assured him that yes, I was very interested. I still had plenty of Diet Coke, and besides, the sun, that tinted truck, Texas, the sprawling emptiness of America and the day ahead – these were all, in that moment, wearisome. Better to stay here and let Steve provide the answers. He rubbed his forehead with the back of his forearm – a gesture I guessed had more to do with the ordering of thought than heat, given the coolness of the Milky King – before continuing.

Steve told me about the evils of the meat industry and chemtrails and how the UN had purposefully started a war in the Middle East to ensure the destruction of the recently discovered remains of the Garden of Eden. The more I listened, the more his speech sped up. His cleaning motions became more animated, jumping from small round table to small round table. He began to clean those a little closer to me. It felt as though we were heading for some climactic revelation. Suddenly, after a particularly enthused 'wow!' from me he stopped talking and pursed his lips, perhaps suddenly aware of the possibility that I might be mocking him (was I?). A silence ensued.

Tentatively, after a pause, again studying the walls and noisily sucking the last of the liquid out from cracks between the melting ice, I asked Steve about one particularly large image on the wall. It was an oversized paper photo of dollar bills – clearly printed on a shitty low-res printer – with red Sharpie-markered fangs coming down either side of a wide, grinning mouth scrawled across the surface.

Steve had moved away from me and was now crouching down to wipe the already gleaming glass of the ice cream display counter. Keeping his back to me, he muttered with a quiet venom that I had not been prepared for: 'Y'all are caring too much about dollars these days, they've made 'em addictive, makin' people think there ain't nothing else left worth living for ... they've laced 'em with something, cocaine or heroin or something worse we don't even know about yet ... it's a goddamned *epidemic*.'

I told him that I genuinely agreed with him, that yes, people did care too much about money these days and that yeah, it was a bit of an epidemic. Even from behind, I could tell by his body language, a slight softening in his shoulders, a slowing in his hand's circular motion across the gleaming glass partition, that he was pleased with my response. I wondered if maybe, with a better diet and a few more years, he could grow into something close to handsome, or at least – alongside all of his burning conviction – fuckable.

Steve now walked behind the counter, rifled a moment out of sight, and then popped back up. 'Here.' He thrust out his hand, offering a flyer. In all this time, even when I walked over so he could hand it to me, he never once made eye contact.

As I glanced over it, he stared at his handiwork on the walls with a frustrated expression, as though bursting to explain it all with one perfect word, for me to comprehend it all at once. It was as though he wanted conversation to work like visual art, in immediate atemporal splatters. Or more like a dick, or a gun – for his thoughts to enter me with one single epiphanous shot. We were standing closer than we had thus far – just the two of us there, enclosed within the cool, clean, humming Milky King. Below the waft of disinfectant and the constant sweetness of the ice cream, I could faintly make out a pleasant savoury scent emanating from his body. I could just feel the soft but constant heat that radiated from his skin. His fingers, resting on the counter between us, fidgeted with the damp ragged washcloth. Glancing surreptitiously from the page to look at them, I could see that his nails were bitten to the quick, as were his cuticles, which looked red and sore and swollen. For some reason they made me wonder about his family, his mother and father, if they were good to him, loved him, and what car he drove and whether he'd watched *Sesame Street* as a kid like I had and whether he'd ever come close to having a girlfriend, somebody who wanted and understood him. In my mind there floated up a hotly humming empty street, single-storey houses, an open gate, an unkempt lawn and a screen door, and I wondered about what he used to eat when he got in from school, and just how bad the bullying had been.

The flyer, which I endeavoured to focus on, was a hand-printed advertisement for Steve's new book. 'Yeah, course,' he said dismissively, annoyed at having to tell me at all, 'I've writ plenty of books ... I got a lot to say, I've got wisdom to share, if anybody'd listen.'

The book was called *Don't Give Into Your Monkey Brain! A Guide to Avoiding the Cultural and Moral Pitfalls of Modern America* by Stephen R. Mitchell. A grainy photo on the flyer showed one of the interior walls of the Milky King with Steve standing broodingly before it, arms crossed. In the photo, he was still wearing his uniform. I wondered who'd taken it and if Milky King headquarters knew about it, but said nothing.

'Your monkey brain, interesting ... oh, like a reptile brain kinda thing?' I asked.

There was a pause, and Steve looked me straight in the eye for the first time. '*No*,' he hissed emphatically. 'No, nothin' like a goddamned "*reptile brain*".'

His tone wasn't outright aggressive, but it was enough. I suddenly found myself noting the exact distance between my body and the glass front door. I could feel the effects of the cool Diet Coke filtering through me. I was sufficiently fortified, I realized, by this and the relief of the air-conditioning, to re-enter the outside world; to flee. I decided that, actually, today would not be the day I joined Steve's cult, or any cult for that matter. I would instead continue my search for Dioralyte or – even better – go home and lie down on Charles's couch and watch Netflix for an hour or two, or maybe all afternoon, until ten minutes before he was due home from work; at which point I'd turn it off, take out a book, and pretend I'd spent the whole day reading.

I was wondering how I would make my escape while Steve, taking out all the ice cream scoopers now to wash them down, was preparing to launch into a rant on the perils of the monkey brain – which seemed to have something to do with Hindus, whom I quickly gathered he *despised* – when, to my utter delight, the door behind me dinged. It was the driver of the truck, my latest saviour, a mustachioed Mexican man with a baseball cap and a faded blue Abercrombie t-shirt stretched over an enormous protruding belly. Steve halted mid-sentence, taken aback. There was a moment of suspension between the three of us, a held breath, and then the Mexican guy, glancing a smile and small nod at me, sidled up to the counter, jangling his keys as he reached for the wallet in his jeans' back pocket. I took my chance.

'Huh, yeah, well, that's so interesting, well, oh, oh well, I guess I'd better go – but yeah, I'll definitely pick up the book, so interesting, thaaanks!'

Steve blinked, as though waking from a dream and then, realizing what was happening, shouted something after me, stretching up on his toes from his position behind the counter, his voice reaching for me over the head of the Mexican man. But I didn't hear him – I was already gone.

The bus to Houston took an hour and cost two dollars. I rode that bus six times – three journeys into the city and three journeys back. Each time, it was virtually empty, with at most four or five other passengers on board, usually spaced out so as to be as far from one another as possible. Mostly, people wore headphones and stared out the windows at the highways, avoiding eye contact.

Once, a crazy old white man who reeked of piss, spent the entire trip yelling to no one in particular about how he was going to 'git, L. Ron Hubbard, you betcha, gunna git 'im good!' Every now and then the bus driver would look into his rearview mirror and shout for him to pipe down, and he would be quiet for a few minutes, muttering under his breath, before forgetting the injunction and raising up again into his wailing crescendo; 'you think I ain't gunno get 'im? Well I gotta tell yuh, you wrong! Cuz I is!' It was only as he alighted ahead of me onto the white glare of a Houston sidewalk, that I realized he had no hands – in their place were rough, mottled stumps.

To get to the bus stop from Charles's place, I had to walk the residential roads under a shadowless sun. The only sounds were those of my own crisping steps; the occasional whoosh of a passing car with perhaps a trickle of music muffled through glass; the crickets hiding in the bushes planted in neat, suburban formations across the lawns; and the startlingly efficient 'chut chut chut' rhythm of someone's and then someone else's sprinkler, keeping everything an unnaturally luminous misted green.

Three men, broad-faced and dark, sat in the back of a pickup truck alongside detritus and gardening tools. Utterly still and silent, they seemed to be waiting for something. They watched me pass. I shuffled along, sweat slicked between my thighs, in the creases at the back of my knees and all along my back where my backpack pressed, and I wondered self-consciously whether there would be a damp patch on my dress.

After a few minutes, I sensed an engine slowing alongside me, and turned. A smiling black woman, large and kindly, with glistening curls of synthetic hair and a pretty baby-blue silk scarf tied above her navy pantsuit, pulled up on the road beside me, leaned across, and asked: 'Y'all looking for God's Kingdom, honey?'

Confused, unsure, I said 'eh, no? I don't think so ...' (was I?) and she, smiling, said 'oh, that's alright sweetie, it's just you walkin' right on their lawn.'

Sitting outside a café in downtown Houston, I heard him before I saw him.

'So purdy,' he said. I looked up, met his eyes: an enormously fat man balanced across a tragically small bike. *A child's bike?* Eyes of mild insanity. I had been deep in my book and was unprepared. 'So so purdy, like somethin' from a magazine.'

'Ha, ah well, thanks.' Forced smile but book open, *keep book open, disengage, disengage.*

'Where you from? Not here, I knows that!'

Parked before me, not too close, but close. Feet to the ground, stare.

'Ireland.'

'Ayerlund! That's like England, right? Yeaahh, Ayerland ... like Bono, right?'

'Yeah, that's it, exactly, like Bono.'

'Right, right ... and what you doin' here in Houston? Other than lookin' so purdy ...'

'Oh, just visiting ... Visiting the South ... I have a friend here.'

I am not alone, I have a friend, it will be noticed if I disappear.

'Oh yeah? Well welcome! Welcome! Houston, greatest city on the earth, no doubt, no doubt ... greatest city on earth ... you know Beyoncé?'

'Right, yeah! Yeah ... '

'Yuh, she from here, you know that? And Solange, her sistuh – you got Solange in Ayerlund? She's her sistuh.'

'Yeah, we have Solange ... but she's not as big as Beyoncé.'

'No, no, no, not as big as Beyoncé! No, huh huh! Nobody big as Beyoncé, not even Bono! Huh huh huh.'

His chuckling tipped the bike a little and he tilted his bulk forward to grab the handles. He slowly twisted the front wheel side to side, side to side in place, like a child, waiting. In the corner of my eye I felt another presence, glanced – it was a security guard from the bank two doors down, come to hover close by: *saved, saved, saved.*

'So y'all like Beyoncé in Ayerlund? I seen the family, they still come around here ... '

'Oh yeah?'

'Oh yeaaah, yeah they always comes back to Houston, always comes back, for holidays, for Thanksgiviiing, Christmaaass ... now they got them twins, and Blue too, you know? You know Blue? Her daughter, her name's Blue Ivy see ... purdy, ain't it?'

'Yeah, really pretty!'

'Yeah, not as purdy as you though, huh huh huh ...'

That smile spread, a gaping wound creep-crawling, all for me. The security guard stepped closer, a pointed step. My admirer looked up, considered. A gun holstered on the security guard's hip. He twisted his bike wheel side to side, side to side, staring.

'Well ... I guess I best be goin' on ... best be gettin' on ... you enjoy Houston, purdy lady ...'

Free free free free free free!

'Thanks! Thanks, I will ...'

'Best city on the earth, y'hear?'

'Ha, right, yeah.'

Cycling away, legs bent too high up, such a tiny bike, fat all in motion, slow, slow, weaving slow. Then over shoulder, that smile: 'See y'all in my dreams, purdy lady, huh huh!'

And he was gone.

I thanked the security guard with my eyes and breathed deep in my nose, a relief smile, and he nodded, a smile too, a 'what can you do?' shoulders mouth and eyes, before retreating to his post. I waited six minutes and left in the opposite direction, even though my bus stop was the way he'd gone.

Upon renting a car for the first time, in Houston, TX, to drive to Austin, TX, alone:

... First chance I got I turned off the road into a Burger King and drove up to the drive-thru, terror a hunger in my belly (*eat eat eat be better be safe*), trying to judge all the reversed distances, everything backwards, car to wall, road markings to car, trying to figure how to roll the windows down, to stop (!), and then, achieved, money green *take it, take it*, relieved, paper bag smell wafting, '*have a nice day now!*' twisted the wheel turned to park (how do I? Oh, 'P' for park) and sat and stuffed my face in sweet piggy ecstasy in the car park, spilling condiments and shards of limp lettuce all down my dress and not caring. The fries were thin and salty and savoury and crisp, and my fingers grabbed them in greasy bunches and pressed them hard against my tongue, relief. I was out of breath from eating, but not caring because I was in American heaven, this was it, the dream, I was so *free free free*, on my way now, really gone.

Calmed, heart slowing, chew slowing, breaking for breath, sip of Diet Coke, I listened to the preachers on the radio tell a parable about a goat and a man and a banjo and learned from it that I'd probably end up in hell too, actually.

*

Notebook open before me, I was sitting outside Royal Blue Grocery, a coffee shop on Congress Avenue, when an older man from West Texas woke me from my daze and asked to take my picture for his photography blog. He was big and sturdy with combed white hair and brown eyes. He wore a neat pale blue shirt tucked into equally neat slacks, and his belt buckle was of shining silver and shaped like bull horns. He was too perfect, and I conceded.

His camera was a Nikon, modern and bulky, and was attached to a strap around his neck, also Nikon. He lifted it before his eye, squinted his other eye, and told me to just do what I was doing (*but what had I been doing?*), yes, that's it. I heard the click and whirr of a flurry of photographs digitally recording. When he lowered the camera, smiling, images safely captured, he shook my hand. After hearing my accent, he said he could tell straight off that I was Irish. He said yeah, way back – O'Connell – but his family had been here for generations. He told me that they were in the oil business in West Texas. 'Like in *Giant*?' I asked. 'Exactly! Exactly like in *Giant*!' he agreed enthusiastically, waving a finger at me. I pretended that yes, I had seen it, rather than mentioning having fallen asleep ten minutes in. He seemed impressed, and sat down one table over. He told me that he was now retired, his nephews ran things, and he'd taken up photography. I found myself appraising him, wondering if he was still as healthy as he looked, and just how much oil money he might be worth.

He delicately removed the strap from around his neck and placed his camera beside the coffee cup on my table, before fumbling for something in his wallet. His daughter was a writer too, he told me, living in New York. He said the words 'New York' with trepidation, as though just saying them would unleash all the city's unknown evils on her. He found what he was rooting for, and handed me his card, and I immediately pictured us fucking hard, me on top, with a fizzing champagne bottle in one hand, in an enormous, low-lit, cowboy-themed hotel room. He told me to check the website listed there in a day or two for my photo.

(When I got home to Ireland, I realized that I'd lost his card, and forgotten his name. And so now I must know that there is yet another photo of me on the internet, some record of me, of a passing moment of my life, that I will never see.)

He left, and I forgot what I'd been thinking about. It was too hot to read and my coffee was finished. A homeless man, white, skinny, with matted hair and clothes that all blended into pale grey-blue in the too-bright sunlight, muttered something about the Second Coming as he walked by. From the tree above me, whose leaves offered some little slips of swaying shade, the sound of a great-tailed grackle's cry was cut short by the wail of a passing siren.

I felt restless in Austin, as though I were waiting around for something or someone that wasn't coming, and so I decided to leave early, skipping the one meeting I had set up with someone I vaguely knew – the brother of my friend from home and his young family. We were supposed to go for food and happy hour drinks in a bar not far from the house where I was staying. The prospect of his bringing his wife and children had already put me off the notion (it all suddenly sounded so polite, so staid, so *here-hold-the-baby*), and so it didn't take much for me to email him to tell him sorry, actually, I'd decided to get on the road a little earlier to drive a circuitous route back to Houston. He expressed mild surprise at my intention to drive through back roads but, not wanting to seem rude or sexist or condescending, said he was sure I knew what I was doing (I didn't) and the best of luck to me.

The couple I'd been couchsurfing with were both still in bed when I left the house, although it was past noon. She had clearly slept through work in spite of insisting, repeatedly, when we were out drinking and getting high on their porch the night before, that she had to be up for eight-fifteen to cycle to work for nine. She spoke about her early morning as though it were a badge of honour – some unimaginable achievement for myself, a travelling writer, and her partner, a filmmaker, whom she adored and demeaned in equal measure (as nervous women with low self-esteem seem impelled to do).

She worked for Facebook in the Customer Care department but hated it, while he – being, as I mentioned, an 'independent filmmaker' – was essentially unemployed. She had just bought him a violin, because he'd said once in passing that he might like to learn. Now she teased him performatively, all smiles and jabs and 'look at us, the quarrelling couple!' in front of me, for not being able to play it yet. I directed my eyes elsewhere and commented on the neighbourhood, their cat, the weather. He sipped his beer and smiled vacantly. They had only been dating two months when they moved in together. The house was a cutesy ramshackle bungalow, decked out in thrift store furniture, home-stitched cushions and lampshades, fairy lights, cat hair, his photographs, more cat hair, and her little cartoonish paintings of beach scenes, woodlands and animals. As the evening dwindled, the empty bottles at our feet multiplying, the squashed grey butts of joints

in the bottles also multiplying, she began slapping imagined insects off her thin, white arms with increasing force,
leaving red marks. 'Got it! Oh, wait … Got it!' She kept
forgetting what she'd been saying, and when we couldn't
remember either, she instead segued into telling me yet
again that she'd never seen snow. 'Can you believe it? I
mean, I like, work for Facebook, I'm a Democrat and I
drink fucking almond milk, y'know what I mean? And
I've never even seen fucking snow.'

As they slept in, I got up, dressed quickly in what
I'd worn the day before, ate a bruised banana from my
backpack and, tiptoeing as quietly as I could across their
creaking floorboards, filled my water bottle from the
kitchen tap. The water spluttered and spewed noisily, and
I cursed below my breath. Their cat plonked itself on the
floor to my left and mewed, fat and grey and fluffy, its
tail snaking back and forth. It looked hungry. I listened
for sounds of waking from the bedroom, giving the cat a
stern 'shut the fuck up' look. I heard nothing, only his soft
snore, and crept back to my laptop in the living room to
map out an alternative route back to Charles – no, *Houston*. Back to Houston, where Charles happened to be. The
cat followed me but stopped mewing, just watched me
accusingly, as though it could read my thoughts regarding
its sleeping owners.

The plan was to make my way slowly, on the back roads,
taking in small-town Texas en route, for photographs and
general impressions. It felt silly – nay, unbearable – on a
trip of exploration and discovery, to return the same way
I'd come. Also, it would be embarrassing to get back to
Charles's place too early. I'd map out my route carefully
and arrive in Houston by midnight.

*

In the car, air-conditioner blasting, I found a channel pumping out terrible yet delicious chart music on the radio and drove and drove, out of the main city through thick traffic, singing along, tapping the beat on the steering wheel, out onto the freeways and then off the freeways onto two-lane roads, single-lane roads, then down to dirt tracks.

I had been driving for three hours when I allowed myself to realize that I had reached the exact pinpointed middle of nowhere. The sun was just beginning to lower, casting long shadows from barns and barn-like houses dotted at intervals along the road; dried blood-red, with dirty white outlines, crumbling roofs and broken window frames, hanging screen doors, with rusted-out tractors and dust-covered, flat-tyred pickup trucks parked in random formations across yellowed brittle lawns. As the empty spaces between these wooden structures grew, the shabbiness increased.

If I'd been seeing it on TV, or perhaps if I hadn't been lost, I might have found it beautiful. It grew dusky and I turned on my side lights. I drove as fast as I dared, which was slowly, because I didn't want to catch the car's tyres in one of the many deep potholes. Pale yellow dust drifted up on either side and out behind as the car trundled down the road, creating a haze all around me. I could hear the enormous 4x4 before I saw it, as it caught up and then, allowing itself to tilt precariously into the ditch along the roadside, furiously overtook me. I had to grind to a halt entirely to wait for the dirt it had sent swirling into the air to disperse and settle.

Suspended there for a moment, surrounded, I couldn't see a thing. Panic rose in my chest and stomach. This was not a place I wanted to get stranded. I tried to be just fine, to not notice the deep-rooted fear dropping like thick cement into the bottom of my belly; to ignore, determinedly, frantically, the explosion in my mind of the word 'LOST LOST LOST' repeating like a siren's wail in darkness. I tried not to catch even the slightest glimpse of the image of my mother's face, my father, my grandparents, all probably asleep in their beds at that moment, safe and unsuspecting.

The dust cleared and I drove on. To my left, a quarter mile or so further along, another disintegrating house emerged. Four white men sat on fold-out deckchairs along the roadside, drinking beers. The house itself was way back and I wondered why they would sit here, so close to the passing engines, with the dust and fumes in their faces. Then I realized it was to see people passing – people they knew maybe, or people lost, desperate people, like me.

As I passed they watched, unspeaking, beer bottles in hand. They were all strong but weary-looking, their faces resting in soft, resigned frowns. Just as I was right alongside them, one of them adjusted his body as though about to stand, and I, panicking, hit the accelerator, causing the car to emit an audible roar. Caught by the sound, he froze, but as I passed by, watching him watch me, he smiled widely. Perhaps he was trying to be friendly, perhaps not. It was only then, revving furiously, that I thought to check the petrol – in all my driving, I hadn't stopped for any yet.

I glanced down and choked back a whimper: the red light was on and the meter, jiggling a little with the bumpy motion of the car, read a millimetre off empty. I swallowed salty sharp despair and, hand trembling, turned off the radio. It was crackling now anyway, too far from a signal, but that wasn't why I did it. It was because when I'm truly afraid, I need to be able to hear what's coming. It's the same reason I take my earphones out when walking home alone at night – to hear the rush of footsteps closing in. I tried to be calm. This was what I had wanted, I told myself. An 'experience', somewhere 'far away', somewhere 'different'. This is what happens when you insisted on being a lost person.

Now, if this was fiction, I couldn't really write that a mile or so up the road – just as I was thinking of trying to park the car somewhere hidden overnight, to see out the blackness, windows locked, rather than risk seeking assistance in the boondocks (*the actual fucking boondocks*) – there emerged from the solid dark, like a lighthouse through a storm, the illuminated outline of a gas station. If, for some reason, I felt it necessary in a fictional story to invent a scene that included a gas station, I'd have to leave out the bit about actually being in desperate need of petrol. Really, I'd have to forgo the whole idea altogether and instead, having placed the character out there in the middle of nowhere, have her either befriend a kindly local, thus having her preconceived fears overturned, or allow her to be murdered.

But this isn't fiction. I'm still alive, with my preconceptions intact. This is just how it happened. I saw those men, who to my frazzled mind looked like people who might have been simply *too scary-looking* to be cast in *Deliverance*; and at that very moment, accelerating away from them, I noticed I had fuck-all petrol; and then just up the road, at the point of giving up, found the one and only petrol station I'd seen since the freeway. Sometimes (in fact, more often than not) that's just how life goes. Most lives lived for any significant length of time are, at best, made up of a series of near misses, good and bad. Then the rest of those lives are spent idly wondering what might've happened if things had gone the other way.

In my entire time staying with Charles, the nights before and after my road trip, he never told any of his family that I was there. He actively hid the fact of my presence. His people were Methodists and proud Texans. He had been in the church choir growing up along with his sisters, and had played the church piano for all the congregation's special occasions – Christmas, Easter, weddings and even funerals. His grandfather had been a preacher and his direct ancestors were one of their church's four founding families – their last name was carved into the wall, In Memoriam. His parents were not quite Republican, but they hadn't voted for Hillary either – they'd sat the election out, allowing fate to take its course.

Even back in New York, when I'd heard Charles Skype his mother in his room while I read or cooked or cleaned up or sent emails at the kitchen table, I could tell that I was quietly but firmly disapproved of. Over the months and years following our sudden break-up, I sometimes found myself wondering whether this disapproval had contributed to Charles's decision to end things. Visiting now, having to stay quiet while he was on the phone with them, whether we were at home, or in the car, or at a bar, or the supermarket; hearing him lie about where he was, what he was doing, so as not to alert them to my presence; I wondered again, and in the moment of wondering despised his sensible practicality.

Another night, another hick bar, this one off a freeway near Charles's apartment. Charles excused himself to go to the bathroom, stumbling slightly, and almost immediately a short man whose skin audibly hummed with sexual energy appeared beside me. I was perched at the counter, thighs crossed. His head came up to my shoulder.

Charles and I had spent the evening thus far – after an increasingly giggly dinner in a Mexican restaurant, trying to identify the subjects of the truly *woeful* paintings of celebrities that covered all of the walls, done by the proprietor's son – ordering a beer and a shot, a shot and a beer. I can't handle shots and neither can Charles. It was probably a bad idea, but then, this was our last evening together. It was now or never. I had that feeling one has on the lingering tip-top of a rollercoaster, just before the inevitable crashing down, that this night could go anywhere. I was suspended in the utter unknown, the *who-knows-anything-let's-go* of it all. I was hot, tired, confused, elated, a little aroused, nervous, and on my way to woozy.

We'd been out the night before too in a bar in a strip mall near Charles's apartment that was not a hick bar – in fact it was oddly trendy. It ought to have been in Bushwick or Brixton or Kreuzberg, but had been lifted like Dorothy's house and dropped in suburban Texas between a laundromat and a Korean beauty parlour. When it closed up for the night, we'd bought more beers for the road. After an hour or two sitting close on the couch watching music videos, with Charles saying over and over 'well, what d'ya wanna do now?' he'd passed out, open-mouthed, his head against my shoulder. I'd placed his arm around my neck, cooing gently and, stumbling under his warm weight, half-carried him into his room, dropped him on his bed, removed his shoes and hovered for a moment, considering, before thinking better of it and retreating to the living room to make up my own bed on the couch.

Over breakfast, Charles said half-jokingly that he genuinely wished someone could've overheard or maybe even recorded our conversations at the bar, because they were that damn interesting. He said he hadn't had conversations like that in years. We laughed into our coffees, but he meant it, and I silently agreed. Tonight, I made a special effort to look good. My dress was low cut *and* short. I kept my lipstick close at hand so I could keep topping it up as it smeared off on each beer glass. After the first three drinks, I had to consciously balance on the stool.

The man who'd appeared beside me was, I reckoned, in his early forties, but physically extremely well kept. I could see him doing press-ups and pull-ups in his garage, listening to eighties metal before furiously masturbating. I pictured the width of his hand to be greater than the length of his erect penis, but that didn't make his presence any less potent. Before I had time to adjust to him, i.e. to make him feel unwelcome, he launched into what felt like prepared questions. He reminded me of a terrier dog: bristling with confidence, with bright eyes, a clean black shirt and a cowboy hat. I tried to discern whether or not he was bald beneath it. He was clearly a local, and had the drinking persona of someone who would equally happily fight or fuck given one or two more bottles of Bud, but *must* end up doing one or the other.

'So y'all from around here?' Oh yeah, he'd guessed not, so how'd I find myself in this place, oh really, well, welcome (!), it was the best place in the world, yeah Texas (!), of course Texas (!), the food, the people, well I'd surely see for myself, so on and so forth. He was just in the middle of expressing the eyebrow-arched, whistling disbelief I'd come to expect from Texan men upon learning that I'd managed to drive to Austin all by my lonesome, when Charles returned and stood right in close beside me. Charles's hand went to my waist – loosely, automatically – and hovered there, not quite gripping but warm and protective. I felt my crotch light on fire and shuddered with pure want. I could feel every cell of his tall looming body pressed against mine as I sat there on my stool. He swayed a little and swayed me in turn like the pull of an ocean. My mind leapt to thoughts of fucking him back in New York, the feel of him inside me, on top of me, almost crushing me with closeness, the motion of our bodies in sync, and I had to close my eyes a moment.

I came to my senses, to our new reality in the present, and gently tapped his back, indicating for him to sit – *no threat here, we're okay, careful now, steady*. I felt him consider, and acquiesce. He plopped, with a screech of wooden leg against floor, onto the stool beside me. The guy eyed him up smugly. Unlike Charles, balancing on his long skinny limbs, this guy looked like the kind of man who could drink a litre bottle of tequila and still sleep solidly on his feet.

'So you two together?' he asked brazenly, his tone suggesting disbelief, gesturing vaguely at us with his bottle. Caught off guard, I mumbled that no, we were friends, although it was clear from my stilted explanation and the charged body language between all three of us that there was more to it than that. The guy tilted his head and stared Charles down, occasionally glancing at me with an expression designed to communicate *Really? This guy?*

As I spoke, a middle-aged woman, short and tanned with curled brown hair, tapped the man's back, trying to get past him to her friends further down the bar. Obliging, smiling gallantly, he shuffled in closer to me, placing his hand for balance against the bar beside me, effectively encircling me and cordoning me off from Charles. When the woman had squeezed by, thanking him, he glanced at her departing ass and then lingered where he was, in no rush to pull back. He looked from her ass to me, smiling pointedly, then straight up at Charles, daring him to intervene.

I felt Charles's body stiffen, felt him consider leaning forward, then slacken and sink back. His hand, which had hovered comfortingly at my waist all this time, gently fell away from the encroachment of the guy's strong, taut arm between us. My stomach hollowed and I felt suddenly sober, all too sober. The bar was too loud and too crowded, and I wanted to be home – not home to Charles's apartment, not anymore, but home to the house of my father, all across the sea. Not tomorrow, but now. This was not what I had come for.

There was a slight pause, and the sound of vibrant life – the bar, clinks and loud clanks, shouts and murmurs, whoops and hollers and hell-yeah-why-nots – pulsed their way through, infiltrating our charged little trio. I knocked back the end of my drink and gestured behind me, silently, for another.

'So *y'all* from here?' the guy asked Charles over the din, a hint of sarcasm in his voice. I could smell a faint tang of sweat rising up from beneath the guy's armpit, the beer on his breath, and I glumly found myself wondering if he'd at least have the decency to lick a woman out. Vengefully, I adjusted my body ever so slightly to include him more in the conversation, and I sensed immediately that Charles had felt it.

'Yup, born and raised,' Charles replied.

'Oh really?' The guy's eyebrows again arched theatrically. 'Whurr 'zactly?' Charles gave the guy his credentials.

There was another pause as he took it in. Then: 'So, y'all college educated?' Checkmate. Shoulders lowering, a physical sigh, Charles admitted yes, he was, yeah, New York, yes Columbia, yep, engineering major, minored in music. The guy whistled, smiling victoriously, and took a last gulp of his beer, 'Music! Well now!'

It was only then that it hit me that this was where Charles was actually *from* – that these were his people, that this was his *home*. This was a trip for me, a step behind the curtain – like watching a strange and entertaining play and being brought backstage, or visiting the circus and being picked out from the audience to assist the clowns. I remembered, all of a sudden, a story he'd told me on an early date back in New York, sharing a pizza in the booth of a Greek diner, about one of his sisters, the older one; about how when they were younger she'd been rebellious, had stolen money from their parents and run off to teach English in Asia. I also remembered that Charles had never told his parents about his tattoos. He hadn't been able to go to the beach with them since he was nineteen. He'd always had to feign illness when the possibility of a family trip to the shore came up.

I also remembered him saying that, even though he hated it, didn't want it, he knew he was their favourite. He was the boy, the musical prodigy, the golden child. All their expectations, really, rested on him. Suddenly, crushingly, I felt his weariness – his terrible, voiceless isolation – and regretted, painfully, having shunned him. I tilted my body back towards him, compassion swelling in my chest, friendship, love, everything, but too late. Charles was a statue, Charles was gone.

Havana

On the way back to the hotel they picked up a six-pack of cervezas from the corner shop and drank them on their balcony overlooking the hushing blue sea, with the glass double doors open behind them and the scented air lazily swirling over their skins and on inside across the crumpled white sheets. They only moved to make love, to piss, and to eat the complimentary fruit from the bowl, growing soft quickly in all that wet heat. As dusk fell, he'd given her head right there on the balcony as she dozed, hooshing across gently on his knees, resting his head on her lap first, before easing her warm thighs apart and waking her open with his tongue. She'd caressed his dark sea-salted hair while he held her legs firm, for support, bending down low into her on the pattern-tiled balcony. She'd looked out, not really seeing the evening surfers; the last of the straggling sunbathers dragging towels, inflatable beds, baskets; the ice cream man walking back down the beach one last time with his cooler, his long, black feet dusted white, and she'd come, almost silently, her body convulsing in little rippling waves. It was perfect; a completely perfect day between them.

That's how Lucy remembers it now, at least. Although the recollection squeezes tight her insides, making her strangely restless.

My Life as a Girl

I

Girl in a room. On the right is a couch, a small coffee table, a TV facing the couch across the coffee table. On the far side of the couch is a standing lamp, facing down, illuminating the armrest. On the far side of the coffee table, against the back wall, are bookshelves. A standing unit, or just one or two shelves screwed into the wall. The coffee table has a remote control on it. On the left is the door and, beyond that, a kitchen unit running around the corner from the left wall to the back wall. The kitchen contains an oven, a sink, cabinets, a fridge, a microwave on the counter and, beside that, a fruit bowl. There's an apple in the bowl but it's turning, softly crinkling at the skin. In front of the kitchen unit, but not impeding the walk from the couch to the door, is a small round table with two chairs. Above the table is a low-hanging bulb that illuminates the table and casts shadows on everything else. Maybe there's a lampshade. The place is slick or scruffy, big or small, expensive or cheap-looking. It's all the same.

In the centre of the far wall is the window. It has no curtains. It's a circle, like a porthole. It's big. It has one large pane.

*

II

Girl is on the couch. Strewn, legs open, one up, one down, skirt hiked up around her waist. She's reading under the lamp. She reads for a while. She scratches her crotch gently, absentmindedly. Reads some more. She breathes out slowly and audibly through her nose. Vaguely, she swats a fly. (There is no fly.) Reads. Rests her book on her chest, and looks around for the fly. Pauses. Pauses as though listening intently, ear cocked. Lifts her head aloft as though intently watching a fly. Follows the path of the fly a while, eyes wide, until her gaze rests on the empty wall to her left, behind the couch. Suddenly, she whacks the book against the wall. Holds it there a moment. Lifts it away carefully, and looks at the back of the book for a while, as though studying a squashed fly. (There is no fly.) She flicks the back of the book. Pauses. Yawns. Reopens the book. Reads. As she reads, she continues to rub at her crotch, initially scratching, then just absentmindedly touching, feeling the shapes of her own outlines through her underwear. There is no hair there. After a while, her touching becomes more rhythmic, and she is no longer reading the book. She rests it against her face. The open book is covering her face. Pages and ink wetly warmed by her breath. Using the middle and forefinger of her left hand, she rubs herself in small but forceful circles for two minutes and twelve seconds. The muscles in her legs contract, lift a little, then loosen. Hand falls, body slackens.

Girl drops the book to the floor beside her, slowly. There comes the sound, faintly, throbbing louder, of a huge party. Flickering on the blackened window appears the moving image of a party, 1920s-style, a swinging ballroom with an orchestra and chandeliers and small round tables and sweeping shots and close-ups on couples smiling and hanging out of one another, talking, laughing, drinking, cavorting in black and white. It throbs a while, sound and image, crescendos, fades. Girl turns her head to the side sleepily. She slides slowly off the couch and crumples to the floor on top of her book. She lies on the floor a while, face down. A siren sounds out the window, far off, louder, then extremely loud, passing right by, then fading. Blue lights flicker briefly through the window as it speeds by, flashing on the ceiling. She sits up. She looks to the window. Makes a sudden move to get up, hand on coffee table, legs tensed and back straight, to see where it is going, for whom, but knows she is too late, and slumps back down into her sitting position on the floor between couch and coffee table.

III

Girl studies her upper right arm a while, as though checking for spots or moles. She twists it, studying each side, and feels up it with the fingers of her left hand, searching. She picks at something, squeezes, and jerks her arm away. She has hurt herself. Pauses. She sniffs the fingers of her left hand. She looks down to her side, sees the fallen book. She is about to lift it when she spots something else, something small, perhaps the squashed fly. (There is no fly.) Her body tenses like a cat. She pauses, then pounces on it. She picks it up between finger and thumb, studies it in the light of the lamp. (There's nothing there.) She sniffs it suspiciously, sniffs it again. Then she pops it in her mouth. She chews, mouth closed. (There's nothing there.) She gulps. She exhales a breath of satisfaction. Pauses. Using couch and coffee table, she stands, picks up the book, flicks through it as she sidles to the bookshelf. She leans against it or against the wall beside it, reading. Reads a while. Through her top, her left breast appears to be leaking milk. A wet patch spreads outwards, darkening the pale blue material.

IV

Girl stands by bookshelf in same position but in slightly different clothes. Now the material of her top is cream, although there is still a stain of milk spreading darkly from her left breast. She is leafing through a book. Increasing in volume from a whisper, the sound of a woman pleading with a man not to leave her. He says he must. In the window, an Asian boyband in silver clothes dance in sync in a large mirrored room with a disco ball. The camera moves in and out with fast cuts from the sides, front and back and close-ups on their smiling, singing faces. Their expressions are cheeky and inviting. We hear footsteps, a door closing. The woman's gentle sobs. The light in the room changes from regular yellow hues to greens and blues. Head still facing down into book, Girl makes a farting noise with her mouth, long and distended and wet. She snaps the book shut. The image disappears. Silence. She places it back on the shelf. She studies the spines of the books, runs her fingers along them, head tilted, considers taking one out, pulls it, abandons. A phone vibrates loudly. Her head snaps towards the sound and she runs to the couch. She throws off the cushions until she finds it. It is still vibrating. Her actions are frenzied, desperate. She is like an animal. Cushions fly everywhere. The vibrating sound stops. She finds it stuffed deep down the back. Held in both hands, she peers. The window lights up as though it is her screen. The words *Missed Call – Mom* before a stock background image of green meadows and a blue sky. Her shoulders slump. She blackens the phone screen with a press of a button along the side, and the window darkens too. Girl throws the phone back down and, standing slumped facing the couch, scratches below her right tit for a while.

V

Hip hop music starts up, as though coming from the open window of a car parked on the street. Girl has been lying on the floor in front of the kitchen table, curled on her side. She hears the music. She stands and walks groggily, rubbing her eyes and stretching. She stares out. In the window, we see appearing, flickering from darkness, the illuminated image of two beetles fucking in a meadow, close-up. Girl shifts position. Quickly presses her back to the wall to look out over her shoulder, like people do in action movies. She mimes removing a gun from the back of the waistband of her skirt. Holds pretend gun aloft in her right hand against wall beside her. Brow furrowed, staring out. Pretends to remove the safety catch on the gun. The image of the beetles fucking is overlaid with the highly sexualized hip hop music coming from below, lots of women's groans and bass beats. It is getting louder. Men's voices below shout something over the music. Tone of a question, a laugh. She turns suddenly to face the window and points her imaginary gun out, downward. Her shoulders move up and down as though she is breathing heavily, adrenaline. She gives no indication that she sees the beetles fucking. An engine starts up below the deafening music. Headlights sweep across the window and through the image, like a lighthouse, blinding Girl. She covers her eyes with the crook of the arm holding the imaginary gun. Receding down the street, engine and music fade to silence. The beetles finish fucking and, extricating itself carefully, the top one waddles away. The image flickers and fades to blackness. Girl stands up straight. She lifts her imaginary gun to her mouth, and blows the end of it, as though blowing away smoking gunpowder. She returns it to the waistband of her skirt. Through the wall to her left, behind the door – muffled footsteps. She jumps, frightened. The light changes, darkens, a dim mustard yellow. She pads quickly and quietly to the door and presses her ear. More footsteps, the jangle of a key further off. A man's stifled cough. Girl's face lights up. A door opening and closing. Silence. Between outspread hands, Girl turns her head from the side so her forehead rests against the door. Stays there a while. Years pass. Through the window, as though seen from a submarine, appears from darkness the ocean, pure water, grey and empty, sloshing.

VI

Girl sits on couch, takes up remote and switches on TV. Window lights up. A game show. A tanned host with a glittering orange suit and a toupée and a bow tie. He is smiling a lot and speaking to camera, but all that can be heard is construction site noises – engines, digging, hammering, drills. Sweeping shots of the studio: contestants consisting of couples in matching sparkling outfits coordinated by colour, standing on podiums; laughing audience sitting on tiered bleachers; swooping spotlights; a big illuminated screen showing scores. Suddenly, after a big red X has flashed on screen, we see one couple waving as they walk tearfully off their little podium. They are the sparkling green couple. He has glasses and is short and she is also short and fat and blonde but does not have glasses. We see the host blow them kisses, mime rubbing a tear from his eye, blow more kisses. We see them ascend the big staircase at the back and centre of the studio stage, surrounded by dry ice smoke, or real smoke maybe, the staircase to the big black entrance (exit) through which we can't see. The sparkling green woman stumbles and the sparkling green man catches her elbow. At the top of the staircase they turn, just as they were instructed to do that afternoon, just as they have seen so many other couples do on their own TV at home. Then they walk through the door and disappear into the blackness and the camera cuts to the audience clapping and the host smiling and already talking about the next section of the show. The drilling and construction sounds are becoming achingly loud and shake the walls of the apartment. Girl sits in middle of couch, legs crossed at the ankle, eyes trained on TV, mouth hanging slightly open. Her left breast is still leaking milk, now creating the dark, wet stain on a peach-coloured top. Girl picks her nose and, finding something up there, eats it without looking. She goes back for more. The contestants are putting on sparkling wetsuits and diving gear in their special coordinated colours. Host's face up close, smiling and winking words, and then the screen cuts to a commercial, an animated lamb running through a purple field smiling amongst also-smiling sun and flowers. It is for chocolate, or sanitary towels. Wiping her picking finger on her skirt, Girl lifts remote and switches off TV. Window turns black. Noise stops. Girl opens her mouth wide and squints her eyes tight, but no sound comes out, only rose petals and butterflies.

VII

A cat is in the room. It is white with orange patches, or orange with white patches. It has yellow eyes. It walks across the room from right to left. It sits. It mews, tail curling. It mews. Looks around as though it has spotted a fly. (There is no fly.) Lies down. Rolls on its back a while. Flips over again and settles on its tummy. Squints its eyes, purring. Mews. No sign of Girl, although there is a sound of screaming, screaming in agony for help, please help, anybody, please, muffled and far off. Maybe it isn't screaming though. Maybe it's nothing. Probably nothing. In the window, a herd of wild antelope seen from above run wildly across the plain, kicking up a storm of thick yellow dust.

VIII

Apartment is empty. Apartment is tidy. Books on their shelf as usual, TV, coffee table with single remote. Fruit bowl, now in centre of kitchen table, filled with fresh fruit. Out the window, a street in sunshine, view of apartment building across the way obscured slightly by branches of a tree. Stays like this a while. Down below, sound of an ice cream truck. Kids' voices. Far off, a hint of construction. Pouring in through window, light fades to glow of evening, golden butter-warm. Muffled sound through wall to left, a man's tones, Girl laughing. Silence. Then the rattle of a key in the door. In walks Girl. With her is a man. He carries two blue plastic shopping bags. They are smiling. They are talking and laughing but they are muffled, as though being heard through a glass pressed to a thick white wall. They are unpacking. They are teasing and tickling, moving around the kitchen. Then they are kissing and petting. Halfway through unpacking the shopping, plastic bags left sagging and cupboards open, they move across to the couch, entangled in one another, smiling laughing kissing, undressing and almost tripping, and begin fucking slowly and passionately, then fast, then slow again, then fast again, in various positions. Cat walks across the room left to right, and watches them a while. The muffled sounds of two people fucking – slaps and groans and moans and wetness. But the sounds of fucking do not align with their fucking. It is the muffled sound of a different couple fucking, in a different apartment, somewhere else entirely.

In the window (which is growing larger, expanding outward across the whole back wall, the whole wall of the apartment block, the city, the country, the continent, the world), images appear: Times Square; a sparrow on a branch; a woman from an African tribe sitting on the ground, a huge brown disc in her bottom lip; a nightclub seen from above, pulsing bodies lit in flashing lights of green and blue; a sandy beach; a volcano exploding; a samurai doing samurai moves to camera in a red room; Venus; two stags locking antlers near a river, their heavy breaths showing up in misty clouds; the set of a serious political talk show from the seventies, white men in suits with cigarettes and crossed legs; a blonde white woman snorting coke off a bathroom cistern; four boys running as fast as they can down a street in America in the fifties; a black guy tying a tourniquet on his arm in a shoddy, low-lit room; a goldfish circling in a bowl surrounded by family and graduation photos; sneakers hanging from phone wires; a woman climbing on a huge pile of rubbish some-where in Asia, a child strapped to her back; ham being sliced quickly in a factory; a champagne cork flying from a frothing bottle held by a chortling fat man in a three-piece suit; a snail on a footpath; an old woman lying alone in a hospital bed, face turned on her pillow toward the window; an empty wheat field, dry and swaying slightly; a tadpole wriggling in puddle water; a close-up of a glow-ing cigarette being sucked; stubbled chin; empty cinema seats; a church steeple from below; a kid jumping into a swimming pool, body curled in a ball, seen from the kid's perspective; a microwave dinging; a wolf padding across a snowy expanse, pausing to sniff, continuing on; a scalpel cutting into the underside of a woman's breast with thick black markings on it; an empty office block lit up; a brass band in sunglasses and suits leaning forward in unison; a walking stick laid on the grassy bank of a river; a snaking traffic jam on the outskirts of a city; a boy teaching him-self guitar in his room, walls covered with posters; Girl lovingly breastfeeding a baby from her left breast, looking up to camera with teary-happy eyes; a mushroom cloud exploding; a stained toilet bowl; a group of ethnically diverse teenagers giving the peace sign to camera for the opening of a Nickelodeon show from the nineties; melted cheese squishing out the side of a sandwich; a man twisting a pheasant's neck; a still lake reflecting mountains; a man writing at a beautiful mahogany desk facing a window that overlooks a green and floral garden; a highway sign for a brothel in ten miles; rice being scooped into bowls by the hand of a small Asian woman; cards being dealt; a dog bounding ahead happily towards a forest from the boot of a car; then a close up on the man's face, tightly strained, beading sweat, moving forward and back, serious from fucking; then Girl's face, tightly strained, beading sweat, moving up and down, also serious from fucking, both appearing to look straight back in through the now-enormous window. Muffled sound of another couple fucking has faded to silence. No sound. Silence.

Cat lies down on its stomach, facing the other way, bored by them. Squints its eyes, purring. The golden evening light outside fades to dark night, and the streetlight comes on – a false yellow, illuminating the room. All this time, they are fucking. Now he is sitting in the centre of the couch, facing the TV, and she is on top of him, blocking the TV with her body. Finally, it is almost totally dark and they orgasm together, her thrusting up and down above him, tits rotating circles, slapping against one another on the inner turn. Both man and Girl are drenched in sweat. They appear to be screaming out in pleasure. Silence. Slow down gradually like a train stopping, panting. Stillness. Cat mews, sits up, begins licking itself, stops to look up, mews again. Outside, far off, growing louder, deafening, then fading, a siren. Blue light flickers in as it passes. They don't seem to notice. The blue lights and, after it has passed, the yellow streetlight, illuminate the bones of her spine which bulge out from beneath her skin.

A phone vibrates in his trousers, crumpled on the floor. Girl moves to climb off him. She does so in a way that prevents cum from dripping out from inside her onto the material of the couch, crouching over his leg and then standing hunched. He sits back, arms spread out. She pads to the kitchen, knees bent, attempting to clench in the cum. Grabs some kitchen roll and places it between her legs. Leans against the counter. His phone is vibrating. It is loud. Girl removes the kitchen roll from between her legs, throws it in the bin, and slowly walks to the window. She stands naked before it, looking out. His phone stops vibrating. Eventually he lifts his head. He looks around the darkened room. Looks at her. Seeing her, standing there, his face is stricken.

IX

Girl walks to kitchen area. Opens fridge. Takes out sliced white bread, mayonnaise, a packet of wafer-thin sliced ham, lettuce, two individually wrapped slices of yellow cheddar cheese, a pickle jar. She makes a sandwich. She is methodical about it. She cuts off the crusts. She is in a frilly pink dressing gown. Frills on the cuff, the hem, along each side's opening. Tied at waist. Her head is shaved. It is bleeding in places, and there are still little tufts of hair here and there. She spreads the mayonnaise and cuts the crusts off and divides the sandwich diagonally into two neat triangles with a barber's razor blade. The blade still has blood on it, and dyes the mayonnaise and the edges of the sandwich pink. The cat runs over to her because it is hungry. It mews. Licking her left hand's fingers, with her right hand she drops the crusts to the cat, as well as two slices of wafer-thin ham. Girl watches cat eat. Through the window, a child is being born. Horn-led jazz music fills the room. Girl sits at table. Small rivulets of blood from her scalp run down her face and the back of her neck. She eats sandwich. Cat is finished first and watches her and mews. Girl ignores cat. Cat mews more. Girl ignores cat. Cat mews more, plaintively, tail curling. Girl takes a gun from inside her dressing gown and shoots cat. Blood and guts and fur fly everywhere. Girl puts gun down on the table beside her sandwich and continues eating. She pauses to fix herself a glass of milk. She sits back down. Alternating between milk and sandwich, she finishes her meal. Her left breast is leaking milk, creating a dark wet patch on her pink dressing gown. In the window, we see the baby emerge covered in blood, shit and mucus from the vagina. The mother is crying with pain, relief and joy. The camera work is flitting and confused, from mother's face to still-seeping vagina to baby being wiped down to doctor in blue to wall and back to mother. The mother is passed the baby. She holds her baby. The baby is crying too. It is red and scrunched and howling. It's wrapped in pink. It's a Girl.

Don't Pretend You Don't Know

AWAKENING

Her first morning waking up in Oaxaca, she holds a drinking glass over the open flame of the gas burner to heat water for coffee. She can't tell if this is genius or unspeakably stupid. She wonders if the glass will suddenly explode and send glass shrapnel into her chest, belly and eyes. She doubts it, but still, it's a thought. She wonders if the bottom will crack off and melt onto the burner itself, rendering both destroyed. This feels more likely to happen, and less likely to garner sympathy with Emilio, Christian and Omar, her Airbnb hosts or, as they put it, sitting all around her in the jangling little Renault Clio from the airport the day before at dawn, her *familia mexicana*. They're the ones who didn't think she might need pots, or a wardrobe, or shelves, or a table and chairs, or even a cup. They have either taken minimalism to its absurd end, or they're exceptionally tight.

She holds the glass at a tilt, but still manages to lightly burn the skin of her thumb. It's only 5.30 a.m., and she wants to write since, apparently, that's what she came all this way to do, but it is cold before sunrise in Mexico, and she can't write without the warmth and caffeine of strong coffee. At least, that's her justification. There are a lot of preambling justifications before she can get going, and even after she goes through them all, there's no guarantee.

As she stands over the flame, watching the first small bubbles form, rise and disappear, she thinks about the loose-toothed man with eyes facing two different ways – both the wrong way – hovering outside the front gate of her apartment building last night. He strained his head around to watch her enter and she, also looking back, caught him watching before he snapped his head behind the wall, out of sight. She checked behind when opening her apartment door, and listened out. As soon as she got inside, she triple-locked it. One of the locks, she noticed, looked as though someone had once tried to kick it in – the wood around it was flaking. She also locked her bedroom.

Now she hears a few groaning engines starting up, the rumblings of the buildings, pipes and brick-aches, a plane overhead maybe, but not much else. That weight the air has, she thinks, heavy with dreams and stillness, when all around people are sleeping. As she was waking, at around 5 a.m., a man in the apartment next to hers coughed inter-mittently, little guttural expulsions, and every now and again gathered phlegm in his throat thickly, and spat. She wondered if he was spitting on the floor, or had some sort of system. Newspapers laid out, maybe. Then she heard shuffling, and the strong, definite stream of a man piss-ing into the water of a toilet bowl, and she felt an old, familiar pining for the men she's known – the safety of them. Her father, bustling downstairs somewhere, one of her many uncles, off to fix a fence or a car, or a boyfriend, soon coming back to bed, skin cold and dimpled from the world.

She loves the sound of men pissing, she decided, and formulated half-asleep thoughts about this, lying tightly foetal on one side of the double bed. Unformed, dreamy thoughts of how to write about it, what its significance might be. Then the man started his jazz-coughing again, punctuated with those thick, throaty ejections of phlegm, and, remembering herself alone, in an unfamiliar place, she felt the warm comfort seep from her belly, and decided to get up.

She swaps hands and sucks her hot, slightly hardened thumb. It tastes sweet. When the glass is too hot to hold any longer, she removes it from the flame and stirs in two heaped teaspoons of granulated coffee she bought cheap in the little OXXO shop across the road yesterday afternoon, after landing. Coffee, milk, oats, natural yoghurt, toiletries. She thinks now of that strong smell the OXXO shop had; the rotating hotdogs and the coffee machines and an unidentifiable milky sweetness, a bit like Yakult yoghurts. This, she will grow so accustomed to, she will forget to smell it. Much like the garbage piled on the roadsides, the sewage floating up on hot days from the grates, the stench of raw meat wafting from the taco stands, the scent of maize lacing all the cobbled streets.

She had to hunt for bananas, since none of the corner shops she tried had fruit or vegetables – instead, they seem to prefer produce that can sit on the shelves for weeks and years: nachos, moist little packages of cakey treats, stuffed to the brim with preservatives, beers, fizzy drinks and tinned goods. Finally, she found a market just around the corner from her apartment building, swarming with sounds, colours and bodies. Never before, Lucy thinks now, had she been in a place so packed tight with bodies so utterly unlike her own. Never before, at least not when entirely alone, had Lucy been so apparently the foreigner, the visible outsider. Their eyes seemed to ask Lucy what on earth she was doing there; the women, unimpressed; the children, curious; the men, hungry. But, she tells herself, admonishing her weakness, she will grow used to this. This is what it is, to be in a foreign country. This is what she came for.

That market, she thinks now – it shall be the first of her known places. Finding known places, regular spots, is one of her greatest pleasures, when arriving somewhere new. She arrives in new places a lot, and understands that it is the creation of little routines that makes this bearable. It is finding faces that recognize yours, and, after a few visits, smile, say hello, maybe comment on the weather. Otherwise, Lucy knows, a person could very soon drown in lostness.

She yawns, her whole body suspended up, up, up, then sinking back. She is tired, and looking forward to her coffee. She is proud of her ingenuity in making it, and smiles a little to herself, as she pours in the milk, watching it turn from black to swirling, pale brown, before taking her first sip.

CARLOS

Carlos is smaller even than your average Mexican. His body is tight under his clothes – stocky, but tight. He appears healthy, although his skin glistens more than it ought. He has wide eyes – almost like a child's toy, a Furby maybe – and a nervous face, one equally prepared to smile or flinch. He spots her from the street. She is two storeys up, sitting on the restaurant's balcony with a beer and a book. It is her second day in Oaxaca. Next thing he is beside her. He wants to introduce himself. He can speak

English, you see. Carlos is proud of his education and his travels and his interest in literature. He came from nothing and yet here he is. He is an avid reader, he tells her. He is proud, too, of his confidence in coming up to speak to her. He doesn't say this but it's clear. He has the demeanour of someone who believes themselves to have recently overcome the curse of ugliness. He holds his small body well. He stares at her as though he does not quite believe in her face.

Carlos tells her of his trip to Ireland. He takes his phone out of his jeans pocket to show her photos of him smiling in a beanie cap and scarf and zipped-up rainproof coat before green cliffs, beside water, in green fields with sheep, before other cliffs, green, also with sheep. 'Is very green, Ireland.' She agrees. She tells him, unthinking, that Mexican people look wrong in rain gear and he sort-of laughs, not quite comprehending, wary of insult. Now she must be friendlier than she'd like to compensate. She sips her beer. She is still limply holding her book, keeping her page with her thumb. If she puts it down completely, he's in, so she is careful not to do so.

Carlos's hair is slicked and his black button-up shirt has a slight sheen to it, not unlike his skin. Had she passed him in the street without interaction, she might have assumed he was gay. He tells her he is a world-class cumbia dancer and offers to give her lessons. He tells her that he taught classes when he lived in Canada, but that actually now he is a botanist. She raises her eyebrows and tries to appear moderately impressed. She thinks but does not tell him about how she once wanted to become a gardener – she doesn't want to encourage connections between them.

He is carrying a book on plant life in his hand which he shows her, telling her of his fascination with natural medicine. He tells her the Zapotecs, the ancient people from this region of Mexico – has she heard of the Zapotecs? *Bien*, yes, well, they understood the medicine in the plants all around and used them, but much of that knowledge has been lost or is only remembered among the traditional people, the people outside the cities. His ancestors are some of those people, he tells her. They still live there now at the edges of the woods at the base of the mountains, he says, pointing. Maybe she would like to come and see his village some time?

The sun is beating down on them and, mixed with the conversation and the beer and all the general startling newness, it is wearying her a little. She can hear the voices of the people walking down below, down where he had been, wafting up to meet them. They mostly speak in Spanish, but every now and then she can discern US-inflected English. It is the most central street in the city, and from the balcony it is possible to see Santo Domingo, and beyond the great church, all those lushly green sky-piercing mountains towards which Carlos is pointing now but not looking. He is looking at her.

She has not yet grown accustomed to their beauty, those mountains, and can't keep her eyes from darting towards them from her book, and now from Carlos's hopeful, wide-eyed face. He tells her he lives in a house there with all his family – his parents and his *abuela* and all his brothers and sisters, and now some of their children too. She smiles and he, gesturing to the empty chair opposite, sensing his having landed on a subject compelling enough to engage her, asks may he sit down. She baulks, picturing his hands reaching below the table for her leg, or worse, the two of them simply conversing for hours. Sitting up straighter in her own chair, she tells him that actually, sorry, but she was in the middle of reading and writing and she really should continue. She watches him deflate, his shoulders visibly lowering, but he says he understands, of course. He then continues to stand beside her, blocking the only way off the small balcony back into the shadowed restaurant.

There is no one else in the restaurant. It is early evening, and the two waitresses, older skinny Mexican ladies, stand around chatting, leaning on the counter with cleaning rags hanging loosely from their hands. Pop music plays – now it is 'Malibu' by Miley Cyrus. Before that it was 'Shake It Off' and before that, 'Cry Me A River'.

Carlos asks her what is she writing – is she a journalist? And she says no, no, she has actually been writing poetry today, but she usually writes essays.

'For the newspaper?'

'No, no, eh, for magazines or, eh, books, maybe, but mostly just for me … I am going to write about here, about Oaxaca.' Over the coming months Lucy will always say this when asked, both to justify her being there, seemingly just lounging about – *classic* imperialist – and to hopefully make them implicitly understand that she isn't rich; that it is a sort of working holiday, even though she has no idea if she'll ever manage to actually write about any of it, and certainly won't ever earn any money from it; and even though, in their terms, she probably *is* rich. But saying it aloud – that she's there with the implicit intention to write something about it, something presumably significant, shoots arrows of anxiety straight into her belly.

She takes the last swig from her bottle as his eyes widen even more. Carlos leans forward a little over her and says, breathlessly, that he too writes poetry. He is standing so close to her now that she can smell his masculine, incense-like deodorant wafting up from his stocky torso and underarms. There is a pause.

'That's great,' she says, forcing a smile. She is suddenly overwhelmingly tired and wants nothing more than to go back to her cool single bed, to climb between the white sheets and sleep. 'That's really great.'

EARTHQUAKE I

Standing by the bed, ready to resettle, she feels one of those little itches on her left hand and looks down to see a tiny maggot lurching its way up beyond her thumb toward her wrist. She flicks it off in a panic and checks for another, or a bite mark – anything, anywhere on her skin. It must've come from the bin she'd tied up and put in the hall. It was starting to reek. Could they burrow into skin? Could it have lain something, infected her somehow? Do maggots do that in Mexico? Probably. She scratches furiously, leaving red streaks, and studies all up her arms, turning them over and over, storm still raging outside. No sign, no marks, but that means nothing. It could still have gotten her, could still get her even now. She regrets flicking the maggot away and turns on all the lights to find and kill it. But she can't find it; it is impossible to see the tiny white creature against the huge white tiles. Maybe it has burrowed into the sole of her foot? Some delicate place below her ankle? Finally she gives up and climbs into bed and lies there in the dark, listening to the thunder and the heavy rain, remembering the photo on her newsfeed of the bridge to the airport in Oaxaca flooding, cars submerged up to their roofs. She imagines the maggot crawling up the bedsheets to find her, to burrow in between her toes. She has been in Mexico exactly a week. She's alone, unnerved and exhausted.

Awakened by the shaking. She doesn't really under-stand. Whole room shaking, the noise of it the worst thing, she'd realize afterwards. No space for thought now, too much shaking. The rumbling inescapable noise of it, like the whole world is raging. That, and feeling utterly out of control – helpless to stop it, her whole body shaking, her limbs, unable to grasp, to stop, please, out of control, the shaking.

It is, she would tell people later, like very bad turbu-lence on an aeroplane, except that it is everywhere.

When it finally stops, the silence is eerie. All she can hear is a child crying down the street and the rain still falling, but lightly now, pattering against the corrugated roofs all around her. The rest of the world seems to be lis-tening out too, waiting for what next. Nothing, she thinks. Nothing, stop being silly. A storm, just a storm, nothing, she tells herself. She forces herself to believe it was just the thunder, that she is being ridiculous, and makes herself go back to sleep and not think about it; the shaking, the flood-ing, the maggot, still coming, always coming to get her.

She is awakened again, this time to her phone vibrating on the small wooden bedside table. Groggily, she picks it up, the brightness of the screen a shock in the blackened room. Missed WhatsApp calls from her father, and a text:

Dad: You ok after that strong earthquake? (2.10 a.m.)
MISSED VOICE CALL (2.16 a.m.)
MISSED VOICE CALL (2.32 a.m.)
MISSED VOICE CALL (2.36 a.m.)
MISSED VOICE CALL (2.49 a.m.)
MISSED VOICE CALL (3.16 a.m.)

Her: Hey   (3.17 a.m.)
Her: Sorry asleep!   (3.17 a.m.)
Her: Yeah I'm okay!   (3.17 a.m.)
Dad: Jesus. News full of earthquakes   (3.18 a.m.)
Her: Here or everywhere??   (3.18 a.m.)
Her: It just shook the room like mad   (3.18 a.m.)
Dad: Always text after natural disasters,
u feckin eejit.   (3.18 a.m.)
Her: I didn't know it was a big deal!   (3.18 a.m.)
Dad: Biggest Mexican earthquake in a century,
all over the news here. 14 dead.   (3.19 a.m.)
Her: WHAT   (3.19 a.m.)
Her: Holy shit!!!   (3.19 a.m.)
Her: Oh my god!!!   (3.19 a.m.)
Her: That's scary   (3.20 a.m.)
Her: Jaysus   (3.20 a.m.)
Dad: Off the coast of Chips ass and Oaxaca
                                            (3.20 a.m.)
Dad: Ducking autocorrect, *Chiapas   (3.20 a.m.)
Dad: *FUCKING, Christ   (3.20 a.m.)
Her: Wow   (3.20 a.m.)
Dad: Check about tsunami warnings   (3.20 a.m.)
Dad: Are you far from the coast?   (3.21 a.m.)
Her: Yeah   (3.21 a.m.)
Her: Yonks away I think   (3.21 a.m.)
Her: You're freaking me out though   (3.21 a.m.)
Dad: 54 miles off the coast there, 8.4   (3.21 a.m.)
Her: 8.4 what?   (3.21 a.m.)
Dad: If ur ok, that sounds like u are ok   (3.22 a.m.)
Dad: Magnitude   (3.22 a.m.)
Her: Oh wow   (3.22 a.m.)
Her: Jesus. That's acres   (3.22 a.m.)
Her: *scary   (3.22 a.m.)

Dad: Sorry, 3 confirmed dead.   (3.22 a.m.)

Dad: Not 14. That was the recent storm   (3.23 a.m.)

Her: The storm in Mexico?? Or that hurricane?

(3.23 a.m.)

Her: It's been stormy here but just mad rain

(3.23 a.m.)

Dad: Check online. Sounds like ur safe. Susan called and I've just been trying to find out more online

(3.24 a.m.)

Her: Well tbh it's half three, I'll sleep now and look into it in the morning   (3.25 a.m.)

Dad: Waves up to 10 feet expected after quake

(3.25 a.m.)

Her: Stop dad!!!!   (3.25 a.m.)

Her: Jesus fucking Christ   (3.25 a.m.)

SANTIAGO I

Lucy meets Santiago in the one small record store in Oaxaca. He is passive-aggressively polite to two tourists from the States, both with different Asian origins (perhaps Indian and Chinese), both small and pretty, both with performatively flirtatious American voices. They are asking Santiago in a teasing manner for a discount on a record they want to buy, and he, smiling with only his mouth, says it is not up to him, it is not his store.

'So, like, you just work here?' the Indian-looking girl with ombré hair asks with seeming disbelief. She is wearing only short shorts and a crop top, while her friend sports a floral low-cut summer dress, a top bun and a nose ring.

'Yes, I just work here,' Santiago says carefully, looking directly into her eyes.

'Aw, man,' she persists, leaning herself slightly across the counter towards him while her friend giggles behind her hand, 'can't you just gimme, like, a few pesos off maybe?'

One of the girls has a Calvin Klein backpack and both wear pristine Nike sneakers. Santiago has dark skin and a slight frame with apologetically curved shoulders, darting eyes, thick lips and a crop of curly hair.

'No, sorry,' he says blankly. When the girls wait, expecting some further explanation, he shrugs and then averts his eyes to the computer screen on the counter.

When the girls leave, having bought nothing, Lucy – who just that morning on Skype was advised by her mother not to let herself become too isolated (since loneliness is, she must admit, already beginning to discolour her vision, giving everything in Oaxaca a deep, reddish hue, as though there is too much blood in her head, perhaps worsened by the constant, ebullient sunshine) – resolves to speak to him. She wants to engage with him, partly for herself and partly to identify herself as different to those awful gringo girls.

She picks up a Coltrane record, sighs, studies the back and returns it. She does the same with a Chet Baker record. From the corner of her eye, she confirms that Santiago is watching her, although he is pretending to do something on the computer. As the song playing on the shop's stereo system ends, he darts out from behind the counter, grabs a record, and sticks it on the player. He turns it up, then twists his body around towards her, his feet still facing the player.

'Mexican jazz, from Oaxaca,' he tells her, pointing upwards, when the first blasts of the horn kick in. Lucy smiles and raises her eyebrows enthusiastically to convey her 'listening face'. Returning quickly to his space behind the counter, conscious of how she is nodding her head along gently, Santiago starts to tell her something else, but the music is playing so loudly that he has to shout across the small shop, and so Lucy comes over to him at the counter at the same time as he darts back out again towards her, tripping slightly on a box of CDs on the floor. They meet in a rush and then, in sudden proximity, smile shyly.

Up close, Lucy is almost a head taller than Santiago. He wears loose-fitting jeans like a teenager in the nineties, tattered old dress shoes of ruddy brown leather, and a tan-coloured airtex t-shirt. He leans up and in towards her ear, not too close, nervous, warmth of skins, cupping his mouth.

'Friends of mine, the jazz – it's a sort of, eeh, how do you say, "fusion"?' He leans back out to face her and raises his voice further. 'Latin rhythms, see, cumbia, there, hear that? *¿Sí?* The beat and jazz, Mexican brass, all coming together, you see?'

Lucy nods, smiles, nods. She says it sounds amazing, wow, amazing, and Santiago, staring at her, his face indicating 'listen now, this bit', pointing up again at the music filling the warm cramped air of the shop, smiles too.

The sound crescendos to a heady end, and in the pause before the next track, Santiago speaks quickly: 'You want to come to a gig tonight, maybe? Jazz in La Nueva Babel, a friend of mine, friends of mine, we could go see?'

'Yeah,' Lucy says, flooded with the relief of acceptance, of prospective companionship, of not being alone again this night. 'Yeah, sounds great, yeah, thanks … I'm Lucy, by the way.'

'Santiago,' he says as the next song starts up, brass and cymbals flaring. He is grinning widely. She proffers her hand and they shake. His palm is soft and clammy.

DOG

That female dog with all those drooping tits, the one who lives on her street, who followed Lucy to the *lavandería* that day – she sits now just below the apartment block entrance in direct blasting sun, too tired to move. The skin around one of her eyes is red and sore and rotting. As Lucy walks by, she sees the dog's side inflate and deflate quick in the noontime heat and, shocked at the sight of her suffering, Lucy feels as though she wants to cry. She cannot believe the openness of the dog's pain, right there in the street, and she wonders, walking on, what she should do (bring her to the vet maybe?) while knowing really, reaching the apartment building's front door and turning the key in the lock, that she can do nothing. For a while, putting away her groceries, the image bothers Lucy. She puts on a podcast, and dispels it from her mind.

LA POPULAR

La Popular restaurant and café is open to the world on two sides, supported only by a pillar at the building's corner. Breezes rustle through, scents and sounds. Dogs sit and sprawl on the warm pavement out front, dozing, biting ticks on their haunches; the younger ones alert, ears pricked, hoping for scraps. The café is positioned on the sloping corner of Jesús Carranza and Calle de

Manuel García Vigil, overlooking the trickling end of the aqueduct in front of Templo del Carmen Alto, built with greenish-hued cantera stone mined from the surrounding mountains and used all over Oaxaca. This church in turn stands just up from the open-air market selling local weaves and trinkets to tourists: necklaces, brooches, hand-blown hash pipes, dreamcatchers and pirated DVDs.

Before entering La Popular, Lucy quickly scans the room for faces she might know, good or bad; acquaintances, vaguely recalled faces from bleary nights out and then, if all is clear, she steps in to find a table, a chair, a space. For the rest of the evening she can sit and be admired by passing eyes and enjoy and despise it, and talk to whomever happens to be accompanying her this time. (Company in this place for Lucy is simply a means to drinking more and hearing herself say impressive-seeming things aloud – or, in truth, just hearing herself speak aloud at all, the vibrations of sound on the warm night air a confirmation of her continued existence in the world.)

There are three plain waitresses and one beautiful one. Lucy always hopes to get the beautiful one because Lucy is an artist of sorts, or something, and so she appreciates aesthetically pleasing things. Watching the waitress approach, smiling, Lucy smiles too, feeling a special kinship, and tries to decide what it is about her that makes her so astoundingly attractive. As the waitress hands her the menu and wipes down her table, Lucy decides that it's her eyes, or her nose, or her lips, or her ass bending over there, or her small round breasts, or her teeth maybe …

Lucy has always admired beauty, but she is beginning to notice that there is something different in how she admires women here in Mexico. She appraises them in a way she had previously reserved for paintings, or

201

bouquets in vases, or prettily arranged plates of food. It is as though, Lucy realizes uneasily, she is considering whether or not to purchase or consume them. She seems to be *leering*. She has, more than once, had to stop herself from whistling under her breath.

Lucy orders a Victoria and an *espadín* and then, calling the beautiful waitress back, a glass of water, in an attempt to pace herself. This rarely works, but it looks mature and besides, is probably good for her skin, or something. The room is low-lit at night (which is the only time Lucy goes, because in daylight she resolutely forswears both drink and people) and buzzing with conversation, and there are paintings and photographs by local artists covering the walls.

Sometimes if there are too many people in La Popular, Lucy and whomever she has brought with her must share a table with strangers, which is welcomed or resented depending on whether she is the one joining or being joined, respectively.

Lucy is always with a man. All of her friends in Oaxaca are men because they are the ones who come up and talk to her, and all of these men have pictured Lucy fucking them. She knows this because they make it painfully clear, usually three *espadines* in, or after some cocaine, or maybe after just a couple of beers.

The one she was with in La Popular the other night, Rafa, asked her how often she masturbates. She had been talking about Virginia Woolf. When she told him daily, he grinned and told her, using a hand gesture like a giddy Nazi salute, that in that very moment he'd gotten an erection and that it was pointing right at her. Rafa has a successful mezcal and general lifestyle brand that organizes music festivals all over Mexico to which he has invited Lucy to accompany him. He is very into money and *cosas* and technology and has a smart-vaping device especially for his weed. The first time Lucy agreed to let him buy her dinner (a six-course tasting menu in one of Oaxaca's top restaurants), he told her he wanted to take her to Paris to see the Eiffel Tower, and she had to pretend she was choking on her *mole*.

Lucy felt the hand gesture, which had been grand enough (sweeping towards her across the table, almost knocking his glass of Mexican red) was a little optimistic – Rafa is small and heavy and wears very tight, very revealing jeans. But she just laughed flirtatiously and drank some more and hated him enough to let him pick up the tab, again, which is what she's learned to do here to attempt to justify submitting herself to these demeaning dynamics and thus to control her rage. When he then insisted on walking her home and when, as she was saying goodnight, he put his foot in the door and lunged forward to steal a kiss, simultaneously trying to feel her up, she had to lie that she had her period and assure him, coquettishly, maybe next time, next time.

If Lucy has cocaine with her in La Popular, in her skirt pocket perhaps, she will, once the drinks have been served – a respectable, carefully calculated amount of time after arrival – excuse herself to go take some in the bathroom. Cocaine makes Lucy feel incredible, free, without fear or anxiety, and she eats less and feels less sleepy so it's a win-win, other than all the depression and all that adverse health stuff down the line. But in Mexico, Lucy is not living for down the line. She is only just coping with the days, the hours, the minutes as they come. If she makes it to the end of the trip, if she makes it home, that shall be more than enough – more than she feels she deserves. For now, in La Popular, the night is only the night and she is still relatively young and doesn't have any other time – no past or future beyond surviving as well as she can in the right here right now – to consider.

Other than Rafa, Lucy's friends here are mostly male visual artists or musicians and so, once she has stripped away enough self-awareness with the *espadín* or cocaine, she talks openly and pretentiously about art and her intentions and her ideas and dreams and pretends to be far more successful and together and productive than she really is. This is Lucy's self-narrativization in full swing. It is – if she were able to watch herself from above – pathetic and embarrassing. But she resolutely avoids watching herself and so has (mostly) no idea. At least not until the mornings after.

She doesn't, for example, ever mention the five-hour lie-down she had that day to watch Tasty videos and listen to podcasts while swiping idly through Tinder in her little single bed, just to avoid working on a shitty poem. She doesn't mention the spots on her arse or how hairy she is or the family-pack of tortilla chips she wolfed in bed the other night either.

As the men pretend to listen, subtly checking their phones or glancing surreptitiously around the room for other people they might know, Lucy talks about what she thinks art ought to be – a seeking and accessing of universal truths, a way to know ourselves better through others, to startle one another into a recognition of what we didn't know was true of ourselves – and she tells them that this is what she is trying to do. Even hearing herself say it she sometimes feels kind of sick, but she puts this feeling down to thirst and so drinks some more, which works, since it also drowns out the sound and meaning of her own empty clichéd words. Eventually she shuts up, and then all there is to do is wait until it is time to go home, which she does when the night begins turning either sadly or menacingly sexual.

Either that or, depending on the male artist friend, he will take her ideas as a prologue to his own, and the rest of the night shall be him talking and talking and talking and feeling no shame at all. When the night goes this way Lucy can be comforted in remembering, sipping and nodding along, that no matter how awful a person she is, she's probably not the worst.

VISITING THE ARTISTS' STUDIOS

Visiting Pedro's studio, the first word she learns is *dolorosa*. She has been asking about pain because this is what one does when entering an artist's studio. Art, she thinks, is a show, really, for all that other stuff. Like love or loneliness or being overwhelmed by nature or mortality. Or fucking, of course. A way to talk about to access to share to distract from to kill time until getting back to all that other stuff. But *especially* fucking. She is not sure if this idea of art is insightful or radiantly stupid, but in the moment, in the heat, in the studio, she really doesn't care. She thinks it's because she is lonely and horny, tired and scagging from all the cocaine and mezcal and half-comprehended conversations in Spanglish the night before. Right now, there is nothing in the world Lucy wants more than to be touched – touched in a way that reminds her body of the existence, somewhere, of love.

She learns 'painful' from the smiling fat woman with eight languages. She knows the woman has eight languages because Pedro (the artist she is supposed to be visiting to write about his work – only twenty-four, pleasant, warm, from Mexico City, here on a scholarship to draw) tells her so in his own broken English. The fat woman is an artist too, apparently, with a tattoo (don't stare) in faded red and blue in the centre of her décolletage pointing down between her breasts (it is hard not to stare).

They don't know – these artists, here in the sunny studio, making pleasantries – about all the times Lucy has been fucked just next door. It is funny, she thinks, standing there in the friendly heat, surrounded by such earnest art, to imagine all that filthy coke-fuelled fucking. On the couch, on the mattress, on the floor. Juan, whose studio is next door, is an artist too, although all she's ever seen him do is drink and snort and fuck. She knows he is an artist only because of his having a studio, because of how he is treated like a god everywhere he goes in the city, and finally because of a video clip he showed her, still sweating, lying on the floor right after the first time they fucked, of his being introduced to camera by a towering Anthony Bourdain for an episode of his TV show being shot in Oaxaca.

Lucy and Juan started sleeping together two weeks before she visits Pedro's studio and it has proved an enormous relief to her. They do not care for one another, are destined to quickly forget one another, but sleeping with Juan has prevented Lucy's body from closing in on itself. Now all of Lucy's drunken nights either start or end with Juan on top of her, or on his knees behind her, grunting and thrusting. The sex is not good, not at all, but it is warm, and it is a means to being touched, touched deep, and for now this will have to be enough.

Pedro is a friend of Juan's but he does not know they are fucking. It is easier to keep it a secret. This is because

Lucy needs to fuck Juan for her body, but if the others were to find out they would lose interest in being her friend, and she needs their friendships for her heart and mind. It is a delicate balancing act. Now Pedro is rifling through sketches to show her, stored in a black folder down behind a large grubby table. He tells her he sleeps only three hours every night, here in the studio. His grant does not cover room and board. If he doesn't manage to sell any work to the wealthy gringos who wander through, he must live on just two hundred pesos a week, which works out as about eight or nine euro.

Later – when they are eating clear soup with chunks of meat, and warm maize tortillas for dipping, and salsa and limes to squeeze in, at a long plastic trestle table covered in colourful linoleum cloth for Juan's birthday celebrations (in yet another friend's studio, this one just across the road) – Pedro tells her conspiratorially that he sees a therapist, based back in Ciudad de México (these days he speaks to him by phone), and that his art is *oscuro, muy oscuro*. She hadn't really noticed but she nods, yes of course, dark, very dark. He smiles, believing her to understand him, and reaches across the table into the crate of twenty-four to grab out two more cool sweating bottles of Modelo. He opens one with his key chain and hands it to her before opening his own: *¡Salud!* It is only then Lucy realizes that he is convincing himself he is falling in love with her. Juan, sitting at the other end of the table, watches their interaction and smiles.

Pedro is soft and gently creased when smiling – which is most of the time – and full of the belief and hope of youth that she is in the process of losing. That belief that things will undoubtedly be fine. Good, even. It is startling for her to bear witness to – Lucy had forgotten what it looked like, all that blind, fretless hope. She finds herself blinking a lot up close to him. Later, when the dregs of day have descended into black Oaxacan night, all stained and flavoured with desire and brass and mezcal, when Pedro actually tells her he loves her, she will tell him he is too young and he genuinely won't understand, and the irony will be that he won't understand because he is so young.

The very first time they met, Lucy told Pedro (drunkenly, obviously) that she would write 'a poem of his art' and so here she is. She just said it so he would take her seriously and understand she wasn't just another western slut. But he believed her and thought she meant it seriously (she hadn't then taken into account that he is young, and so still believes things that are said) and now she supposes she'll be forced into the act of actually fucking writing something.

Back in the studio, she studies Pedro as he takes out his *dibujos* for her to see and she knows – watching his careful motions, his gentle consideration, those soft kind hands – that she could eat him up.

'Is "dry point". Is with ink, see? *Sí* … I like my, ah, process …'

The music in the studio too is soft and rhythmic and Latin American and all so desperately *pleasant*. It makes Lucy itch, and this makes her think again of being fucked hard on the floor by Juan – just next door, just the night before – and she marvels at how close to pleasant the purely ugly, the desperate, the painful and awful can be, lurking right there, through thin skins and walls. Then, as Pedro scrolls through Instagram on his phone to show her more of his work, just as a siren streaks by up the road outside, she realizes that she's being silly, that it isn't a marvel at all. That this is at the heart of most things, actually – their constant proximity. Life and death, all of it. The whole thing is just more stark here, she thinks, more bristlingly violent, and so harder to ignore.

'Black hole, *sí? ¿Cómo se dice en español? ¿Qué? ¿Cómo se escribe?'*

She must make it look like she is taking useful and important notes for her upcoming, breathtaking poetry: '*Sí,* okay; H-O-J-O N-E-G-R-O? *¿Sí?* No? Oh, eh, okay, could you ...? H-O-Y-O N-E-G-R-O? Ah, okay, *¡hoyo negro! Entiendo, okay, bien, bien, gracias ... tu símbolo, sí, entiendo, muy interesante.'*

How many times can she say '*muy interesante'* before she seems like she's taking the piss, she wonders?

Oaxaca is all artists' studios, especially the street she is currently on, Porfirio Díaz, which cuts right down through the heart of the historical centre of the city. Studios and cafés and churches and bars for getting lost in afterwards. Living here she has been drinking too much and this along with the heat has made her perpetually confused and even writing this she is drinking again. After all, she thinks (again and again and again): surely there will be a time after now when things are supposed to get better?

Pedro is clearly enjoying talking *Art* to her in the studio, although they do not speak the same language and it is something of a struggle. Still, there is some strange comprehension. Perhaps, she thinks, feeding off his optimism, their mutual understanding is being enhanced by the shortage of language to muck it up between them. Grunts, smiles, loose gestures. Lots of nodding. He seems to believe in her, to treat her as a fellow artist, although whether due to race or language or gender or ego (or all the echoing other stuff), he does not ask her anything about her writing in return. Perhaps because he couldn't read it anyway, being written in English, or perhaps because he just isn't really interested.

But it doesn't matter, she thinks. Not now, not here. She is just happy to be in company – to be safe. Besides, she reasons, we are all selfish in different ways, performing in different ways to get what we want. She is nodding along with him, smiling. She knows. She is selfish too, performing too. It's terrible but also refreshing, in a way. A relief, listening to the young artist explain the meaning of his works, to not be, in this self-interest, alone.

Sometimes we simply fulfill our prescribed roles, she thinks, cooing over a large sketch he holds up under the window's light. And right now, for him, she is the admiring woman. If she were to allow him to enforce it upon her, she would become a sort of semi-intellectual muse. Another kind of mirror. Oh well, she thinks. For now, she is too tired to fight. And too alone here. All she has the power to do, here in Mexico, is to appear to acquiesce while, at best, quietly taking note.

HORSE

On the bus through the mountains for a weekend on the coast, Lucy sees a horse in an enclosure no more than three times the length of its body, a strip between the road and the mountain's edge. Its front legs are tied together with rope. It is trying to move forward and is lurching, hooves tied tight together, and getting nowhere. And before Lucy can even really register, the bus has sped past around a corner and she doesn't know what to do, she doesn't know what to do, should she say something? But how, in Spanish? And what would they do? What should Lucy do? And the moment passes the bus speeds on they are already too far now and she doesn't have the language and what would they do anyway and so she does nothing. She does nothing. She puts on some music and tries to banish the image of the horse, hooves tied together, in that small enclosure, getting nowhere – lurching along in pain and getting absolutely nowhere – from her mind.

SANTIAGO II

Santiago invites Lucy to a birthday meal for one of his many aunties, being held in his parents' house. Lucy meets him at the old aqueduct which he has been wanting to show her.

'Beautiful, no?'

Lucy has already seen it, but she doesn't want to ruin it for him, and so she marvels.

'You want a photo?' Santiago asks, unconsciously imitating someone holding up a camera.

'No, no, that's okay, I don't like having my photo taken.'

'What? Why?!' Santiago makes a point of looking disbelieving, eyebrows arched. 'I thought all ladies liked, no?'

He is half-joking. He winks. Lucy has grown used to this mild chauvinism in Mexico and pretends to laugh along.

'Haha, no no, I don't ... I don't know, I guess I never look as good in photos as I'd pictured myself.'

'Ha,' Santiago laughs forcefully, dropping his hands, 'of course.'

It is extremely hot out, thickly silent but for distant engines and the hum of insects. The water in this part of the aqueduct runs weak and discoloured, although it ought to be flowing heavily. Lucy thinks of the rivers of home, the waterfall in the Devil's Glen in Wicklow where, at the base, she and the dog swim naked in summer when there's no one else around, her clothes strewn in a messy pile on the warm grey rocks.

As they walk, Santiago tells her loose, general facts about the Spanish and their arrival in Oaxaca, emphasizing the violence. He intersperses this account with stories about himself. Over the month or so since they met, Lucy has learned that Santiago loves nothing more than talking about unhappy things, and that this category includes himself: his wasted potential, his unappreciated talents, and all the myriad ways in which he has been wronged. He hates lots of things that it has never occured to Lucy to really think about. But then, as Santiago patiently explains, Lucy does not have to think about these things because she is a beautiful white woman. He, on the other hand, is a Mexican man – not only that, but his father is a *mexicano negro*, a black Mexican.

His father, Santiago has told Lucy more than once, is a descendant of the African slaves brought to Mexico, and still looked down upon by other lighter-skinned Mexicans. 'See, the Pope, he told the Conquistadors – do you know "Conquistador"? *¿Sí?* Yes, *sí*, see the Pope told them that Mexican people, that they have souls, *sí*? And so they could not make us into slaves, the *mexicanos*, and so they had to bring the Africans here, to be slaves here too, *sí*? And my father, his family, they come from those slaves, that is why I am so dark, you see? See, just look at you and I!' Santiago holds up his arm. Lucy, uncomfortable, holds up hers alongside. She has known many men like Santiago – embittered men, self-pitying men, men who feel as though the circumstances of the world prevented them from being the kings they ought to be – but she has never before had to take race into consideration in her dealings with any of them. Santiago makes race an ever-present, glaring issue and, it being too delicate for her to dismiss, Lucy is forced into a wary pity for him.

Santiago's forearm, she notes, has two long pinkish scars at a forty-five degree angle from one another. She wants to ask him about them but something prevents her.

'See?' he persists, excited, rubbing his arm against hers slightly in a way that, if pressed, he could claim was due to the motion of their walking. 'My mother, she is like you, she is Mexican, but she is very white, *sí*, like you – you will see.'

Lucy lowers her arm. When the path narrows on the bridge over the aqueduct, he goes first, and she, walking behind him, sees the sweat patch spreading across his pale blue t-shirt from the base of his back. Down below them, trees flourish along the banks, their canopies coming up to meet their feet. Lucy listens vacantly to the unfamiliar song of small birds darting between their red and purple flowers; song that is then drowned out by the building up and softly fading sound of a motorbike engine speeding past them, carrying a man, woman and child. After they cross, Santiago veers uphill to the left and they enter a cobbled street lined with squat shadowy houses. A dog barks angrily from a rooftop across the road, startling Lucy. She looks across and sees but cannot hear a woman talking into her phone, standing half-obscured in the shade just below it. The dog and the woman stare at Lucy and Santiago, who stare back, an anomalous pair made stranger by the heat.

After they have passed by the woman – who, Lucy sees, looking back at her as she steps out from her place in the shade to better watch their ascent, is young, in her early twenties maybe, with dyed blonde hair, thickly black-lined eyes, low-rise tight jeans with diamanté at the hip, a purple V-neck t-shirt, also tight, and black, strappy heels – Lucy, feeling herself burning, thirsty, mumbles something about Santiago being lucky he doesn't have to wear suncream. He, who had been lighting a cigarette between his lips, makes a point of stopping in his tracks, forcing her to also stop a few paces ahead, to look back at him, and to see his eyes widen in faux-disbelief, before simply shaking his head slowly, at the wrongness of her statement. She, growing a little weary, gives him no reaction, instead looking past him down the hill towards El Centro, feeling the sweat bead on her brow below her fringe, the warmth rising from the road, the haze, before turning and continuing on. He holds out a moment longer, willing a stronger reaction, a small and righteous scene, then relinquishes and walks briskly to catch up. Ultimately, their friendship means far more to him than it does to her.

'What should I bring?' Lucy asks after a few minutes of silence, rooting in her shoulder bag for her water bottle as she walks, feeling herself still not quite ready to look directly at him, to forgive him, although for what exactly she isn't sure (it is hard to think clearly, she reasons, in this heat).

'Oh, nothing, nothing, you do not need!' Santiago says, sucking in and then waving his cigarette in his hand dismissively, trailing smoke.

An old bow-legged man, carrying a blue plastic bag filled to bursting with oranges, emerges from the cool darkness of an alleyway to their left, making Santiago flinch. Lucy suppresses a smile. The man is dressed in a tucked short-sleeve button-up and slacks. He pauses, looks at them a moment, then tips his hat to Lucy, indicating politely for them to walk on. After a few seconds, she can hear the creak and wheeze of his old body shifting into motion behind them.

Insisting she could not turn up to his parents' house empty-handed, Lucy stops at a strip of small rickety shops including a florist, a laundrette, an abandoned dust-filled shoe shop with bare mannequin feet still displayed in the window at jaunty angles, and an OXXO store. She picks up a bouquet of yellow roses (which, Santiago immediately informs her, were wildly overpriced, but still, yes, good, very good, very generous of her) and, on his recommendation, a six-pack of Corona, which he promises his parents would prefer to the bottle of wine Lucy had originally picked out.

When they get to the party, Santiago's demeanour immediately changes. He becomes sulky and strangely reticent, not unlike a moody teenager (he is thirty-four) in the presence of his various aunties and mother. His father remains upstairs, only coming down to collect a plate of food, nodding without smiling to Lucy and Santiago, and waving vaguely towards the women around the table. In turn, the women (his mother and all six of his sisters), speaking in loud, enthusiastic Spanish too quick for Lucy to follow, utterly ignore him. Later, Santiago tells Lucy in English, which the women can't understand, that his father used to beat his mother when he and his brother were kids.

His brother, he tells her, now lives in California, and has invited Santiago to go too, has offered to get him construction work. But Santiago hates stupid Americans, and doesn't want to work construction, and also doesn't really like his brother.

'I love him, you know, because he is my brother, but we are not the same – he is more, how you say … he does not read books, like me. He does not love jazz, music, art, all these things, you see, like you and me, see? He has pale skin too, like hers,' Santiago adds in almost a whisper, tipping his bottle towards the fair-skinned figure of his mother, standing at the head of the table, ready to dish out food from a large clay pot she has just carried in from the kitchen.

His mother brings out many steaming pots and dishes over the course of the evening and, smiling graciously, laughing and chatting in Spanish, tops up glasses and refills waning plates. Not once does Santiago ask if she needs any help, nor does she ever ask him.

Over the course of the next hour, Santiago drinks five of the six-pack of beers Lucy has brought, while she, ashamed to say yes to the proffered wine without having brought any herself, sips the sixth. When they have eaten his mother's gazpacho, homemade shrimp tacos and the caramel panna cotta made by the fattest of the aunties for dessert, alongside strong black coffees, Santiago – who skipped the coffee and is growing louder, more brash, and increasingly expansive in his movements – rushes off to his bedroom to retrieve his accordian. Returning to his chair with a screeching thud against the white-tiled floor, legs spread wide, he starts to play traditional Mexican gypsy-style music. It is too loud to continue conversation, and so, after a time of polite listening, realizing that he is not now going to stop, his aunties and mother clap along, click their fingers, trill their tongues, and finally – shrugging across the table at one another in good-natured resignation – pull each other up to their feet, to dance in pairs, cumbia moves, all hips and arms and laughter, in the tight shadowy corners around the table.

It is at this point in the evening that it becomes clear to Lucy that Santiago's mother, his aunties, perhaps even his father hiding away upstairs, are all used to this behaviour from him – that he is treated by them delicately, as someone known to be gently problematic. Soon after she finds an excuse to leave, and insists to Santiago, standing too close to her in the narrow hallway, that she will be fine to walk home herself – that no, really, she would prefer to walk home herself. He gives her an unfocused, pointedly questioning look, shrugs, and shuts the door with a bang behind her without saying goodbye.

That night – lying in bed, tired, showered and relieved to be alone – Lucy receives, toppling one upon another, eight apologetic messages from Santiago telling her that he is so sorry, that he is never normally like that, that he was not a gentleman, that he was too loud, can she ever forgive him, and she, startled, spends the next half hour reassuring him of what a lovely time she had, until he is somewhat appeased and she is free, at last, to fall asleep.

GUN

One night, over two months into her stay, Lucy leaves Rafa's house to go meet Juan. She had been smoking weed with Rafa's ridiculous smart-vaping device (which, for reasons Lucy still can't comprehend, could hook up to his smart TV and be controlled by remote control) and watching Netflix when Rafa started running his hands across her body. She'd told him she was tired and ran out before he could find his shoes.

Juan is drinking mezcal and beers on a rooftop bar with some old friends from the outskirts of the city. Friends from his life before he became a 'big shot artist'. He has been texting her asking her where she is, and she loves this, this being wanted by him, and she tells him she's coming now, wait, she's coming, she's coming.

When she gets there, she sees Juan and four other men sitting around a table at the edge of the rooftop with a view overlooking Santo Domingo. It is truly beautiful. As Lucy walks in, the small French DJ, the only one bopping away to the techno tunes, purses his lips at her. She joins the table and Juan, trying to hide how drunk he is, carefully kisses her cheek.

The friend sitting directly across from Lucy, a bald man, maybe in his late forties or early fifties, has his head down on the table. Sensing a new presence, he raises himself up and focuses his bleary eyes on Lucy. On his upper-left cheek is a teardrop tattoo. He does a double-take. He lunges at her and she darts back. Sorry, sorry, excuse me, he says in Spanish, waving his hands. He has misjudged his motion. The other men, half-watching, laugh and tease him in Spanish that Lucy doesn't understand. He wipes his mouth where a little spittle has escaped from when he was lying on the table. Then he moves to take Lucy's hand. Lucy allows him to do so, shakes, then pulls her hand back. He looks confused. He asks her who she is and she says her name is Lucy, that she's a writer from Ireland. Leaning into her, pretending he can't quite hear, he says okay, but who *is* she, and she says that she's with Juan. At this, Juan looks over from his conversation a little blurrily, smiles, and rubs her back. The bald man's eyes travel slowly from Lucy to Juan, Juan to Lucy, and then harden unhappily.

At that moment, one of the young boys selling sweets, condoms and single cigarettes comes around to their table.

The bald man is overcome with a bright idea. He grabs the boy's arm before he can move away and fumbles to extract his wallet from his pocket. He buys Lucy a round strawberry lollipop. Lucy, who at this stage has turned towards Juan, feels the bald man's hand take her shoulder a little too forcefully, and turns with a start to find the lolly held right up to her face.

'Oh!' she exclaims, and the others around the table, noticing the interaction, again burst out laughing. There is a pause. 'Em, oh, thanks!' She takes the lollipop and holds it a moment, acknowledging the gift, before putting it down on the table.

'You no want?' he asks her, seeming annoyed.

'No, sorry, no, *el azúcar*, the sugar ... *¡Pero gracias!*' Lucy says, smiling as sweetly as she can manage, before tilting her body back toward the safety of Juan. She is not about to start fellating a lollipop. She is excited to leave, to get away from this old drunk and for her and Juan to go to bed together. But with Juan, as with Mexico, there is always one more drink, just one more.

The conversation lilts on slowly, with long pauses in which the men check their phones or swig their drinks or nod to men at other tables whom they know. All of a sudden, the bald man perks up again and takes a new-looking iPhone from his leather jacket pocket.

'You and me, we, we have picture,' he says, gesturing at Lucy to join him. He stands up expectantly, holding the iPhone ready.

'No, no, haha, *gracias*,' says Lucy, waving her hands and shaking her head. The last thing she wants is to give this guy an excuse to press himself against her.

His expression changes. He is frowning at her now. '*¿Que?* What? No, you and me, now, photo, come here, photo, *sí.*' He gestures more quickly, as though instructing a particularly dim child, or an animal maybe.

'No,' Lucy says, her will quickly materializing like a shield before her, made from diamond-hard quiet rage. *'Gracias, pero no quiero una foto.'*

He stops moving, and stares at her. The other four men around the table are silent and still now, not drinking, just watching. There is a mounting knife-edge tension and Lucy can feel it, she understands, but in this moment she does not care. She will hold her ground no matter what. Fuck him, fuck this, fuck all of them.

'No?' he whispers menacingly, swaying a little on his drunken feet.

'Nope!' Lucy replies, staring straight back at him.

There is another held breath of silence, and then the bald man gesticulates to Juan. In Spanish he says: 'If she won't come to me, you come here and take the photo and I will go there to where you are.'

Juan hesitates and Lucy, feeling his hesitation, turns to him and whispers that if he even thinks of moving, she'll kill him. She means it, she says, unblinking – she'll kill him in his sleep.

He raises his eyebrows, goes to smile but, sensing her desperate rage, turns back to his friend. He sits up a little straighter in his seat, and says in Spanish: 'No man, sit down, relax – she doesn't want to be in the photo, she doesn't like photos, just relax, chill, sit.'

The bald man stares at Juan a moment, disbelieving, and then lunges across the table towards Lucy again. Juan and the other men at the table all jump up to hold him back, but mid-lunge the bald guy, perhaps realizing himself outnumbered, tilts back and falls down into his seat, scraping the leg of the chair against the roof's cement floor.

The other men remain half-standing, unsure, and the bald man forces a laugh, staring at Lucy, and mumbles something in Spanish – something along the lines of 'Okay, fine, the lady doesn't want a photo, fine'. Lucy nods, says nothing, but her chest is on fire. She wants to cry, and she also wants to take a knife, cut off this guy's dick, impale it on a lollipop stick and force him to suck it bare.

A few minutes later, when the other guys are chatting again and Lucy is considering giving up on Juan and going home alone to eat mashed banana on toast and listen to an *In Our Time* podcast in bed instead, the bald man cautiously rises to his feet again, holding his chair for balance, and takes out his phone. There is a collective sucking in of breath before he says: 'Okay, okay, you take us then?' He is addressing Lucy, gesticulating in a circle at the other men with one hand, and with his other hand holding his phone out towards her. 'You take us photo, *sí*?'

Lucy exchanges a look with Juan, who raises his eyebrows again. 'Okay, sure,' says Lucy, fed up but also, in a depressing way, amused. 'Sure, why the fuck not.'

'*Sí, sí*,' he says, watching her and grinning. He motions for all the others to gather around him, barking faux-jovial instructions in Spanish, and so Juan and the others clamber to their feet and walk around to him, all five of them standing close, doing drunken Mexican-macho poses: hoods up, chins up, devil horn signs with their fingers.

Just as Lucy is about to take the picture, the bald man lifts his backpack up from his seat and, using his body to block the other guys from seeing, takes out a gun which he points straight at Lucy. Lucy, who had been in the middle of counting down from three, stops. She is holding the phone out before her, and there, in the screen, and in real life, is a gun, a silver, boxy handgun, pointing right at her stomach – pointing right at where her womb must be, she finds herself thinking.

She looks up into the bald man's sadistic, drunken eyes, staring right back into her, and she holds his gaze, silently and unflinchingly pouring into it every ounce of hatred she has inside her, all the rage she's ever had, built up for years and years, a silent piercing scream sent to him straight from the bullet-hole centre of her. She holds his gaze for just long enough to let him see, to let him feel it, before – smiling pleasantly and batting her eyelids as prettily as she knows how – she resumes her countdown: 'Tres, dos, uno ... *CHEESE!*'

HANDS, MOUTH, TONGUE

Interestingly, when Lucy is finally attacked in Mexico, that night walking home by the outer wall of the church grounds in Xochimilco, five minutes from her home – a warm night, a pleasant, humming night – she is not shoved against the wall as she tells people she was, afterwards. Apparently, according to the account of it in her journal, written the moment she gets home – still out of breath, skirt torn where he shoved his fingers in her crotch, neck still wet with saliva from his licks, his mark-leaving bites – that detail is an embellishment.

The thing is, Lucy actually *remembers* it happening that way now, because she has told it so many times, and has told her mother, her few trusted friends – told herself, in repeating it in her mind, over and over – that she was shoved against the wall. This seems now, Lucy thinks, like nothing more than a small assertion of unconscious will, a human peccadillo in the face of the reality of the situation;

a situation that actually happens to Lucy, that is forced upon Lucy, disgusting and frightening and beyond her strength to control or to prevent.

CHIPMUNK

Lucy is spending the weekend in a house in Puerto Escondido, a village on the coast. It is off-season, so she has the whole place to herself. She sits in the garden overlooking the ocean. The garden is hidden from any neighbours and so she lets the towel that was wrapped around her body fall to the grass. As she snoozes, thinking of nothing, the small squirrel-like creature who she had been studying in the flowerbeds at the garden's edge earlier that day, who has been studying Lucy back, comes over to her in fits and starts, fluffy tail curling and jolting, and hides itself in the folds of towel down to her left. It wraps itself in it, and Lucy can hear it muttering and squealing in delight. She, too, is delighted, and she chats to it about the light, the sea, other things.

After half an hour or so Lucy reluctantly rises, careful not to disturb the towel over her little friend, and walks inside to pee. She tells it not to worry, she'll be back in a minute. Inside, she checks her phone, charging on the bedside table, and there is a message from her father: 'love you kiddo, hope all's sweet with you, x'. She decides to take a photo of the sunset for him, and of her new best friend, which, she decides, is a chipmunk. She and her father are both equally crazy about animals, and when she is home they can wax lyrical for hours upon hours about the sheer amazingness of the dog.

Still naked, she goes back outside, and immediately sees an ugly huge raccoon, with one damaged eye, pale

223

blue, stalking near her empty chair. Her heart rises, panicking. She sees, through the towel, the little body of the chipmunk quivering as the raccoon approaches, sniffing. She shouts, her voice breaking a little, and stamps her feet, but she too is scared when it looks at her, and she finds she is not moving any closer. She doesn't know what to do. She turns to find something to throw but when she turns back, the chipmunk, thinking itself abandoned, has made a run for it, and the raccoon has leapt into action, and Lucy cries out but it is too late, the raccoon has it just before the edge of the garden, just before the cliff that leads down to the ocean. The little chipmunk, struggling, is grasped between his claws, and it is squealing, crying out, it is piercing, and Lucy's heart is tearing, she is gulping for air, she can't believe this is happening.

In one hand she holds her phone, and in the other she has picked up her shoe, a Nike trainer, but she doesn't know what to do; if she throws it, she will probably miss anyway, and then it may go over the edge of the cliff; and then, she reasons, she'll only have one shoe; and just as she decides to throw it anyway, the raccoon takes the chipmunk firmly in its mouth and, glancing at Lucy, pads quickly off to the side and through the brush to some place down the cliff, out of sight. Lucy could see the little chipmunk's fluffy tail hanging, swinging side to the side, from the creature's jaws. And now she can hear the cries of it, being eaten alive. Tears streaming, she half-heartedly throws the shoe, although she doesn't know why – to know that she did maybe, to be able to say that she did this at least, in the inevitable retelling. But she throws it so gently that it barely reaches the middle of the lawn, let alone the edge.

In a state of shock – still able to hear the desperate sounds of the squirrel crying, being torn apart, her little friend – she proceeds, dazed, to walk to the edge of the cliff, raise her phone and take a photo of the sunset before it fades to darkness, to send to her father back home. 'Wow, paradise!' he replies.

EARTHQUAKE II

There are two more significant earthquakes while Lucy is in Oaxaca. The first of these happens while she is at her kitchen table writing in her nightdress. It is around noon. She finishes her sentence before stumbling out-side, hands to the walls for balance, and stands on the street until it stops. More than anything, she is irritated at having been disturbed. Car alarms are going off, dogs barking, voices yelling. A woman weighed down with two heavy shopping bags trots as quickly as she can past Lucy down the street, no doubt to see if her home has been damaged. Perhaps, Lucy thinks, she has left an infant sleeping.

The guys in the garage up the way are smoking out front. When Lucy emerges they smile at her, shrug at the earthquake, whisper to each other and then smile down her way some more, teeth bared. She covers her chest with crossed arms and faces away. As soon as the rum-bling ends, she goes back inside. She doesn't know about aftershocks or, if she does, she decides she doesn't care enough.

Later, down at the market stall where she eats her torta for lunch most days, the TV that hangs in the corner above the drinks fridge will show the wreckage from Mexico City: the death toll, footage of skyscrapers shaking and tumbling, the smoke, people running and crying and, repeatedly, images of a playground – where children had just been evacuated from inside – suddenly collapsing beneath their feet.

EARTHQUAKE III

The last noteworthy earthquake Lucy experiences happens a few nights before she is due to leave Oaxaca for good. It happens in the night, much like the first one, but this time she runs out of her apartment and down into the street as fast as she can. The bottom step of her apartment block has crumbled away and, stepping over it, she hears herself whimper aloud.

Outside, children wrapped in blankets wail in their parents' arms, dogs bark on leashes, people chatter nervously, shifting and staring around from clustered groups, and old women in long cotton nightdresses, hair askew and leaning on the arms of young men, cry silently into handkerchiefs. This time, Lucy finds to her surprise that she is crying too. She doesn't want to be here anymore. She doesn't want to be alone in a place where even the earth can't be trusted. She waits on the street until the very last chattering stragglers have gone back inside. The sun is just beginning to thin out the darkness of the sky into a deep and fervid indigo – a colour so beautiful it seems to Lucy discordant, seen after the night's events. Turning to re-enter her apartment building, she hears the first birds' waking song and finds the sound unreal.

Inside, Lucy switches on all the lights, then gathers up her passport, phone and wallet and puts them in a clear ziplock plastic bag, propping it up against the serviette holder in the middle of the kitchen table. She considers the bed a moment, swaying, then turns back to the kitchen, makes a pot of coffee, and sits down: not reading or writing, not doing anything, in fact, other than staring vacantly at the ziplocked package, thinking about what home – that place so far off, that still place, cool and green and quiet – might, at that moment, be like.

SANTIAGO III

Two weeks after his aunt's birthday celebration, sitting in La Popular, Santiago tells Lucy that reading her writing was the first indication he ever had that women had the potential to think like men. He means to be as intelligent as men, as well as to be rational and funny. He says this like he is joking but he is not. To justify the terrible things he says, Santiago opens his sentences with 'I know I am an asshole, *but* ...' Now that he has discovered that Lucy might have some intelligence lurking under her white skin, he speaks a little differently. He sits up straighter. Now he is intrigued and a little frightened by Lucy, and approaches her with the tentative curiosity of a dog sniffling in circles around a coiled snake.

One night, towards the end of her stay in Mexico, Lucy goes out dancing and runs into a friend of Santiago's, with whom she dances some more, and laughs, and snorts cocaine through a two-hundred-peso note (the green one with a nun on it) from the top of a toilet cistern in the secret social club downtown called Patio, a place where Lucy has become a weekly fixture. The next day, Santiago – who has become one of Lucy's closest friends in Oaxaca, in spite of his underlying sexism; his hatred of foreigners; his hatred of Mexicans, especially of *fresas* which is his term for Mexican yuppies (meaning 'strawberries'); and his resentment of, concordantly, the general successes of others – texts Lucy, and asks her how her night went. She, still lying in bed, reading a novel, says fun, fun, and then mentions having met his friend out – what's his name again? – and says something about what a nice guy he seems to be. This is Santiago's reply:

Fuck	(12.02 p.m.)
I'm gonna beat the shit out of him	(12.02 p.m.)
It is not about you	(12.02 p.m.)
It is about you	(12.03 p.m.)
But he is supposed to be my friend	(12.03 p.m.)
I have beaten people for him	(12.03 p.m.)
For	(12.04 p.m.)
Sorry, Lucy.	(12.06 p.m.)
This guy is being an asshole	(12.06 p.m.)
He is interested in you	(12.06 p.m.)
Aswell	(12.08 p.m.)
Lucy	(12.12 p.m.)
Did you ever stopped to think that I was interested in you as a woman?	(12.13 p.m.)
How can you tell me you like my friend	(12.13 p.m.)
Even as a friend	(12.14 p.m.)
I know what that means	(12.14 p.m.)
It is pure logic	(12.14 p.m.)
I told him you are crazy	(12.15 p.m.)
BTW he told me he fucked you	(12.21 p.m.)
That is why I got so mad	(12.21 p.m.)
I respect you	(12.22 p.m.)
Lucy	(12.23 p.m.)
Sorry for going so crazy	(12.28 p.m.)
Lucy	(12.37 p.m.)

Later, Lucy would find out from another friend that when Santiago was a teenager he killed a guy, something to do with drugs, and that the real reason he had come back to Oaxaca from Mexico City two years before wasn't to take care of his mother, like he'd told Lucy, but due to a restraining order he'd received for beating the shit out of his girlfriend. Apparently, the friend told her, scanning the room and whispering into her ear, the girlfriend had needed nine stitches above her left eye.

A few days later, Lucy flies home to Ireland, fingers tightly gripping the armrests as the aeroplane takes off.

AWAKENING (contd.)

That first morning, and the dawn begins to filter through the opaque glass windows. Men out in the corridors shout what she hears as the word *huevos*, but she's sure is not. They are probably selling water, or bread, or ice maybe. Or maybe it's a warning of some sort.

Her first glass of coffee is finished, and she wants another. It worked, the experiment of the glass, it was sufficiently tasty and warm, and she feels the beginnings of a buzz. Things are looking up. She is not really writing yet, more coasting through articles, flipping through books, but she believes herself to be on her way. She is waiting for an idea to hit her.

She stands over the cooker again, more relaxed this time – a pro – and as one hand holds the tilted glass over the flame, the other scrolls through her phone. Titbits of news, recipes, dog and cat videos, photos of two best friends in a hot tub in the west of Ireland, a voice message from her father, another voice message from another friend, living in New York, requesting photos of the Mexican food she eats that day.

Reading absentmindedly, something about Trump's hair now, a little video of it blowing in the wind as he boards an aeroplane, the glass in her right hand suddenly explodes. Water splashes out the gas flame with a hiss. She gasps, but doesn't move. It is a mixture of the two scenarios she pictured; no shrapnel in her belly, but also more widespread and shattered than the bottom of the glass simply plopping off neatly. She stands still a moment, adjusting to the new situation, then she places the warm, now brittle-feeling neck of the glass into the sink. The cracked bit at the bottom is scalding, and hisses when it touches against the wet, cold metal of the basin. She hadn't noticed it getting so hot. Lucy turns off the gas, and considers the wreckage. The remnants are still steaming, and so she'll have to wait to tidy up. Well, come on, she thinks. She knew it was going to happen, really. It was inevitable. She's neither disappointed nor relieved, but is, even as she tries not to openly acknowledge the feeling, a little disconcerted. Did she really put a glass directly into a flame? What could she have been thinking? The men beyond are getting louder, getting closer. 'Don't worry, it's okay, you're okay.' She only realizes after she hears it that it's her own voice speaking.

DUST

Sometimes, Lucy remembers now, on especially hot afternoons – those afternoons too hot to do anything else – she would sit out in a chair in front of a café in the Zócalo, or on a bench up by the Guelaguetza stadium on the hill, and watch the soft movements of all the endless dust that coats the streets of Oaxaca. In an instant, picturing it, even now she is there she is with it she is swirled away; swirled a white dust into all the adobe mud walls into fields of maize, into the open windows of all the cars parked along the roads, into the hair the mouths of all the lovers in all the backseats, into the children's playground the funnel of their instruments pouring out brass in the mornings before school, into the swollen eyes and ears the fur of all the full and hungry animals and into the vats in which they ferment mezcal; into the paint of all the artists, the studios and the drying murals in the streets she swirls her way into all that coke and gets sucked up all the people's noses and slicked onto pretty ladies' gums; she circles around the warm walls of Santo Domingo as the bells clang heavy through thick noon air and gets blown and kicked down to the markets – so much dust! – into the ladies shouting 'empanaaadaaas' and a little of her is caught and settles in the fish tanks or gets embedded in all that pungent leather, sandals, satchels, boots and briefcases; some of her is kicked up by passing feet and swirls and lands on the pigs' trotters, the feathers of the chickens and on the curling strands of the tentacles of an octopus unfurling across the ice, a little speck of her in every sucker. The last of her is carried on those gentle winds into the surrounding mountains to dance around the woodlands, on and on around circling the valley, coating gently all the leaves, the animals and walkers and teenage drinkers, she is dusted silently falling across all the quiet, struggling rapes, pinned bared legs kicking up leaves, dirt in hair, hands over mouths and, in the evenings, she finds her way into the deep creases in the faces of the old tortilla-sellers, those women who've lived there their whole lives, who've known nowhere and nothing else, emptied baskets loose-balanced on their heads, long thin plaits swaying down behind their thighs, plodding slowly home; darkness seeping through, frowning, frowning, weary, a silent sigh, through all that dust returning dust to home.

Le Rêve

A young woman moves to New York to live with an older man, to whom she gave a James Joyce walking tour in Dublin, back in August. At the end of the tour, after her grand finale, in which she reads that bit about the snow falling all over Ireland in her most poetic brogue, he asks for her email. She gives it to him, and half an hour later he contacts her, then again later that day, then again that night, at four minutes past midnight. The emails contain thoughts on literature, Joyce's legacy, Dublin, her exceptional ability as an orator, an intellectual, her beautiful hair and lips, as well as descriptions of his own life; the many international cities he has visited, his damning opinion of Donald Trump, his reputation as an educator, his special interest in disadvantaged students and/or students from immigrant families, his salary at its height, his current take-home pension after taxes, his cat, his favourite recipes, with many uses of the words 'fresh', 'light' and 'delicious'. The emails also contain poems – both those of other writers as well as his own humble compositions.

Initially, she ignores him. It is late summer, and she is young and alive. Then her life begins to fall apart and, one night, when her ex again fails to text back to her messages, she replies. She does so 'ironically' at first, then in earnest. His unrelenting praise helps her to feel okay about herself. To feel incredible, actually. Walking around in the daytime, in the cold streets of Dublin, blindingly shiny with rain, or boarding cramped trains, or doing the grocery shopping in the local Tesco, or scrubbing stuck spaghetti from the bottom of the pot, she sucks on his adoring vision of her like sugary lemon sweets, flipping them round and round with her tongue and savouring their sweet tang.

Gradually, their correspondence becomes heavy, passionate, highly sexualized. She neither encourages nor discourages, once he has pushed it a little further, the incremental progression of their intimacy. She accepts his love unreservedly because, from an old coot like him, she believes she deserves it. Her ego, so starved, devours everything he offers, and grows fat and rosy-golden on his adulation. As he makes clear, he is old and alone and wizened – if with a pretty healthy life-style and a lot of accumulated knowledge and wisdom to impart – while she is young and beautiful, with all the world before her. For both of them, she is, by far, the more wonderful.

The next step comes after an aborted night out one Saturday, when she comes home crying and ends up sending him nude photos. She takes one of her body, open-legged, lying across the bed, and one of her ass, bent up into the air, her vagina and asshole up close in the foreground. It is a difficult angle to achieve, and she has to take over ten shots to get it right. At one point she very nearly rolls off the bed. But she has just had a Brazilian wax and, she reasons, otherwise, no one will even see it. At his request, she also sends him a recording of her voice over WhatsApp (which he has downloaded solely to communicate with her). He tells her that he wants to hear her pretty voice, begs her to give it to him, and so she records some gentle, high-pitched moans as she masturbates (purportedly to thoughts of him, but in fact to thoughts of this very situation – that is, of herself, arousing him). It is barely audible, he says, with a sad emoji, and she tells him she has to keep her voice low, so as not to wake her father. This seems to drive him all the more wild. He says he'll use his headphones to listen properly – they are noise-cancelling, he tells her. Afterwards, he pronounces himself 'completely enraptured' with her, 'overcome'. As she stumbles into her pyjamas, and sneaks downstairs for a piss, her phone, abandoned in her bed covers, silently lights up with messages from him, saying he'd love to paint her, likening her to Maud Gonne, and finally, at four in the morning her time, when she is already fast asleep and snoring, he signs off with:

'well, i imagine u're asleep now darling ... Sleep well with dreams of me, utterly ADORING u, kissing u, mind & body, sweet angel xxxxxx ...'

She doesn't see his final seven messages until the morning. She turns off her phone, and goes walking in the mountains with the dog. It rains, the walk is arduous, and she gets soaked through. The mountains are steep and misty, and she almost gets lost. When she finally gets home, she is cold and tired and aching. She showers, the heat stinging her face. She makes scrambled eggs and beans and toast, with sausages for her dad and the dog. It is only when she is in bed again, in the silent dark, that she switches on her phone. Twenty-three messages.

Finally, on a damp, grey Tuesday, with nothing to do and her dad already out somewhere in the car they share, maybe for the whole day, she agrees to come to New York to live with him. He is ecstatic. He sends lines and lines of happy emojis. He uses the one with the excited hands up on either side of its face. The next day, flowers arrive for her at her house – a dozen red roses. 'Fancy,' her dad says, winking at her.

And next thing she's here. She's done it.

The steps a person takes to change their life entirely are surprisingly easy, she thinks, waiting for her luggage at the carousel. A bit too easy, in fact. There ought to be tests, or conversations with professionals – like those required for plastic surgery. But there are none. She is a free woman, free to make her own choices. That is what women fought and died for. Went on hunger strikes and broke windows for. That is what allowed her mom to leave her dad all those years ago, and it is what has allowed her to make the decision to come here. And now she is here, and he is standing on the other side of security with a sign that says 'Céad míle fáilte!' waiting for her.

Her friends tell her she is lucky – a new life in New York, with an older man, and free accommodation. Too good to be true! This is what they say to her face, at least. Work accepts her two weeks' notice, and offers her luck in her new life. Her boss, a small man with two young children whom she kissed once at a Christmas party two years back, buys a bottle of prosecco and a card, which everyone signs. They drink it in the office on the last day, under the posters of Beckett, Wilde, Shaw and Joyce. They all emigrated too, someone says, jokingly. Yeah, just keeping up the tradition sure, she smiles. Her dad gives her a hug beside the car at the airport. The engine is still running, and a large bald man with rosary beads hanging from the rearview mirror is impatiently waiting to pull into their spot, edging closer and tapping his steering wheel. Tearing himself away, her dad wipes a tear from his eye, and tells her he's proud of her, terribly proud of her.

He lives on the Upper West Side, although he has, in their recent, almost constant stream of emails and voice messages and texts, been talking of selling up so they could move to Brooklyn, if she likes, in a year maybe, to be closer to the 'scene'. She feels obliged to pretend to know what he's talking about, when he alludes to a 'scene', and says sure, that sounds exciting – whatever he thinks. She tells him she trusts him. She knows he likes that.

He has never been married, but prides himself on his ability to keep home, solo. His place is therefore full of dark wood furnishings, mustard yellows and forest greens; African and Asian ceramics mixed with late-modern European art, broad brush strokes and bold colours, bought on tour in France, Italy, Spain; hardback books, a record player, records (lots of classical, some jazz and, deeper down the pile, a few offerings of alt and mainstream rock – the Beatles, Zeppelin, Springsteen, one Red Hot Chili Peppers 'best of' album, as well as the soundtrack to *Les Misérables*); in the kitchen, spices in a blue-painted spice rack with sell-by dates from three years prior, perhaps evidence of a previous female inhabitant; cat fur on the rugs, the couch, the armchairs, dust covering all the shadowed, untouched spaces and spiderwebs in the ceiling corners. The bedcover set is beige and still creased from sitting a long time somewhere, poorly folded. Over the bed, she notes, putting away her things in the drawer he has cleared for her, hangs a Picasso reprint – one of the moderately sexual ones, of one of his muses. She has seen it before, in a museum somewhere, in some past life, but she doesn't remember when and where exactly, nor does she remember the title, although she wishes she did, so that she could mention it to him in an offhand way, as though she is au fait with important artists and concepts. Now, no longer communicating through the internet, she cannot feign knowledge she doesn't actually possess with a quick Google search, and this makes her nervously reticent.

She doesn't know if he has taken Viagra, before or during dinner maybe, but his penis is stiffly erect when he presses himself into her behind in the kitchen, just as she is placing the dishes in the sink. For dinner, he made a lemony chicken and pasta dish with parsley, penne, Parmesan and pepper. It is one of the meals he had described to her in his early emails. To be fair, he has never actually lied to her, she thinks.

Out the window before her, a dark New York street. Cars pass slowly, street lights aglow, headlights growing and fading, briefly illuminating in sweeps the cold, scrunched faces shuffling along the sidewalks. Down the way a little to her left, someone hollers a name she doesn't recognize. She can feel, even in the warmth of the apartment, from the proximity of the cool pane before her face, the hint of snow in the air. On the radio in the car all the talk had been of a storm coming in across the sea tonight. Apparently there'd been a rush at a lot of the big Manhattan supermarkets, Whole Foods, Trader Joe's, but he'd told her it was nothing, not to worry – this happened every year.

Beneath the sounds of John Coltrane coming from the living room, a horn blows. Another responds, layering over the held note of the first, before a third joins in. In the distance, a siren. His breath is hot on her neck, and she can smell the food they ate, and the wine, and something else, older, unpleasant. She had forgotten until this moment, noticing the same smell when he spoke to her after her tour, back in Dublin – the day they met.

The plates, which she has relinquished, clatter softly into the sink, their knives and forks slipping down beneath the pots and colander already soaking there. For some reason, the sound embarrasses her. She tries to relax. Across the way there is an old brownstone wedged between many other brownstones, just like their own, with the lights on but cream curtains drawn. As he begins rubbing himself up and down against her, groaning slightly, hips thrust forward, his hands, first gently placed on her hips, then gripping harder, now moving up to hold her breasts, to pull himself tight against her, searching over and then slipping under her shirt to grip between each forefinger and thumb her nipples, twisting them into stiffness, she finds herself wondering who lives there. Now, they will be her neighbours. The small shop, windows caked in bright cut-out pictures of Coke bottles and fruit and veg and sandwiches and cigarettes and booze, that she'd seen on the corner from the window of his car – that will be her local shop now, she marvels. That will be where she goes to buy milk, and eggs, and bread, and unfamiliar American chocolate bars.

Naked, his skin hangs off his bones less than she'd feared it would. She has seen old men's bodies before in films but, in comparison, his is relatively tight and compact and strong. He still retains his summer tan. She can see the muscles flex and relax along his arms and legs. The hair on his chest, stomach and groin is coarse and has turned a yellowish-blond colour, and his gut is not at all large – in fact, it is small and neat, like a baby bump, she thinks, but sagging downward.

His apartment is on the third floor, and is as spacious as he'd promised. The cat, much spoken of and seen in candid photos and videos on WhatsApp, to which she'd replied with heart-eyed emojis, has kept itself hidden since she first spied it, ears back, spine curved and wide-eyed, lumbering in the door behind him with the rest of her luggage. She would never have to work, he'd said – not, that is, unless she wants to. He is all for equal rights, and wants her to do whatever makes her happy and ful-filled, here with him, he'd said, followed by lots of love hearts and kisses. He had hinted, early on, that he had no children, not even any nephews and nieces, to leave this lovely apartment to. There is just him, the cat, with all this room for love …

When he fucks her, she must spit liberally in her hand, twice, and rub it all over his cock, so that he can enter her without it tugging at her, and hurting. His cock, she notices, surprised, is the most youthful thing about him. There is very little difference between it and other cocks she's known. This, she tells herself, is a blessing.

Moving above her, his face low in the pillow beside her own, she can tell he wants to whisper something in her ear, that his lips are pursed and ready to do so. But, perhaps from shyness, perhaps exertion, or perhaps from not knowing exactly what it is he wants to whisper, he refrains. With a final thrust and gasp, he just manages to pull out in time, and comes in a few, rhythmic spurts across her stomach. She is on the pill, which he knows, but they have not yet discussed much in terms of sexual logistics, other than their both being STD-free, and so his pulling out is a courtesy she appreciates.

Afterwards, in that panting lull, he, on his knees above her, eyes closed and mouth open, raises his head to the ceiling, and releases a low and quiet groan. She finds herself wondering how long it will be now before she is allowed to sleep. Slowly, he turns his face back down to her, opens his eyes, smiles, and collapses beside her. 'Wonderful,' he whispers, chest rising and falling quickly, 'just wonderful.' He reaches for her hand, finds it nestled in the covers by her side, squeezes it, and then keeps a loose hold, fingers interlaced, as they lie there for a while, in the half light. His hand is hot and clammy, and has the texture of her grandmother's.

The record has ended, and she hears it clicking in the next room. She must be calm. Beneath the faint mustiness of closet storage, the sheets, she notes, breathing deeply through her nose, smell of synthetic lilac. He had told her, as they were texting furiously back and forth while she awaited her flight at Dublin airport, that he was in the process of putting on fresh ones for her. That was today, she realizes, amazed.

He also washed the bathroom, he'd told her proudly, and bought her favourite shampoo and conditioner, and bath salts, since he knew she loved a bath. When she'd arrived, a few hours ago, she'd discovered that he had also bought Irish teabags and the film of *Ulysses* on DVD online, for them to watch together, since he remembered she'd told him she had never seen it. It would be impossible, of course, to tell him now, that her never seeing it had been intentional.

His kindness is strange and startling to her, and all this is not his fault, she reminds herself now. It is not her fault either, she tells herself soothingly, although it *is* her fault that she is here, now, with his cum on her stomach. It is her fault that she told him that yes, she loves him too, that yes, alright then, she would come and be with him, share

241

his life with him, here in his apartment, where he has been living for the last thirty years or so, here in New York. He has been living here, she realizes, for longer than she has even been alive.

'Are you okay, sweetie?' she hears, coming across to her from some place far off.

Lying here, in his bed, in his slightly too warm apartment, all the way across the dark, sloshing Atlantic – all this way from home, miles and miles, from her dad, the old stained teapot, the stove, the broken kitchen chair; from her friends, her old school, the cobbled streets of Dublin at night, from the giggling raucousness, the feeling of pure possibility, of how anything could happen, the sounds of music through doorways, the steamy-windowed, little pubs; from the empty beaches, the seagulls screeching, the chimney smoke rising of an evening, from the crisp, green air of the woods, with all the trees above her, hushing, creaking, asway … She closes her eyes carefully – she is suddenly dizzy, nauseous, unsure of the balance of her body on the bed. She grips his hand, and he, taking this as her answer, immediately returns the pressure.

She breathes deeply, and brushes thoughts of home from her mind. She is here, it's done, as was intended. And it's true – it is just as they'd intended, even if they had never said it outright. She is here, with him, they are both breathing the same air, into the same silence, which must mean that they two, at least, are no longer so alone.

Acknowledgements

I would like to thank the following:

The Arts Council, Brendan Barrington, Lucy Luck, Cormac Kinsella, Declan Meade, Sean O'Reilly and Rob Doyle, for their professional encouragement and support.

Anna Morrison for the beautiful cover, as well as Emma Flynn and Kirstin Campbell for their copyediting and proof-reading.

Eric Savoie of Savo Photography, for the press photos.

Tess Byrne, Siobhán Savoie, Manus Sweeney, Georgie Sweeney, Oisín Sweeney, Cilian Byrne, Maureen Brennan, the Syborn family, Cormac Creed, Bethan Phillips, Rachel Noble, Ellie MacNamara, Róisín Linnie and Mollie Guidera, for helping me through.

My grandparents, Aileen and Terry, for letting me run off to Connemara to write.

My aunt and uncle, Mick and Liz, for facilitating the same, down in West Cork.

Dublin Area Rapid Transit, for being so slow, and letting me read.

The James Joyce Centre, Dublin, where I worked on at least half of these stories.

The Wicklow Mountains.

Max the dog.

Banshee Press, specifically Laura Cassidy, Eimear Ryan and Claire Hennessy, for their unfailing (and unflinching) championing of my writing.

My mom, Cathy Sweeney, for submitting my first story. And all the rest.

My dad, Paul Byrne, for giving me music, and movies. *And* comedy.

David, for finding me.

BANSHEE
PRESS

Banshee Press was founded in 2014 by Laura Cassidy, Claire Hennessy and Eimear Ryan to publish exciting and contemporary new writing from Ireland and around the world. *Banshee* literary journal is published twice a year, in March and September. *Paris Syndrome* is the publisher's first book.

WWW.BANSHEELIT.COM | BANSHEELIT@GMAIL.COM